THOSE BELOW THE TREE HOUSE

MATT HAYWARD

POLTERGEIST PRESS

POLTERGEIST PRESS

ISBN: 978-1-913138-36-3

Artwork by Ben Baldwin

First Edition

www.poltergeistpress.com

For Cooper, Tom, and Colin.
Three of the best friends I ever had, taken far too soon.

ACKNOWLEDGEMENTS

A special thank you to Anna Hayward, Melissa & Fionnuala Hayward, Tim Meyer, Robert Ford, Kelli Owen, Alicia Stamps, Lane Heymont, Jamie Goecker, Brian Keene, Mary SanGiovanni, Bryan Smith, Jennifer Smith, Richard Chizmar, Simon Clark, Patrick Lacey, Mark & Emer, Martin & Reete, Paul Goblirsch, Aaron Dries, Glenn Rolfe, John Quick, D Alexander Ward, Kevin Lucia, Os Andres, Kevin Liffey, Ivan Byrne, and everyone who gave this book a chance. Except that one guy.

CHAPTER ONE

THE WORLD FIRST bared its teeth when I turned thirteen, starting with a drunkard on a riverbank.

I sat in my mom's car with the man I hated, bobbing at each pothole and turn, still soaked from the night. Smoke clouded the vehicle, seeping from the cherry of his cigarette, and the fumes churned my guts.

"I'm cracking a window."

He grumbled, flicked some ash, then squinted at the intermittent flashes of road the wipers permitted. How my mother turned a blind eye to Jack's darker side, I'd never know. He'd collected me from the arcade only for the booze run, and my mother pretended not to notice. Being my birthday, I asked to spend the day there just to get out of the house, out of Riverside, even leaving Jacob behind. Jacob's lisp drew attention like a fatty rabbit would a fox, and as much as I liked my friend, I didn't want a black eye from a city kid as a birthday present.

No raised voices, crashing plates, or bad looks. Some relief from the madness, if only for a night.

With a bottle of cheap rye poisoning his system, Jack's fists jittered on the wheel, the smell congealing with his Marlboro to turn my mother's hatchback into a puke-inducing box on wheels. I saw things in that man my mother didn't. When it came to partners, kids usually had that power. Jack masked his booze with mouthwash to the effect of a duvet over an elephant, and I'm damn sure he'd beat my dog. She'd run away a month before.

"Seriously, Jack, I'm gonna get sick. The stink in here..."

I cranked my window, and fresh air billowed inside with a hiss. A splatter of droplets tickled my arm. I sighed.

"Say to let the window down?"

His eyes left the road, and my chest lurched. The deluge and alcohol conspired to make my chances of getting home null, but getting home was all I wanted—not too much to ask for my birthday, surely. Tonight was the night I'd convince my mother to get this asshole out of our lives for good. He'd done all the work himself, after all. With his eyeballs almost in their opposite sockets, she'd have to face the truth. Much as it pained. She needed some dignity after my dad's death and I intended to make it happen.

"Watch the road, Jack."

And don't you come back

"Fuck off, ye little shit."

I shook my head as a humorless grin twitched my lips. *There* sat the monster my mother would finally meet, the hidden daemon infecting our home. As I would soon find out, he'd ruin us—all of Riverside—in ways no one saw coming. Not even him.

Like I said, it started with a drunkard on a riverbank.

Jack cocked his head, indicating the mouthwash in the glovebox. "Pass it 'ere."

I ignored the request and wriggled back into my seat. Grey smoke invaded my nostrils.

"*Fucker*, seriously. Now."

Each word filled me with simultaneous hurt and happiness. Hurt because adults weren't meant to talk to kids that way, at least not in the movies or books I knew. Happiness because my mother would finally see. Tonight everything changed.

Jack hissed and dropped his cigarette as his boot slammed the brake. The tires squealed and my neck whipped as my palms collided with the dash. The engine ticked. Rain drummed the roof.

"What the hell you doin'?" My voice quivered as I brought my injured wrists to my chest, bones throbbing, my hands seared red. He shushed me, wide-eyed and frozen.

"Not see him?"

"See who?"

"Paul Osmond."

My mouth dried. Osmond had slipped from Riverside the previous week—a staple in the streets, always a bottle in hand and a slur of unwanted advice. Most folks palmed him change and forced a smile, having grown up with him, and five years ago, after the mill closed, he'd practically melded to the sidewalks. *An accident,* he'd said, but still, better that than the chipper like my father. I swallowed as the night returned to the cinema of my mind, same as always: Officer Richardson knocking the door, my mother collapsing and crying so hard my hair stood on end. Vomiting when Richardson, pale-faced, told us my dad had fallen victim to the metal teeth of the mill. All the while Christmas decorations glittered and the fire crackled...

"Wait here."

Jack popped the door, amplifying the fizzing rain. I almost asked him to wait but bit my tongue as the door slammed shut, locking me in silence. I hadn't seen Paul Osmond myself but wasn't prepared to tell Jack. Let him wander off. Shit, let him get lost and never come back, save me the hassle of the night ahead.

Jack passed the headlights, briefly snuffing the glare, hunkered against the deluge distorting the windshield. The wipers creaked back and forth, back and forth, and I watched him jog to the roadside, parting a matting of ferns. I unbuckled my seatbelt and sat up with a squint, idly unwinding my window to clear the stale air. The car sat on a bridge at the entrance to the mountain, hence the town name, and the headlights illuminated the mucky path up to our home through the woods, only a suggestion of light in the distance.

Jack stomped ferns before disappearing into the gloom, and the idea of running home crossed my mind. I could pop the door and race up the mountain, but decided against it. The image of my mother's hatchback screeching as it gained caused a shiver up my spine. Jack would catch me for sure, and knowing Jack, he'd spin a tale to ensure *I* came out badly. My mother would take his side, too, business as usual. *Know what your son did? Jumped from the car like a fuckin' stuntman and made me chase him halfway home!*

So, no. I needed to stay cool, needed Jack home in his wretched state. Mom couldn't deny evidence like that when confronted. Not again.

Jack yelled for Paul, already further out than expected, as his voice lost a hard battle with the rain. I imagined he'd slipped down the embankment past those ferns, traipsing the riverbank now. I knew better than to do anything but stay put.

"Osmond! Where you at?"

My eyes darted to the woodlands on either side of the car, fear coursing through my system. At thirteen, I'd grown to fear real monsters, like Jack, rapists, and pedophiles, but I also had the added bonus of still dreading vampires and zombies and banshees. Kid's fears, all clinging to the crossroads of youth.

"Hurry up, Jack..."

I imagined a lurching circus freak slipping from the woods, a jagged knife in one gnarled fist, and a *'c'mere...'* motion with a pointed finger. I swallowed the lump in my throat and focused on the rain.

"Paul, it's comin' down hard! You wanna get yourself hurt out here!"

To the left, something rustled in the woodlands. Branches bobbed. My head whipped to the right and back, and I pleaded Jack to return.

Clowns, knives, sharp teeth...Clowns, knives, sharp teeth...

"Oh, fuck it..."

I shouldered the door and stepped into the deluge as a shiver wracked me. "Jack!"

After glancing to the gloomy thicket, I raced to the ferns, hugging myself and wishing I'd worn more than just a teeshirt. I imagined the fire blazing at home, my mom knitting in the glow of Friday night television, and suddenly wished I'd never chosen tonight to cause a fuss. A bath and my Game Boy outweighed the inevitable fight, but I knew I couldn't stop my plan, not now.

"Jack!"

I parted the greenery, ice water racing down my arms, and stepped through to the embankment. I'd slipped on this hill many times before, and now mud glistened in the moonlight, daring me to slide into darkness. Down there, flashes of light shimmered on the river, and its static roar filled my ears. I pictured Jack stumbling along its banks, and knew I had to find him—little as I wanted. If he had an accident, that gave him a free pass to rest up in our home. He'd bask in my mother's sympathy for days.

"Not happening," I muttered, and started forward. I raised my voice. "Jack, gotta—"

My foot whipped from under me and I crashed, slopping down the damn organic waterpark. I grasped for roots, but my fingers found only air as cold mud slopped up my back and I collided with the trunk of a tree. The rain punched my face and shoulders as I groaned and stumbled to my feet, blinking away the fireworks exploding in my vision. Against the darkness, gargantuan pines loomed, circling me and leaving only a patch of clearing by the riverbank. An owl hooted from somewhere overhead, and my breath came in tight bursts.

I wiped muck from my back and, one arm clutched to my chest, I hobbled to the riverbank, keeping a close eye on my footing—one wrong move meant I'd stumble into the drink. Although a shower didn't seem so bad. I stayed a good two feet away from the black water and shuffled through the slop, my vision adjusting to the gloom.

"Jack! Please!"

I hated the whine in my tone, but my voice easily betrayed me. I was lost and frightened, and—asshole or not—I needed Jack as a guardian here. My chest tightened at that fact, but I kept his words in mind—*fucker, little shit*...and, not surprisingly, my original plan stuck.

A noise ghosted on the river roar then, a slopping and wet sound.

The 'adult' part of my mind asked: *boots in the mud?* while the child in me screamed: *fuck outta here, that's a goddamn troll.*

"Jack, can you hear..."

I froze as rivets of rain matted my hair to my forehead and dripped from my nose. As motion came into view, my legs froze.

I'm dreaming. Gotta be...

Paul Osmond, rain-slicked jacket bundled over his hunched form, loomed over Jack thrashing in the mud. The source of the sound became clear: tired limbs slopping the dirt, an exhausted mewling escaping Jack's lips. His dirt-caked head fell sideways, eyes finding mine, and in that moment I learned an important lesson. Adults were not invincible brick-houses, fearless and all-knowing. Here lay a frightened human, same as me, with no damn superpowers in sight. Only the real world existed, gritty and grim.

Prey and predator.

Paul Osmond wriggled atop Jack like a lover as Jack's boots kicked the slop, spraying brown bursts. One shaking hand reached in my direction, fingers opening and closing, *pleading*, and the reason for his lack of energy became clear— his neck had been torn wide, and crimson gunk pumped, mixing with rain. A collection of blood-soaked mushrooms lay crushed beneath the men, glistening in blood and muck.

"Hey!"

The word came by itself, a primal reaction, and I braced for Osmond to drop Jack and leap for me. Instead, Paul appeared content with his catch, attention locked and paying me no mind. I back-peddled, scanned for a rock, hit a root, and slammed the dirt. Air whooshed from my lungs. And Paul dropped Jack.

On my back and vulnerable, I had his attention now. The hobo swayed and started forward.

With a yelp, I fought for purchase to get upright. My palms slipped in sludge thick as old Vaseline. I rolled onto my stomach and used my knees, pushing to my feet before stumbling along the path. Mud pulled my shoes, and one came free with a pop, my sock sinking into the icy mess. Still, I ran.

Wake up, wake up, wake up!

I shook my head, heart slamming, but the world didn't fade. The nightmare remained, and my brain screamed for logic. I threw a look over my shoulder as Paul gained, his stiff limbs reminding me of a mummy from some black-and-white throwback. His outstretched arms swayed, palms flashing, *wanting* me. *C'mere, Tony…wanna show you something…*

In the moonlight, his beard dripped rain, and my heart slammed as I noted one new detail: thick moss and hardened gunk clung to his face like decade-old plaster. I screamed.

Logic told me I'd watched too many late-night movies, that this was some fever-induced dream, but as Paul Osmond groaned—a sound like a man who'd just taken a punch from a steroid-ridden fighter—my skin prickled and my innards fizzed. Real as day.

"Help! Help me!"

Osmond answered with a groan, stumbling after me as my legs pumped, slipping and sliding and avoiding the river at all costs. The fern-topped bank bobbed into view and I pushed my limits, needing to be up there, back on the road and in the car's headlights. Someone would drive by, preferably Officer Richardson, and all this would end.

Can't stop at the car. He'll catch me.

I'd run home. A mile uphill at most.

I leaped at the embankment, my hands slapping into the slop but finding no purchase. A stone came free and I flung it over my shoulder, hoping to crack the bastard's face. I jumped again, and my stomach clapped the dirt. I pulled myself up like a worm, working my whole body. Sludge seeped down my shirt like cold oatmeal, and as Paul reached the bottom of the bank, he raised his arms as if to catch me. A mud slab came free and pulled me with it. I balked. Paul's upturned hands flexed.

Fall to me, Tony...Adults know best.

My fingers worked around a root and I jerked to a stop as the rainwater tried its best to work my fingers free. The root strained. I hoisted my legs up, now sideways on the bank, and dug my right foot into the mud. On the count of three, I let the root go and leaped, gaining more height. Nearly there. Paul began wailing.

My fingers found the ferns, and with their help I wriggled the last stretch, pushing to my feet on the tarmac as my breath burned my lungs. The car headlights comforted me, no longer in the darkness of the woods with a maniac, but I pictured Jack still in the forest bleeding from the neck and shaking as this lunatic prowled the thicket.

Why didn't Paul climb after me? Why wasn't he chasing me?

I didn't much care. Instead, I ran for home with tears streaming down my face and my breath wheezing. A fat stitch gnawed at my ribs and I ignored the pain, focused only on the bobbling lights of Riverside Lane, eight houses topping the mountain I called home, one bookended by an abandoned sawmill that'd taken my dad's life. I'd asked my mother why we never moved. She said their plan was to stay there for life, an idea my dad refused to budge from, and in some way, she intended to honor that. The mill created jobs for a full decade, but these days, only our homes and a few cabins remained, with that entire end of the mountain fenced off with razor wire. The cabins sat off the beaten track, and venturing into the trees wasn't an option, so I stuck to the road and tried not thinking of all the lurking dangers.

Soaked to the bone yet still sweating, I topped the hill and veered left, racing for the glow of houses, one particular light coming from my kitchen window. Steam fogged the glass, and I imagined my mother humming while putting the dinner on. Probably something I liked, for my birthday: spaghetti, lasagna, a fancy dish instead of the usual potatoes and beans. Either way, I never found out.

I banged the door and screamed, skin prickling at the darkness my home kept at bay. With the safety of my house, adrenaline began to wane, and my stomach roiled with nausea.

My mother rushed the door and swung it wide, her eyes bulging.

"Tony, what's happened? Where's Jack?"

I pushed into the hallway, the warmth of the house making me shiver. I clutched my stomach and tried not to vomit as my legs threatened to give out.

"Paul Osmond," I said, and blurted the rest in a quivering, high-pitched voice. I spoke for five minutes, my mother pale-faced and rubbing my back, her free hand to her mouth as tears raced down her cheeks. Her head shook ceaselessly as if she could wish away my words.

"He's hurt," she said. She straightened and pulled her rain-jacket from the rack, eyes feverish. She spoke too quick. "Tony, stay here, okay? I'm running to the Fowlers' to use the phone. I need Dennis Richardson."

With that, she raced out the door and slammed it, leaving me shaking in the hallway. I'd told her about the stuff all over Osmond's face, but even that fantastical fact didn't register past *Jack's hurt*. Being home, I hardly believed the story myself.

I crossed to the kitchen using the wall for support, leaving filthy streaks on the floor. A foil banner greeted me: HAPPY BIRTHDAY. Two balloons lulled to either side of the table, pinned beside a ribboned box. I didn't open that present, and the gift remains a mystery to this day.

I poured a glass of water and tried calming my breath, bringing the glass to my mouth and spilling half of it down my shirt. I tried again and took my time, managing to drink a full glass. The water helped my nerves, soothed my throat and relaxed my muscles, but I still needed to dry off or risk getting a cold. I filled a bath and waited by the toilet, sniffling back mucus and tears. I found myself surprised I wasn't going batshit. Shock, I would later find out, led to all kinds of reactions.

In the heat of the water, the mud swam away from my skin and clouded the bath. I sighed and watched the mirror fog as my pores opened. The clock ticked from the kitchen, and my brain refused to believe such nightmares lay outside. A police car would come screaming into Riverside right about now, as my mother raced down the mountain to find her battered lover held captive by a wood-lurking lunatic. Both my adult and childhood fears—real and fantastic—concocted to one terrifying beast.

"Happy birthday," I whispered, and sunk further into the tub.

After my soak I'd make my way to the living room and wait, distracting myself with the TV and my Game Boy. It'd be two hours before my mother returned and tires squealed on the drive with Dennis Richardson close behind and his blue lights flashing. They'd find me on the floor screaming, my brain finally processing what had just happened, and they'd console me. They'd shush me, then cry themselves. Our statements would come soon after, and wouldn't finish until four in the morning. I'd eventually pass out and dream of moss-covered faces. Then the real horror would begin.

The world first bared its teeth when I turned thirteen, starting with a drunkard on a riverbank.

CHAPTER TWO

THE **BUBBLE BOY'S** older brother didn't click with his classmates. At sixteen-years-old, Lee's interests tied closer to the younger kids', myself and Ben Rodgers for example. Adventures piqued his interest, and (like most kids in '97) his Game Boy, and Saturday morning cartoons. A commitment to science (begrudgingly, I'd later find out) left his peers avoiding him like a turd, but with Bubble Boy for a brother, his enthusiasm was justified. A year earlier he'd introduced me to Deep Purple and underground rock via cassette tapes, and I'd eventually owe him my life for that. He smoked, too, and although I didn't care for the habit (at least, not by that stage) Lee Stapleton was King Shit in my eyes.

"Hey, Lee."

The teen pushed from the wall using his boot and adjusted his leather jacket—two-sizes too big and dotted with patches. He smiled around a cigarette and threw me a salute. "Been waiting all day for you, man. The hell happened at your house last night?"

I stifled a yawn, feeling drained and anxious. "Richardson's still up there in case Jack comes home. He went missing. Has Allie and Nate combing the woods since six. It's a madhouse."

Lee's face dropped, cigarette dangling. "Slow down...The fuck you talkin' about? Jack's missing?"

"Sorry, my brain's scrambled. Haven't slept a wink." I started towards Rodgers' house, setting into our usual Saturday routine. We'd knock there and then move on to Jacob's, scour the woods for points of interest before retiring to Rodgers' tree house with our Game Boys and shoot the shit. Living up a mountain ghost town left little for entertainment. And Lee, as I knew, wanted to get back to his books on his brother's condition, squirreled away from his parents' disapproving eyes. *False hope*, they called it. *Fucking research*, Lee called it.

"You need to keep this to yourself, okay? Richardson says I can't tell anyone because they don't want to scare people."

"Don't want to scare people about *what*?" Excitement took control of my friend and a grin twitched his lips. A spot on his right cheek looked fit to pop. I understood my friend's buzz, though—we'd once found a dead dog and kept an eye on it for a full two weeks as it bloated, attention glued til it burst. Compared to that, last night's events were a carnival, complete with a freak show. "I saw the blue lights, man," Lee said, "heard the tires and everything. Like something from a movie."

I nodded, and Lee made an impatient *'go on, go on!'* gesture. After a breath, I told him everything, taking my time with the stuff on Paul Osmond's face, needing that part to get through. He listened as his mouth did odd twists with each new revelation. Finished, I waited for a reaction as he lit another smoke, digesting the story.

"Very funny, Tony."

My stomach fizzed. "I'm not lying, Lee. I swear it."

"Sounds like you're talkin' about a damn mossy *werewolf*. Paul Osmond...a fuckin' *monster*."

"Believe what you want, asshole. I ain't lying."

The 'monster' concept had crossed my mind—and my nightmares sure used the fodder—but if anyone could convince me otherwise, he now just scowled. "Dirt," Lee said. "Dirty face? The man slept in the fuckin' woods. Pop said he'd made up camp beneath the bridge, can you imagine? Never saw it comin' home from school but I imagined it, all curled up by the riverside. Could've gotten shit stuck to his beard n' face, sticks n' twigs n' such."

I'd thought that, too, but no. How the rain dripped and glistened..."I saw *gunk*," I said. "Like his skin was all deformed and...green. I'm *not* lying."

He studied me a moment, head cocked sideways. We'd reached Rodgers' drive. "Jesus fuckin' Christ...You're really not, are you? At least, *you* believe it. What are we doing out here then? Go back home and don't—"

"Richardson said not to panic anyone, Lee. I'll get in *shit* if you say a word. Allie and Nate and Richardson himself are out there now, they'll fix this."

"Allie and Nate, honestly?"

My friend's skepticism didn't come from nowhere. Allie and Nate walked the mountain of Riverside twice a day side by side, 'deputized' by Richardson (not officially, Richardson just called it that because of Kit and his friends vandalizing the mill and homes). The elderly couple watched the kids' every move, even taking notes some days as we played in the woods, watching from the dirt track we called a main road. I often wondered if they wrote our names and the time and what we were doing. Felt like a goddamn zoo animal most the time.

"If they're out in the woods, explains why Kit and the Doom Patrol are doin' around."

My stomach dropped. The *Doom Patrol* consisted of Tim Meyer and Eddie Pollock, two egregious little shits whose idea of a good time consisted of smacking me and my friends across the head and spitting in our lunches. They visited Kit from time to time, but those outings had become gratefully less frequent over the past year. Mostly due to Kit's father and his 'cleansing' ritual, but out here, no one spoke of that.

Dennis the Menace didn't have shit on Kit Peters.

Dennis never melted a balloon over a cut-off bottle top and fired lead pellets through his principal's car window. That hard plastic solidified the balloon opening like the mouth of a cannon, man, and with projectiles as strong as a bullets. His smirk made me grimace, but with Lee at my side, nothing would happen. Today, at least.

Rodgers' dad opened the door, his face drooping from flu, eyes puffed and red. Still, he was the man who gave me a guitar responsible for so many blisters, and in the process opened a new and life-saving world. Sick or not, Rodgers' dad kicked ass. "Boys?"

"Rodgers home?" Lee asked.

Rodgers' dad stepped outside, scanned the road and sniffed. "Not with you? Went out an hour ago, just missed him."

Lee and I exchanged a glance, and Rodgers' dad squinted. "What?"

"Nothin'," Lee said, hands in his pockets. "Thought we saw him head for Jacob's, actually. No problem."

That seemed to work, just about. "All right. Have him drop home when you see him, will ya? I was meant to take him to the dentist today but I'm still not feeling up to it. Be nice to him, will you? That damn tooth's killing him."

"Will do, Mr. Rodgers. Thanks again."

And as the door closed, my stomach flipped. "Fuckin' dentists, man. Poor Rodgers."

"Well, he ain't going today, and if he's not home, you know what that means."

"Mill?" I asked—like I even needed to. That damned building would be the bane of my existence.

"Come on."

For Kit and his friends, the sawmill had gone from local business to dare-filled delight when left unattended. I'd heard stories they'd stop-watched each other running through its dusty shell, each racing out the opposite side with tales of ghouls and slobbering crawlies. They'd never say anything about the mill in front of me, though—and especially not in front of Lee Stapleton. Whether from fear of getting in trouble or out of respect for my father, I didn't know. But I guessed the former.

"They got Rodge up there, then we gotta haul ass," Lee said, and began jogging. "Come on. Jacob can wait."

I felt bad leaving Jacob at home, especially after ditching him for the arcade, but with Rodgers in trouble, we needed to move. I'd make it up to my friend.

After passing the *faux*-deputies' home, we continued the path until we reached the cul-de-sac entrance of the mill. Trees closed in overhead, making a sun-blocked canopy as if the Earth fought to reclaim this now unused section of land, one now guarded by razor wire. Ahead, the chain-link fence glistened with morning dew and rattled as Eddie Pollock pulled the lock.

"Hey!" Lee shouted, racing forward. I slowed and caught my breath. How Lee ran after smoking so much, I never knew.

The three kids turned and squinted, and a fourth stood off to the side—Rodgers. My best friend held his right arm, red-faced from tears, and the relief washing over him filled me with confidence. Even from where I stood, I could see the welt in his cheek from that infected tooth. Lee jogged to the group.

"The fuck you doin', Kit?"

Kit Peters grinned for show, although when Eddie and Tim went home, he'd soften up and tame his attitude, mostly because beyond myself and my friends, no other kids lived here in Riverside. But with the Doom Patrol by his side? He went full bastard.

"Fuck off, asshole. Go bounce your brother for a while, eh?"

Lee's hands curled into fists, but he took a deep breath and released the tension. We had an unspoken rule when it came to mockery—thou did not talk about Kit's father's 'ritual'. Thou did not speak of Lee's Bubble Brother. And thou sure as shit did not talk about my father.

"Think it's funny pickin' on Rodgers, huh?" Lee stepped forward. "It's three-on-one here, fuckers, whatcha gonna do?"

Kit sighed. "Mind your own business, ass wipe. Nate got a lock on the mill, we're tryna get in."

Lee threw me a look that everyone caught, and heat flooded my face.

"They were gonna make me run through," Rodgers blurted. "Said I didn't wanna."

"Were not!" Kit shook his head as if this were the biggest lie he'd ever heard. "Didn't fuckin' drag you here, fat-ass. Didn't pull you along, you came yourself. Even said you'd try to get the ol' chipper goin' again!"

Eddie snickered at that, and an anvil of pain slammed my gut. Kit could be an asshole, a *real* asshole, but he'd never taken a cheap shot like that...And the words came before I even knew it. "Someday I hope that fuck-nut dad of yours keeps your head underwater for longer than a minute."

That got him. Kit's complexion drained. And Eddie and Tim backed off.

"The fuck you say, Tony?"

Lee pinched the bridge of his nose. "All right, all right. Let's stop before shit gets messy, okay? Kit, you guys do what you want, but we're takin' Rodgers and getting the hell out of here. See his face? Ever have tooth pain? No compassion, y'know that? Stay away from us, and we stay away from you."

Kit didn't answer, only watched me with narrowed, burning eyes that promised the worst pain I could imagine. I gave him the finger. Lee grabbed Rodgers and pulled him away from the group, and the tension in the air was so thick I could've served it for lunch.

"Come on," Lee said, releasing Rodgers as he led the way back to the matting of houses. I followed and prayed a rock didn't crack the back of my skull. A light rain drizzled down, and I remembered the weather warning of a coming storm. The other kids' eyes cut through the backs of our heads as we traipsed the path, and their hatred radiated as hot as the unseen sun.

Rodgers sniffled. "Thanks, guys...Eddie grabbed my arm and wouldn't let go, y'know? Said I'd yell, but he hit me a good one...Arm's still dead." He rubbed the skin to illustrate. "Still, not as bad as the pain in my mouth. Haven't slept a wink with it."

Lee slowed, his breath still fluttering with adrenaline. "Gotta stick up for yourself some, Rodge. You know that."

Rodgers kicked a pebble and stuffed his hands into his pockets. "Why's it me who's gotta change, man? Why can't they? It's not my fault I'm not like them."

"Yeah," Lee said, "well something's gotta change."

I wondered how that happened, then. Did bullies and victims just slowly part ways? Did they look back years later and recall the exact day it all changed? I clapped Rodgers' shoulder, feigning playfulness while the idea of Jack in the woods still plagued my thoughts. "Tree house later? Some Game Boy?"

That got a smile, and he sniffled. "Sounds good...Gotta stay quiet though, Dad's still bedridden. Second day of the flu, can't even move. Meant to go to the dentist's today. Hey, I can't believe you said that about Kit's father."

"Me neither."

Lee shook his head. "That was actually pretty badass, man. Thank shit it didn't come to blows."

"Hope the fuckers die in a fire," Rodgers said. "They can go suck a dick."

As we approached home, dark grey clouds threatened rain, and the sight of my house caused a shiver.

"I'll have Lorraine over within the hour to check on him, but keep him in bed and don't try clean it yourself, okay?" Officer Richardson scribbled something on a notepad before sniffling back a troublesome snot. His hands shook, the situation affecting him unlike a big city cop, but he faked confidence for my mother's sake. "Found him about a mile out from the stream, passed out in a bed of shrooms. Still no sign of Paul Osmond."

I recalled that bed of fungus, and shivered.

Jack's groans cut through the ceiling, making my hair stand on end. I'd left my friends to the tree house, opting for home under the guise of hunger and a head cold. My mom stood by the living room door, and a shaking hand went to her lips as fresh terror glistened in her eyes.

"His neck," she said. "What happened to his neck, Dennis?"

"Already told ya, that's for Lorraine to decide. And to patch. When Jack can speak, we'll know everything, all right? It's not easy, but you need to stay strong here."

"Okay...All right. I can do that."

"Good." Officer Richardson punctuated something in his notebook before tucking the paper down in his pocket. He gave me a forced smile. "Little man, you gonna be good for your momma and look after the place?"

I nodded.

"That's a good boy. Sarah, look, I'll be back in a couple of hours, okay? Goin' back down to Alison and Nate, seein' if they found this asshole yet." He glanced my way in apology for the cuss, not that I cared. "Then I've to run by the station and start my report."

Sarah scoffed. "You haven't *reported* this yet, Dennis? Goddamnit, why haven't you—"

"Easy, easy." He waved his hands in defense. "You caught me at home, all right? It was the middle of the night. I needed to wake Allie and Nate for help too, I just haven't had the time to go to town. *I'm going*, as soon as I have an update from the other two, save me two trips. I'll be back in a few hours, okay?"

My mother sniffled but nodded, clearly zoned out now.

"Okay."

He clapped my shoulder on the way out and eased the front door shut. My mother stared at me that whole time, her eyes wide as saucers and vibrating in their sockets. Richardson's engine rumbled as he took off down the mountain, and, as if on cue, Jack screamed. My mother jumped.

"Tony, help me with this, would you?"

I fumbled my words, and she snarled. "*Tony, please,* I-I don't have time for this!"

She started towards the door and grabbed my arm in the process, her nails biting into my skin.

"Richardson says to let him rest, Mom, we shouldn't go up there."

"Fuck Dennis. I can't stay down here and listen to *that* all day."

Another roar of pain from Jack seemed to agree, and my guts knotted in response. I did *not* want to go into that room, and you better believe I still wanted to tell my mom about his drinking and what he'd said to me.

She bound up the stairs, myself in tow, as my t-shirt stretched in her fist. Each step pushed an involuntary sound from her lips, as if her overflowing emotions were leaking from her mouth. She paused at the bathroom only to soak a washcloth before grabbing me again, droplets tapping the floor.

"Dennis said not to clean the wound," I reminded her.

"It's for his *face*, Tony, his *face*! I am not touching the cut."

She shouldered the door and there he lay—a pale face poking from fresh sheets. His half-closed eyes struggled to focus. Dirt caked his hair and skin, clumps of brown that could've been muck or shit and I didn't know which. My throat tightened as I studied the wound.

"Looks like a knife cut," I spoke aloud.

"It is *not* a knife," Mom said, and she rushed to the bedside. To me, it looked like blade damage—shoved and twisted, corkscrewing a dime-sized hole. Copper-brown stained his throat and shirt.

Jack's delirious eyes found my mother and he groaned, sounding like a brain-damaged geriatric.

Mom hushed him. "It's gonna be all right, Jack. I promise. Stay still now."

I winced as she wiped his forehead and water raced down his face, leaving a visible rectangle of clean skin. Jack moaned.

"Quiet now," my mother insisted, and wiped again. Slow and deliberate this time. "I'll make it all better."

I made to leave but her attention whipped in my direction. "You. Stay."

It struck me then, why I couldn't go. She was frightened. The situation might be uncontrollable, but she could damn well keep control of *me*, and that made her feel in charge. So I stayed.

I watched her clean his ashen skin. When she finished, she sighed and massaged the bridge of her nose. Jack seemed to have fallen asleep by then, and his closed eyes twitched as his chest shuddered. With the job done, some tension dissipated.

"You think it's infection?" I asked. I couldn't pull my attention from the filthy neck wound, my mother restraining (just about) to follow Richardson's orders.

"What do you mean?"

"How he's so out of it," I said. "His eyes can't even focus. Like when I caught a fever from Rodgers...I remember that, not being able to speak."

My mother whined. "Get some food and keep yourself busy, okay, Tony? Make a sandwich. Watch some TV."

The defeat in her eyes hurt. She knew she should take it easy on me but with Jack laid out before her all control had slipped. To lose Jack left only me. I didn't see that as a bad thing, hell, I prayed for it, but at that age, I didn't understand the fears of being alone. I would though, of course, and far sooner than expected, but right then my mother chose a stranger over me. And I hated her for it.

"Fine."

I stalked from the room and grabbed my Game Boy before bounding down the stairs. I considered staying in my room and locking the door but instead chose the living room, the distance giving me peace of mind. I imagined as the night wore on I'd hear Jack groaning and my mother crying as I lay only a staircase away, that fever and infection oozing beneath the doorframe to reach me. I shivered. After making a cheese sandwich, I locked the living room door—*just in case*—and buckled down on the couch. After trying the handheld but unable to concentrate, I clicked the television but only got talk shows and sports. I switched off the set, and my eyes fell to the six-string in the corner.

Rodgers' dad, like I said, built us that tree house two summers ago, but that wasn't the only thing he did for us kids. Six months previous, he'd given me a battered old acoustic with a fresh set of strings, and after being introduced to Deep Purple by Lee, I managed to pluck out a tune or two by ear. I imagined he'd given me the guitar out of pity, knowing my dad always wanted to learn, but either way his intentions didn't matter. Mom called me a natural but my face always flushed when people listened and I'd only play alone. Now seemed like a better time than any.

I pushed from the couch and swiped the instrument, accidentally knocking the body off the TV cabinet. Not to worry, the body looked like shit to begin with, but to me only added character. Each scrape and pock like a soldier's battle wound. I positioned my hands on the frets for an E, and as Jack groaned in agony from upstairs, I strummed. Then I smiled.

The music took me away, brought me to a soundscape where a screaming man and even my own mother couldn't reach. I'd learned a handful of chords from trial and error and ran them with ease, my fingers desperate for a good racket. My pinky slipped and made a quirky chord (what I'd later find out to be a 7th), but right then I only knew it prickled my arm hair. My body hummed with excitement—this didn't sound like any tune I'd heard before, and as a smile spread across my face I came to realize I'd made the melody myself. An idea came for lyrics, and I began to hum. It was the first time I attempted to sing or write.

My hands cramped and the soft pads of my fingers burned but I played on, the possibilities as wide as an ocean, and a new world presented itself to me. A world I created, one I could control. Somewhere nice.

After an unknown amount of time (the fun of music apparently had the ability to warp time and space) a smell crinkled my nose and I stopped mid-strum. The cheese sandwich caught my attention, untouched and forgotten. I frowned as my eyes drew to the window, where dark clouds rolled across the sky. The clock read almost eight. I'd been lost to my sonic world all day.

Jack's moans whipped me back to reality, and any good cheer I had gathered faded fast. I set aside the guitar and ate my sandwich, fingers shaking from both hunger and a lack of sleep. My stomach roiled at the food, but I managed to keep it down. Afterwards, I unlocked the living room door for a piss break.

I crept to the stairs, the darkness of the hallway resurfacing every fear I'd grown to know over the past couple of days. I pictured Paul Osmond busting the front door down and grabbing me as I kicked and screamed and got dragged across the threshold. I wondered if my mother would care and scolded myself for such a selfish idea. With a shiver, my foot found the first step, and the wood creaked. I winced and listened. With no response, I eased myself up using the banisters, mindful of any movement from my mother's bedroom. At the doorway, I stopped and listened.

"He'll be back soon, and then this will all go away, okay?"

My mother spoke in hushed tones, comforting herself more than Jack by the sounds of it. An idea made my stomach plunge: hadn't Richardson said he'd be back within a few hours? That was in the morning. And wasn't Lorraine (a vet by trade, but we were in no position to be picky in Riverside) meant to stop by this afternoon? Neither had shown, and that realization made my nerves fizzle.

"Mom?"

I eased open the door, and my eyes widened. Jack's face glistened in the darkness, strands of wiry hair jutting from odd-colored blotches. His patchy skin reminded me of cheese. As his head shook side to side, my hand fell from the handle.

From his mouth poked a crooked, jagged tooth.

My mom screamed. "Get out of here!"

I spun and slammed the door shut, my bladder threatening to loosen right then and there. I made it to the toilet but only just about. I held the bowl for support, my legs shaking and my breath fast. I *had* seen what I thought, I didn't doubt, and a scream threatened to boil over and rip from my throat. Done pissing, I didn't bother washing my hands. Instead, I bound down the steps two, three at a time. I scooped a steak knife from the kitchen, a blade the size of my forearm, and bolted myself back in the living room, double-checking the lock. Outside the window lay darkness, and I couldn't chance Paul Osmond finding me alone. Paul, I thought, or Richardson, Nate, Allie, Lorraine—god knows who the madman had found by this stage. And if he'd done to them what he'd done to Jack...

That tooth.

"What the actual *fuck*?" I spoke too loud, my own voice slapping this all home: reality had flipped, and no matter how *hard* I pinched myself, nothing would change. I'd never wake. The safety curtain that youth provided had fallen, and only stone cold and heartless reality remained.

Goodbye Saturday mornings watching TV, so long Game Boy sessions with my friends, and farewell to laughter and the tree house and anything else that brought me joy. With a steak knife to my chest and my mother in her room with an abomination, I was no longer a kid.

I clutched the knife and peered from the window at the mysterious new world beyond. A purple-black sky rolled with pregnant clouds above swaying pines, and the highway down in the distance seemed forever away. Lights as small as pinholes twinkled as cars zipped along, never stopping to turn, because why would they? Only folks to venture up Riverside *lived* here, and we were all at home.

A figure shuffled from the left then and I darted to the light switch, plunging the living room into darkness before jogging back to the sill. My breath fogged the glass and I shifted left, clearing a view and breathing through my nose. The man hunched despite the night being clear, throwing one leg ahead of the other as his arms swung by his side, his head lolled back on the stalk of his neck, and his mouth open.

"That tooth..."

The jagged nub poked past his lips like a spider leg the length of my middle finger, coiled and sharp, and just the one. I gasped as his head swung in my direction, briefly pausing. He yelled, sounding like a just-woke drunk, and then, thankfully, moved on. My muscles eased up some. I let out a shaking breath as my fingers relaxed around the knife hilt. I recognized him instantly.

As Paul Osmond crept along Riverside under the cloak of night, I prayed for morning and brightness and my old life back. I prayed for Jack to die and for Richardson to drive into our yard with the dawn, bringing good news and coffee. But none of that happened.

The screaming started an hour later, and at four A.M., Jack fell down the stairs.

I huddled by the couch clutching the kitchen knife as he climbed to his feet and slogged to the other side of the door, the bold sounds painting a perfect picture in my mind. The wood crackled as he leaned against it, breathing heavily through his nose—*smelling me*. He raked a hand across the grains, and pushed and pushed and pushed.

Chapter Three

"Mom!"

She never answered. Jack's attack on the living room door didn't let up. He hadn't tried the handle, or slammed his shoulder and shattered the wood. He never kicked or punched, only *pushed*—and scratched, and moaned.

Braindead came to mind and didn't feel far off. I'd seen Jack angry before, watched him pound his shovel-fists against a table in frustration, and if he'd wanted to, this door made for little work. Yet he only scratched and moaned as we approached the second hour.

The sun painted the sky an orange-pink through the fogged-up window, and I realized he wasn't getting in—or out, for that matter. If he couldn't figure the handle, then the front door's bolt wasn't happening, either. I remembered the backdoor lock, and my skin prickled. The lock broke the previous month and Mom still hadn't gotten around to paying for a replacement. With enough elbow grease, that door was coming clean off.

"Oh, shit..."

But what *might* happen took a backseat to what *would* happen: staying here meant starvation, or Jack eventually getting through. Richardson wasn't coming back. The image of the cop lying in the woods atop a mess of mushrooms with his throat shredded solidified my escape plan. The screams from the other homes continued, but as the hour wore on, they'd shriveled. I pictured Lee, Rodgers—hell, even Kit—with their homes turned to the same living nightmares as mine, their parents the same as Jack. Then I thought of my mom. And of Jack's gnarled tooth.

"*Mom!*"

Jack's scratching grew frantic and I jabbed the blade towards the door. If he could see I'd hope he'd think twice about getting inside.

"Get away from me, man! *Go away!*"

I could race down the mountainside, get on the highway, a half-hour hike through the woods at best. Once there I'd thumb a ride and get the driver to take me to a police station, let everyone know. Get emergency services out here.

I crossed to the window and clutched the handle, the metal icy with morning chill. I squinted through my reflection at the deserted road ahead. Now was as good a time as any.

With a grunt, I pushed the window open and the frame crackled as I eased one knee to the sill, placing the knife beside me. I took a moment, the cold morning spilling across me, and studied the outdoors. A crow took flight from the pines and I envied its freedom. With a count of three, I eased onto the ledge before hopping out, landing in the drive with a thump. Nothing from Jack. Good. I reached around for the knife and clutched the weapon until my hands shook, then I pushed the window shut again.

Scanning the yard, my breath wafted away in a visible pillar. A wind swayed the trees out in the forest, but beyond that lay no signs of movement. My plan could work. I crept to the road, skin prickling at the low temperature, and I cursed myself for not taking a coat. Mom would've scolded me for such foolishness. A hot tear stung my eye at such a simple thought, but I forced myself to move. I'd get warm somehow, but right then I needed only to reach the highway.

To the right lay the other homes, the eight houses spaced widely apart, and movement caught my eye from Kit's. A shape in the doorway shifted, too far to discern.

Then moaning drifted on the breeze.

I turned with my teeth gritted, towards the winding road through the forest and the highway beyond—to where

Richardson, Allie, and Nate now waited. The image of Osmond shuffling past my house only confirmed my fears that the policeman had been caught. Had it been the other way round, cop cars would have swarmed Riverside with blaring sirens. But that hadn't happened. I had, however, seen Paul Osmond.

My best chance lay beyond the woods.

Jogging, I took one last glance for signs of my mom at the house and kept to the grass, avoiding gravel and attracting attention. At the forest I slipped behind a pine and took a breather, listening for movement within the thicket. Wind hissed through the branches, but I heard no steps, no snapping twigs. Osmond and Jack acted clumsily, and if Richardson and his team succumbed to the same fate, I doubted subtlety crossed their infected minds. Which led to another thought: was this an infection? A disease? I believed so, but couldn't allow myself much time to think.

I pushed from the trunk—and yelped as a hand snapped at my face and I tripped and the knife went flying.

I scrambled on all fours, reaching for my weapon as Allie shuffled quicker now, her legs dragging the foliage, one bent at an odd angle, her face a dark matting of slick fur that shone in the low morning light. She let out a groan as I scooped my weapon and scrambled to my feet, jogging backward with the knife raised.

"Get away from me!"

Allie didn't listen as she raised her arms and her head fell back. There I caught a clear view of that gnarled appendage bulging from her gums, the other teeth crooked or gone entirely. Her stiff limbs picked up speed, excited by my presence— *needing* to get me—and I matched her pace for pace.

"Allie, it's me," I pleaded. "Stop!"

That last word came out a shivering mess and tears slipped down my cheeks. The old woman never liked me, never liked any of us kids, but I prayed I could get through. I liked to think I could act brave, like Spiderman or Wolverine in the comics, but at thirteen, I'd only ever been in one fight and that'd left me with a plum eye. I was no hero, and I waved that knife like a madman.

"Allie..."

Something rustled behind me and I spun as Nate rushed from a grove, his outstretched fists pulsing with anticipation, his face the same pulpy, mossy mess as Allie's. I screamed and dashed back towards the houses on instinct, praying Rodgers' dad or some other adult could make this all better. My chest ached from running, the elderly couple hot on my heels as they hauled their rigid limbs through the dry leaves, heads thrown back so those misshapen teeth pointed right at me like accusatory fingers.

Foliage gave way to tarmac and I pelted for the homes with my knife swinging—not like I had the guts to use the damn thing, anyway. I passed my own house, and Jack's outline in the hall drew a shivering breath. The frosted glass hid his features but his jerking movement was all I needed to know my house was off bounds. My mother lay upstairs, possibly bleeding out, and despite her short temper, I prayed she'd lost consciousness. That way would be easier. There was nothing I could do.

Behind me, another groaning mess joined Allie and Nate, shuffling from the tree-line like something from a Romero movie, and I yelled as I noted the freak's clothing. Richardson's voice congealed with the others in one off-key chorus.

"*Help!* Goddamnit, somebody help me!"

A shape shot through Rodgers' yard then, coming to intercept me on the road but hidden by the bushes. I wished for Mr. Rodgers to appear at the foot of the drive with a shotgun raised, just like in a movie, and I prayed he'd keep the monsters at bay while I raced into the house and to safety. The rising sun currently painting the sky pink made the situation all the more surreal.

Instead of Mr. Rodgers, Jacob skidded to a stop in the middle of the road and waved me on, his face tight with fear— the kind of fear no twelve-year-old should ever know.

"Run, Tony," he yelled, the words mushy and joined with spit. "Hurry."

I felt awful having ditched Jacob for the arcade, that he stood here helping me, risking his life in this hell. Ten yards away, he took off back through Rodgers' garden and I followed suit, stumbling across wet grass and almost going over twice. When Jacob raced around the side of the house and not inside, my worries bubbled. Rodgers' front door stood open, darkness cloaking the hall, and the door itself hung shattered and limp on a hinge. I prayed Mr. Rodgers' hadn't turned, not like Jack, but with a better idea of where Jacob was leading me, I knew the real world didn't punish the bad and reward the good. We were headed for the tree house.

Dad's still stuck in bed, I heard Rodgers say. *Second day of the flu, can't even move...*

As I slipped around the side of the house, Jacob panted and slowed for me to keep up. He turned to speak just as the bushes rustled beside him. Lee's father smashed through and snatched Jacob in a bearhug.

Jacob thrashed and screamed and threw his head back, connecting with the man's chest as I skidded to a stop. But Lee's father paid the boy no mind, holding him easy as a cat would a tired mouse, and his head fell forward. I screamed, but it didn't matter, that nasty tooth smashed into Jacob's neck all the same. And the boy roared.

I rushed Lee's dad with my knife, screaming my throat raw and swinging the blade in a vicious arc. The knife embedded in his thigh. I got no resistance as the metal parted skin and muscle, and yet the man didn't react. His groaning became nauseously eclectic as he gorged on my friend's neck.

Jacob turned ashen, eyes fluttering to milky whites as I pulled the blade free and stabbed again, this time sinking the blade into his side. The impact roiled my stomach—tissue tearing and giving way. As Jacob's cries threatened to pop my eardrums, I wiggled the knife hilt, ignoring hot crimson raining across my fists, but the knife wouldn't budge.

"Tony!" Jacob's voice raised an octave, still maintaining a lisp. "Please, help me!"

My friend's final cry gave way to a constant ringing in my ears. I back-peddled as Lee's father dropped the boy like a discarded doll and turned to me now, each movement seeming slowed down to my chugging brain. His grotesque face shone in the dawn, and that knotted tooth dripped red. Blindspots plagued my vision and morning air cooled and dried the blood on my hands, a strange detail to note in my confusion but there it was. As Richardson, Allie, and Nate rounded the corner, Jacob's body began to convulse, and natural tendency moved me. I raced to the back garden, the same yard I'd spent countless days playing and laughing and enjoying my time with friends. The same garden a certain tree house awaited.

Lee's father joined my chase, arms outstretched same as the others, but with my knife still buried in his ribcage. I prayed I wouldn't pass out before I reached safety, as I imagined all those knotted teeth ripping my throat to shreds. However, movement within the tree house window ignited my hope.

I leaped at the hodgepodge of crooked 2x4s in the trunk, a splinter instantly biting my right palm. I sucked a breath and scrambled for the structure above, muted thumping coming from the latch as my friends clamored to get it open. Below, the neighbors slammed against the tree just inches from my feet, four hideous faces with bulging eyes and pulsing palms. They longed I'd fall, slip into their eager grasps.

"Tony!"

My foot slipped and I gasped as my leg dangled a moment before finding a plank and locking tight. My heart slammed and my breath wouldn't catch. My shaking hands whitened around a 2x4, and overhead, the hatch lifted. Lee and Rodgers peered down, their expressions as shocked as my own and clenched with alarm.

"Move it, man, come on, move!"

I clambered the last of the planks and accepted Lee's outstretched hand, my stomach lurching as he pulled me inside the hut. The trapdoor slammed and I rolled onto my back, blinking at the plywood ceiling while my breath struggled. The hardened blood on my hands had chipped and I lay my palms across my chest, the damned splinter now burning like molten lava. Then the tears came.

"It's all right," Lee said. He kneeled beside me and patted my shoulder. "You're here now, okay?"

I nodded but a tea-kettle cry denied my words, my body shaking with sheer force. "My mom," I managed. "She's upstairs and I can't get to her and Jack's in the hallway and Richardson came out of the woods with Allie and Nate, and your dad and Jacob just...Oh god...Jacob..."

Lee sniffled, eyes red, and wiped behind his glasses with the sleeve of his jacket. That jacket appeared too big now, as if it weren't so cool after all, just some cosmetic, defensive cover-up, and I saw Lee in a different light for the first time. Here was a terrified kid, same as me. "We saw," he said. "You don't need to tell us."

"What the fuck..."

I pushed my palms into my eyes, the darkness soothing, and waited until my chest stopped heaving to remove them. When I did, Rodgers sat huddled in the far corner, knees to his chin.

"Your dad?" I asked.

Rodgers just shook his head and closed his eyes. I didn't ask any more, didn't need to.

Outside, more voices joined the slobbering choir, and I imagined every soul of Riverside shuffling about the Rodgers' garden, their deformed faces covered in green splotches as a single, knobbed tooth jutted from every one of their open mouths. I pictured their necks torn to shreds, and their eyes milky and lifeless. Were Jack and Mr. Rodgers out there now, too? My mom?

I shuddered. With Lee and Rodgers both lost in thought, I scooted to the table, our only piece of furniture. Atop lay a scattering of comics, back-issues of *Casper, X-Men,* and *Sandman.* An eclectic collection. A beanbag, faded and damp and found in a dump, sat slumped in the corner. I shifted to it and the beads gave way to my weight. Six Mason jars peppered the shelves running the four walls, each with a single candle inside, the glass blackened from use. Rodgers' dad had warned us about candles, and we took his words to heart, never lighting them for longer than half-hour stints, mainly relying on flashlights we always took home afterward for fear of mold. I wondered how long we'd be trapped here, and prayed Lee had his lighter.

Three sleeping bags lay bunched by Rodgers (our 'cotton worms', as we called 'em), and I felt a moment of gratefulness at the break we'd been granted—little as it was. We had somewhere to sleep. We had shelter. We had each other.

"Jacob..." Rodgers' sudden cry gave me a jump and I shuffled to my friend's side, placing a hand on his back.

"I'm so sorry," I said. "I tried, I did. I had a knife, man, *a damn knife,* and I—"

My eyes fell to Lee and I shut my damn mouth. For everything that could've happened, I never imagined something as bizarre as this...I'd stabbed his father in the fucking ribs.

"You tried your best," Lee said, and relief washed over me. The last thing I needed was him angry at me. How he spoke, his lack of expression, told me shock had gratefully taken my friend under its wing, too, but I worried for Rodgers.

"This happen to Jack?" Lee asked.

I nodded, and after my stomach settled, I came clean, filling them in on the night before. I told them of Richardson's warning.

"But you knew," Rodgers said, speaking for the first time. His brow creased as he shifted away from my touch. "If you'd have told Lee and Jacob yesterday, then we could've stopped all this...We could've gone to the police."

I felt as if I'd been gut-punched. Rodgers was right. I *could've* stopped this. If I hadn't gotten lost in my music and remembered to come meet my friends, we could've formed a plan. Jacob might still be alive, then. Our parents might still be alive.

"I'm so sorry..." That's all I managed, and as Lee patted my back for comfort, more tears came. "I didn't mean to...I-I didn't know what to do."

Rodgers returned his attention to the floor, clearly done with the conversation, and I silently thanked God for not allowing a fight. I didn't want to hurt my best friend. And with Lee to help us now, with all of us here (*except Jacob...*) we'd find a way out.

"The police will come," Lee offered, but not sounding entirely convinced. "They'll have to. No way this can go unnoticed."

"We're up a mountain," Rodgers mumbled, eyes to the crusted floor. He winced as his hand shot to his cheek. "Ever see anyone come up this way except for us? Everyone who lives here? No. Me neither. Richardson is one of them out there...I think I can even make out his voice."

Lee snarled but kept his cool. "Someone *will* come, Rodgers. We have to do whatever we need to until that time. And part of that is having confidence, okay? There'll be time to absorb the shock, but right now we need to stay strong."

"What about food?"

Rodgers' question jarred us both, and we shared a brief look of worry.

"When it comes to it, we'll sort it," Lee said. "For now, we wait."

Rodgers sniffled. "Wait for *them* to get up here?"

I'd never seen my friend act this way, but then again, I'd never seen his life thrown upside down, either. Never so much as a hiccup in Rodgers' short days. I envied him for that, but always remembered I'd benefited from his cushy life, too, having his dad build us this tree house, for example. And for giving me my guitar. A guitar which now sat on the couch at home, gathering dust next to my Game Boy and an empty sandwich plate. A rise from our neighbors crawled across my skin.

"Jesus, will they ever just shut the fuck up?" Rodgers threw us a frantic look, his eyes shining. "Seriously."

"Let them draw attention," Lee said. "Hopefully someone down the mountain will hear."

"That's *miles* away, Lee, for god's sake! Can't even hear the cars on the highway from here, think yelling will help?"

I wanted to hit Rodgers then, wanted to smash the anvil he was strapping to our hopes in his face. Then a bang made us jump. Something whacked the tree.

"The hell's that?"

I shuffled to the window and Rodgers grabbed my shirt. "Do *not* let them see you, Tony, okay?"

I wrenched myself free and adjusted my clothes. "I won't. But if that's someone here to help, we need to let them know where we are."

He nodded and I peered out the window. My stomach plummeted.

Despite their deformities, I recognized each and every face milling about below. Rodgers' dad fell about in an awkward circle, his arms limp and that shining tooth jutting from his tossed-back head. Around him stalked Allie and Nate, lost wanderers lacking in necessities. Richardson, however, stood still, blinking at the trunk, as if the cogs of his mind struggled to move. I wondered what he thought—what they *all* thought—in that state. If they thought at all. They wanted to reach us, but climbing the tree never crossed their minds, or were they even capable of such a feat? I'd watched their stiff limbs quicken as they caught sight of me, but on ground. Jack couldn't even use a door handle. For now, at least, I considered the tree house safe.

Something hit the tree again. A dull *whack*.

"The hell is it, Tony?"

I shushed my friend and scanned the house. Movement caught my eye, but whatever it was darted back around the corner.

"Hold on...Oh, holy shit."

Kit leaped into the backyard as Lorraine, the local vet, chased him with outstretched arms, herding him straight for the gathering by the tree. I noticed the cause of noise then: Kit's homemade slingshot.

As he ran, Kit pulled something from his front pocket, slipped it inside the balloon before pulling the rubber tight. With a yell, he released the projectile and it blurred through the air before shooting through Lorraine and whacking the house. She slopped forward but kept moving, undeterred.

"It's Kit," I announced, skidding to my knees by the hatch.

Rodgers clutched my arm. "The hell you doing, Tony?"

"Jesus, Rodgers, you can't be serious?" My mouth fell open. "We gotta get him up here."

"*No fucking way!* We lost Jacob trying to get *you* up here. Kit's on his own, man."

"Rodgers, goddamnit." Lee crossed the room and grabbed the boy in a vicious hold, keeping him from stopping me. He craned his neck back, avoiding the attempted head-butts. "That's it, wear yourself down, Rambo."

"The hell off me, Lee, he's on his own!"

"Tony, fuckin' hurry."

I nodded and undid the lock, throwing open the hatch. Below me, our neighbors' eyes widened as they shuffled to the trunk, peering up. Heads thrown back, they thumped against the tree, their feet moving in no particular pattern. Moving on instinct. Moving with hunger.

I cleared my throat. "*Kit, hurry it up!*"

A projectile zipped through Nate's neck and the elderly man thumped to his knees as a crimson stream jetted from his wound and painted the wood. Instead of slamming his hands to the gash like a normal person would, Nate simply reached towards *me*, as if he could somehow reach me with just a *little* more luck, as thick, red gunk continued dribbling down his chest.

Kit moved faster than I'd ever seen, launching himself at the 2x4s as shaking hands snatched thin air. He kicked out and connected with Lee's father's head, knocking the man over. Then he scrambled up the trunk, spilling bark on the gathering below. And Allie grasped his foot.

"Kit!"

His eyes found me, bright with panic, and he smashed her in the forehead to no avail. She groaned and pulled, desperately prying him from the tree.

"Goddamnit..." I pushed from the trapdoor and ignored Rodgers' useless thrashing in Lee's arms. The kid could fight all day and never get loose. The bizarreness of the situation refused to register in my brain as my eyes fell to the Mason jars. A bad plan but a plan nonetheless.

"Tony, the hell are you doing?" Rodgers spat. I ignored him and scooped the glass, headed for the ladder. Kit still struggled in the old woman's grasp, and Richardson had now joined the fight. His greedy hands opened and closed just short of the boy's leg.

I lowered the glass out the door, hovered it above the woman's head, and prayed my aim straight.

"Kit, when I count to three, press yourself to the trunk, got it? Need you out of the way as much as you can be."

Kit bared his teeth. "Just drop that damn thing, Tony, for fuck sake!"

"Okay."

I mustered all my strength and pelted the Mason jar. The glass sailed in an arc, suspended in mid-air for a brief second before crashing across Allie's face and raining in shards. She stumbled back, blinking away the specs caught in her hair as Kit clambered the 2x4s and grabbed my outstretched hand. I pulled him inside.

Just like me, the boy fell to his back and panted as I slammed the trapdoor and re-did the lock, my skin prickling. Only a few steep meters and lumber separated us from the mouths below. From whatever the hell our neighbors had become.

Lee released Rodgers, and the boy adjusted his denim jacket before stomping to the beanbag. He glared at Kit panting on the floor, eyes burning with uncut anger.

"Now we've to deal with him, huh?"

I sighed. "Just shut the fuck up, Rodgers, seriously. Just *shut up.*"

Lee folded his arms in disgust. "Think about Jacob out there, Rodge. Would you feel so good if Kit ended up the same?"

The question slapped me with guilt, but I knew we'd morn our friend when the time came. In the thick of it, only the present remained.

"He sure as shit wouldn't save *me* if things were different."

Kit didn't answer, still catching his breath.

"But things aren't different," I said. "None of that matters, man. Can we just get through this?"

"Except Jacob. Jacob won't get through it."

"Right," I said, and my voice hitched. "Jacob won't get through it, you're right. Now where do we go from there?"

Unable to answer, Rodgers turned his rage on Lee. "You. Don't you ever handle me like that again, hear me, fucker? Not in my house."

"Or what?" Lee said, shaking his head in disbelief. "You'll throw us out, that it?"

Rodgers gritted his teeth and folded his arms across his knees. As tears slipped down his cheeks, his eyes faded far away. I suspected the nightmare (as with me) hadn't quite clicked yet. Part of him still believed if he pinched, *pinched real hard*, then he'd snap awake in bed, feverish and panting. All just a bad dream...one caught from his father's flu or from his bad tooth.

But as the day wore on, we learned better. We'd never wake from this.

CHAPTER FOUR

"MY DAD..." KIT wiped his eyes and sniffled. "I locked my room, like every night, just in case he decides to drink too much...But this time...this time he didn't knock the door for hours, that's how it always starts. He just...banged against it. Moaning...Moaning and scratching the wood, *raking his hands down*. Over and over and over and..."

"It's all right," I said. "I had the same thing with Jack."

He let out a shaking breath. "It's just...My sister, man. Josie."

As hitches wracked Kit, I shared a look with Lee and Rodgers. We all knew Josie, the sweet little girl all of six who enjoyed playing out front and sticking her tongue through the gap in her teeth. She never failed to wave at any passing car, missing tooth on show for all.

"I heard her screaming," Kit explained. "But not for long. Didn't take long. Found myself in the hallway, just standin' there, didn't even realize I'd unlocked my door until it was too late...old man came hobbling out of her room with his face messed up and drippin'...Jesus...Someone knocked something over downstairs, then. Didn't care to stick around and find out who. Back in the room I just screamed and he...he raked the door over and over. More dishes crashin' downstairs. Heard all the commotion outside and knew help wasn't comin'. Pieced that together when I didn't see the cops light the place up red and blue."

"You get out your window?" Lee asked.

"Yeah. Same branch as always. Made sure I'd stocked up first." He turned out his pocket, and seven lead pellets rolled about his palms. "Anywhere to put these?"

"Here." Surprising us, Rodgers fetched a plastic container and dumped the contents to the floor. He handed the blue box to Kit before returning to his corner, good deed done. Still, it was a move in the right direction, and my worries about his mental state eased some. The pellets drummed like rain into the container.

"What about you?" Kit asked. "Your mom's boyfriend started this."

"No."

As all eyes fell on me, I cleared my throat. "It was Paul Osmond, man. Found him out in the woods last night. Jack got out of the car and followed him down by the riverbank and he...he got attacked. I saw it all. Ran home. My mom called Richardson."

"But you brought Jack home?" Lee asked, his brow drawn together. "He was okay?"

"Richardson found him, drove him home before going back out with Allie and Nate to scan the woods. At first, he seemed just sick. Then he took a turn. Lorraine was meant to stop by and check on him but she never made it. Richardson was meant to phone it in but..."

"But what?" Rodgers asked.

"But he went looking for Osmond first, wanted to bring him into the station. Nate and Allie were out there with him, too... but I guess Paul found them first."

The moaning intensified from underneath the floorboards, and the image of Paul Osmond ripping into the elderly couple's throats blared in my mind. I squeezed the bridge of my nose and took a breath. Then I said, "There's no one coming."

As we fell silent, my friends' faces paled. We digested the news a moment, and the sound outside became all too familiar. I wondered if we'd acclimatize to the noises, like how people who live out near airports do. Then I wondered how long it'd last. Days? Weeks? Months? I prayed we even had hours.

"I hit my dad."

All eyes fell on Rodgers, and he spoke to the floor. To a person *through* the floor, I suspected. "Someone broke in around two in the mornin'. Fell through the front window pane. I wet my—" He caught himself and took a beat. "I ran into the hall screaming for Pop and saw someone hobble on into his room...Just a shadow in the darkness. Don't know what I was thinking, maybe I could protect him? I ran after them, screaming...when I reached the doorway, *my dad* was screamin'. Never heard his voice so high. Didn't know he could *go* that high...Lying in bed with his hands beating that shadow man's back. Looked like the stranger was *kissin'* him, I swear, but I heard the screaming and knew that wasn't happening. His mouth was clear. Whatever it was, it was bad, though, 'cause I heard this...*slopping...*" He looked to us to make sure we all knew what he meant. We did. "Fuckin' flu, man, had him weaker than an old dog. He couldn't fight back. He couldn't...just screamed and I couldn't take it. I never knew a grown up so *hysterical*. So like me."

Lee crossed the floor and put his arm around the boy's shoulder and, this time, Rodger's didn't fight. Instead, he pressed his head to his knees and sniffled. "Then that man came at me. I slammed my dad's door and held it shut. Didn't need to pull as hard as I thought, though, 'cause the idiot couldn't even work the handle." He let out a humorless laugh. "I just kept screaming for help, pullin' on that door and looking over my shoulder every two seconds, sure as shit another freak'd come up the stairs and grab me."

There it was again, the word 'freak'. I supposed we'd found a name.

"About a half hour later I heard my dad moan and thump from the bed. I screamed his name and heard all the commotion, thought Pops had beaten the man to shit. Thought maybe he'd finally found his strength, y'know?...'Cause that's what I saw in my mind, see. That's what I wanted to believe. But then I opened the door."

Rodgers looked to me, willing something I couldn't give, and continued. "My dad fell out, just collapsed on top of me. I felt all this *moss* ticklin' my face, like Pops hadn't shaved. And the *smell*, this *organic ripe* stench. Then my eyes adjusted in the dark, and his fucking face looks like gone-off cheese, bumpy and wet and wrong. And then this big fuckin' tooth comes out nearly reachin' my nose. Grazed against it." He shivered before taking a breath. "I just about got from under him and then the stranger was chasing me. Stumblin' from the room with his arms out like a mummy in one of those old-style movies. He sure as shit could move when he wanted to."

I recalled Allie in the woods, how she'd shot after me.

Arms out like a mummy in one of those old-style movies

"Got halfway down the stairs when my dad got up and started walkin' the same as the shadow man. Looked like an act, in a way, like they were pretendin'. But I knew they weren't. Pop had really went for my neck...I had my old man's blood soakin' through my shirt to prove it."

He flicked out his clothes in demonstration and we all nodded. Lee went to the window.

"How's it looking out there?" I asked, giving Rodgers a break.

"You don't wanna know."

"Come on, Lee." Rodgers made to get up and Lee's eyes widened. "Rodgers, sit down. *Please.*"

My friend cocked his head and his complexion dulled. "He's...he's out there, isn't he?"

"He is," Lee said, attention back to the outdoors. "And you don't want to see, all right?"

Rodgers didn't give an answer, just curled back up, retreating into himself.

"Who else?" Kit asked.

Lee cleared his throat. "Allie, Nate, Officer Richardson... My...my dad. My mum." His voice rose and his throat clicked, but he pushed on. "Jack, Paul Osmond, too, up near the corner of the house, near Jacob."

"Stop," Rodgers spat. "I don't care anymore, just...stop."

Lee eased from the window, his shoulders slumping. "Sorry. I didn't mean to..."

"It's all right," I said. "Just...hard to hear."

I wondered about my mom, and the idea she might've escaped entered my mind. Could she still be in the house, maybe locked up in her room? She might have trusted me enough to lock myself downstairs and done the same, staying quiet as a field mouse so Jack never found her. My stomach fizzed at the concept, but something deep down told me not to wish too hard. The more my hopes heightened, the harder I'd fall. Still, maybe...

"We could try talkin' to 'em?" Rodgers suggested.

Lee scoffed. "Rodge, I don't mean to burst your bubble, but you saw what my dad did to Jacob. They're not themselves."

"Then who are they, smart ass?"

"I don't know...but they're something else."

Kit adjusted himself to face Lee. "You're a smart guy. What *do* you think's happening here?"

The fact that Kit hadn't called Lee a nerd both pleased and worried me. He wasn't acting himself, and I wondered if that was due to genuine gratefulness on account we'd saved his life, or if he was playing an angle here. For all my life, Kit had berated Lee, Rodgers, and myself. This wasn't normal, but then again, nothing was.

"You know what they look like," Rodgers muttered, "we're all thinkin' it."

Lee blew a breath. "Like if werewolves were made of moss."

"Um-hmm...and like them old black and white *ghoul* things."

"Zombies," I said.

Kit shook his head. "For God's sake. There's *somethin'* wrong with them, but *zombies* and *werewolves*? What about that damn *tooth* they got comin' from their mouths? Lee, you gotta have *some* guess."

Lee picked a splint from the table. "Kit, I'm not a scientist who can concoct some special potion and save the day...we don't live in a fuckin' movie."

"Sure as shit feels like it," Kit said. "But you gotta know something we don't."

Lee eased himself back to the bean bag with a sigh. "Unfortunately, I don't. The only thing I can think of is some kinda parasite."

"How'd you mean?" I asked.

"That *thing* coming from their gums. Looks like a tooth but I never seen a damn tooth that size, so, y'know, like, *twisted*." He illustrated in the air with his finger. "*Could be* a parasite, spreading itself through a bite."

"Anything like that ever come up in nature?" Rodgers asked. A familiar routine took place, and it almost made me feel normal again: Lee in the beanbag, Rodgers questioning him about all sorts of things, fascinated by new knowledge as he tapped away on his Game Boy. Except the Game Boy had been replaced by a blood-stained shirt and desperate eyes.

"There's the damn book." Lee pointed to a hardback by the comics. "Feel free to scan and find out yourself."

"Come on, give us something here."

"*Look for yourselves*," Lee repeated, his eye twitching. "I'm not some fuckin' go-to jukebox of scientific knowledge. I'm *sixteen*, for Christ's sake. And *you*, out of all people, know why I have that damn book here in the first place."

"Speaking of which," Kit said. "Is your brother out there?"

"My brother..." Lee's face twitched as a redness rose in his cheeks. "My brother's in a goddamn *balloon* in our living room, Kit, which you very well fuckin' know. You see him out there? You *ever* seen him outdoors? You know damn well he's not out there."

"Lee, I'm sorry." Kit sounded sincere, but I wasn't quite buying it. Not yet. "Just...didn't mean nothin' by it, all right?"

"Sure." He shook his head and put two fingers on his wrist, pulse-checking. Then he exhaled. "Look, I'm sorry, guys. I have no answers, okay? Moss and shit growin' across people's faces? I mean, I can't even see if it's covering their entire bodies. I have no idea. I don't even know what purpose it'd serve. They sure as shit *look* like mangy green werewolves, but it's broad daylight and that goes against the whole *moon* thing so...I just don't know. And that gangly tooth? All I'm thinkin' is, like, an organic syringe or something, maybe even the parasite itself, spreading to new hosts...Stiff limbs sounds like rigor mortis."

"Rigor mortis?" Rodgers repeated with alarm. "You're saying you think they're *dead*?"

"I don't know what to think. Hearing me? I don't know." Lee enunciated each syllable.

"But we've all the time in the world to figure it out," I added. "Not meaning to bring everyone down here, but no one's coming...and we'll need to find a way out of here sooner or later."

"You're right." Lee fished a crumpled pack of smokes from his pocket. "We do have time, at least, that's for sure."

He lit a smoke, much to Rodgers' dismay, and inhaled deeply. The old phrase 'smoke 'em if you got 'em' came to mind as I watched a grey cloud swirl up to the ceiling, and Lee gave a satisfied sigh. "Soon enough, we're gonna need food."

The thought had come to mind, but I didn't want to be the one to say it. My stomach already ached, my only meal that sandwich from the night before. I imagined it to be around nine in the morning now and wondered how long before hunger *really* kicked. Could we go a day without food?

Rodgers pushed to his feet. "We still got our candy stash, let me see."

"Rodge, your tooth," I reminded.

He threw me a look before pulling open the battered toolbox we used for treats. The blue and rusted hunk with hinges rustled as he shifted the contents about. "Four Twinkies and a Butterfinger...Might do for today."

"It won't," I said flatly. "And if you want that tooth to get worse, then be my guest."

"Just trying to give some hope here, Tony."

"But it's false hope," Lee said. "We gotta think about this realistically, Rodge. We will need proper food. And water."

"And plenty of it." A smirk lifted Kit's cheek. "Plus you'd have them gone in an hour if we turned our backs. Your shit tooth be damned."

The remark, surprisingly, settled my mood—our roles had reverted back to normal. All morning long I'd felt like alien shape-shifters had replaced my pals. After seeing our neighbors, that thought didn't seem unlikely. All except for Lee, who'd kept his cool, even when shit hit the fan. With his brother, he had the experience.

Rodgers doled out the Twinkies, one apiece, and my stomach tightened as I unwrapped the treat. I'd felt hungry before, sure, but the idea that our next meal wasn't promised ate away my psyche. I nibbled gingerly and the sweet sponge flooded my mouth. In seconds I had the candy gone and guilt overcame as I twirled the empty wrapping. My own fears reflected in my friends' eyes.

Then someone thumped against the trunk and we gasped.

"Think they'll figure a way up?" Rodgers asked, keeping his voice low. "Could they?"

Lee chewed his lip. "Don't think so. Couldn't even work a door. I imagine climbing a tree's out of their skill set."

"True. But what if they come around? I mean, what if their senses return but they're still...*that*."

"Rodgers." I said his name louder than intended, and my friend eyed the floor.

"I'm just sayin', Tony. Lee says to be realistic. I'm bein' realistic."

"I don't think that's gonna happen," Lee said. "Going on what we've seen."

"That's false hope," Rodgers muttered under his breath.

Another hit against the trunk lurched my stomach, and I went to the latch. I don't know what I was thinking, but our neighbors' incessant moaning grated through my skull like worms through an apple. I couldn't take it.

"What are you doing, Tony?"

I shushed Rodgers and popped the lock. "Need to see what's going on down there."

As I lifted the hatch, morning air cooled my skin. Jacob crashed against the tree stomach-first, his head lolled back and his arms limp by his sides. Lifeless eyes found mine and he moaned along with the rest, a tiny nub of a tooth jutting from his bleeding gums, neck in ribbons. Short, white fuzz twisted from his pores, his skin greened by patches of moss.

"Jacob," I said, unable to look away. "He's up."

The boy stretched his arms, tiny, blood-soaked palms curling and unfolding, curling and unfolding, hungry to reach me. He'd climbed this tree a hundred times, yet something stopped him. Lee's mention of a parasite lodged in my mind. I hardly noticed the others gather around me, their breathing loud and their combined sweat crinkling my nose.

"Look at that," Rodgers said as curiosity got the better of him. "It's really something, huh?"

"It's disgusting," I said.

"Let me see." Lee wiggled himself between us and leaned forward, one hand to his glasses to stop them falling. The smell of tobacco smoke wafted from his jacket. His face crumpled as he studied the anomaly in Jacob's gums, his own mouth open. "Thing's still small...look at it compared to Allie's." He chose a non-relative purposely, I guessed, and I silently thanked him. "In their mouths, that thing's about the size of my middle finger, but Jacob's is just a nub. It grows fast. Judging by Osmond, if he *was* first to catch this, it seems to stay about that length, 'bout the same as my finger. But look at that...it's red in the tip. Not from blood, but the actual color."

"Why would that be?" I asked.

"I've seen something like it before...watched a David Attenborough documentary about ants...some parasite that grows from the insect's head before it calcifies. Then it pops and spreads spores to the colony to infect the rest."

"You think it's that?"

"I know as much as you, Tony, but I'm getting gooseflesh just thinkin' about it."

A question caught in my throat and I forced it out. "Those ants you're talkin' about, are they...are they dead?"

Lee eased himself back inside with a grunt, the other two moving to take his place and get a better view. "Yes," he said, "they are."

Those words hit hard.I reminded myself that I hadn't seen my mother down there. She could still be alive. It was possible.

"What about the length of that *thing*?" I asked. "Why would it stop growing? In Osmond, I mean."

"Just enough to reach something."

"What?" I asked, and my heart thumped.

"Something in the neck," Kit said absently, still staring below.

"What's in our neck?"

Lee's face fell in a way I'd seen happen before. Something had clicked in his head. "The thyroid gland," he said, "hyperthyroidism. Rapid hair growth..."

"What are you talking about? Why would that *thing* need hair growth?"

Lee moved with speed, cracking the spine of the hardback and falling into the beanbag. He skimmed the pages. "Give me time."

Recalling the small strands of hair and the moss and the disfigured faces made me ill. What could cause such a thing?

Rodgers eased the hatch shut and bolted it slow and deliberate. His complexion had turned the color of cottage cheese, matching Kit's expression. "They're not going anywhere," he said. "They're staying put and no one's coming... Man, there's nothing in their eyes."

My brow furrowed. "How'd you mean?"

"He's right," Kit said. "They're just...lifeless, Tony. I think Lee's right. They're walking around, but...they're dead."

The cabin spun on me, such a confirmation wracking my brain. The moaning from beneath the boards made my breath come fast and shallow, and blind-spots danced in my vision. "We're stuck up here," I said, and my voice sounded far away to my own ears. "They're dead and we're stuck up here and no one's coming and we have no food or water."

My chest hitched and tears flooded my eyes. My friends shared my realization, each shocked into silence. No one pulled any usual jabs to avoid discomfort. Not even Kit.

We were kids, alone in the world, and without a clue. We were terrified.

And the dead moaned and moaned.

CHAPTER FIVE

"**M**Y STOMACH'S KILLING me."

Rodgers clutched his belly, wrapped in his sleeping bag. We'd given Jacob's bag to Kit, and luckily got no protest from Rodgers. The *Ninja Turtles* on the cotton wrenched at my heart, but thankfully the lack of light obscured the images. The sun dipped below the pines outside, painting the sky a deep purple and leaving our tree house crawling with shadows. We'd split the remaining Butterfinger, and now hunger growled from each of us like rabid dogs. The soulless moaning outside didn't help matters, and we refused to light candles in case of drawing attention.

"My tongue feels like sandpaper," I said, knowing the complaint wouldn't help matters but needing to say something. I had no idea how long humans could last without water but it felt like mere hours. "I need something to drink."

"We all need water," Lee said, clear irritability in his tone. "And we're gonna have to do something soon or risk dehydration."

Kit lowered the comic he was reading, thick bags under his eyes. "Is it possible to...y'know, boil our piss?"

A collective eew rang out, and I shook my head. "Boil it with what?"

"I don't know. Just sayin'."

We'd taken turns pissing out the window throughout the day, each of us looking at opposite walls while it happened. Under any other circumstances, we would've found it funny, sure, but right then 'embarrassed' couldn't even begin to describe how I felt. There was nothing more vulnerable than having your pants undone and your back turned to three other boys. On the upside, Kit said he'd soaked Richardson last time, and I believed him.

"Shit." Lee stood and folded his arms, his face unreadable.

We watched him a moment, and once he didn't speak, Rodgers blew a breath. "What, Lee? Just say it."

"You know what I'm thinking."

I did but didn't want to admit it. Still, I asked, "How? I mean, they're circling the trunk, man. There's no way we can get down there."

I imagined trying to sneak out, slipping down the 2x4s as quiet as possible while insects chirped from the woods to mask my sound. I'd watched plenty of spy movies, sure, but I wasn't an idiot. I pictured my foot slipping and my back slapping the grass. Then I envisioned sharp teeth sinking into my neck, and the *groaning...*

"It's impossible," I said.

"Look, we need to try something." Lee peered out the window, his eyes darting left to right. "What about a distraction? How would we get their attention away from here? Give me something."

"Kit's slingshot."

Lee's eyes widened and he rushed to the container by the table, counting out the lead pellets. "Yes. Yes! We've got seven here."

"*I've* got seven there," Kit corrected, getting to his feet.

"Dude, for God's sake, you know what I mean."

"I know, but if we're shooting anything, *I'm* shooting. I'm not trusting one of you to waste what little ammo we have."

I hardly considered tiny spec pellets as 'ammo', but I got the message all the same. And I agreed. We could not afford to be wasteful.

"They know we're here, though," Rodgers added in a small voice. "I think they smell us."

"Or," Lee said, "they hear us banging about and talking and pissing on their heads. That's a pretty good giveaway. We need to try *something,* and losing one pellet in the process is worth a shot if it means us getting food and water."

"He's right." I stood and shook out my legs, circulation cramping my joints. "We need to try it."

It felt good to have a plan, something to give us hope. The gears in my mind jittered into action, and adrenaline pumped through my blood. I hoped Rodgers felt the same.

"And what are we thinking?" Kit asked.

Lee returned to the window, studied the garden a moment. "We've got a sliver of light left here...Not much, but it's something."

"Shouldn't we wait until morning to try anything?" Rodgers asked.

"I don't know about you, but my stomach's cramping like a bitch, and if I don't get some water soon I'll drink my own piss, boil or no boil."

"You're right...but there's no way in Hell I'm going out there."

"I never expected you to."

Rodgers straightened as if slapped but kept his mouth shut. I felt bad for him but agreed with Lee. I never expected Rodgers to try either, honestly.

Lee chewed his lip as the cogs turned in his mind. "Right," he said. "Kit, how far away was Mr. Peter's window when you smashed it?"

A smirk lifted Kit's right cheek. We all remembered the principal's car window being shattered before the holidays, and Kit wore that on his sleeve like a badge of honor. "Across the entire lot," he said. "Fuckin' bullseye."

"And you think you can get Rodgers' bedroom window from here?"

"What?" Rodgers protested. "No fucking way, man, come on."

Kit scrambled to his feet and to the window, eagerly squinting out. "Let's take a look-see."

"Hey!"

"Rodgers." Lee's face fell, his lips drawn tight. "Don't be ridiculous, all right? I hate to tell you this, but there's a high chance none of us will *ever* see our rooms after this. Our parents are fucking *gone*, understood? Your window is the least of our worries."

Gone, I repeated silently, and recollection of my warm bed tightened my chest.

Rodgers mumbled and returned to his sleeping bag, curling onto his side.

"Yeah, I can take it out," Kit said, still eyeing the house. "No problem, one shot...but then what?"

"Then we see if they go for sound," Lee said. "That's all I got. They're moving on base instinct. You've seen how they speed up when they see one of us. Let's try to manipulate that. If they go for the sound, we've got a chance to get down the tree and get to my house. Next door through some bushes, man, that's all we gotta do. Dad's got bottled water, at *least* two crates, stocked by the fridge. Never trusted the tap. Kitchen's at the back, right...there. I can even see the fridge from here." He craned his neck and Kit gave him room. "...I left the back door open, too. Just a matter of getting in and out, back up here before those freaks catch us."

Referring to our parents and neighbors as 'freaks' had become standard practice. Calling them by name only humanized them, and right now we couldn't afford our emotions to sabotage our plan. The job needed doing, and there was no room for error.

"What about getting back?" Kit asked.

"You and I got back pretty fast this morning," I said. "They're not as quick as us, not with their limbs so stiff...It's possible."

"And possible's all we need," Lee said. "It's all we fuckin' got, actually. Kit, if you hit that window, someone's gotta be ready by the trap door, hand on the lock. We can't waste time reloading."

"Or waste a second pellet," I added.

Rodgers stirred. "You're only thinking about water. What about food?"

"Can't carry both."

"Then someone will have to go with me," I said. Soon as the words left my mouth, I realized I'd committed. I pictured myself sprinting across the lawn as neighbors banged against Rodgers' house like blind moths while I prayed none turned and gave chase. With a gulp, I double-checked my laces.

"Tony, not you." Rodgers' shoulders fell, and genuine hurt clouded his voice. "Please. Not you."

"I can get there," I assured, not *wanting* to say it but needing to give Rodgers hope. I could see my own house from the yard, after all, and, if lucky, I could catch a glimpse of my mother's bedroom window. I might see a silhouette...I hid my real reason for going.

"Can smash it and run," Kit muttered.

"That's what he said," Lee added, quick as lightning, and we all laughed. That laughter died as soon as it started, but I appreciated the attempt. My smile faded as I worked my fingers around the hatch lock.

"Kit, you ready to do this?" Soon as I asked I prayed he'd say no and we could wait for help. My mouth dried and I suddenly needed to use the bathroom as Kit nodded, and I took a shaking breath.

"All right then. Aim true."

"Always do." Kit popped a pellet into the slumped balloon and pulled it taut, his other hand pinching the plastic bottleneck. How he'd come up with such a creation was beyond me. With one eye closed, he shuffled to the window and cocked his head sideways. He waited a beat, and my fingers tightened on the lock. My bladder tightened, too. His chest rose and fell, and his hands shook ever so slightly.

Don't miss, I pleaded. *Do not fucking miss, Kit, I swear to—*

The balloon *slapped!* and Rodgers' window crashed to pieces. My heart kicked as I scrambled with the lock, Lee yelling *go, go go!* and Kit skidding to his knees as I got the latch open. I held my breath as our neighbors shuffled from the tree below, instincts promising them easier prey in the house. A house with an open door and few exits.

I went first, my quivering leg finding the first rung as I pushed from the tree house and eased myself down using my stomach. I worked my body lower, searching blindly for the next step and the next as Kit came right after, almost on top of me.

"Move it, Tony, come on!" he hissed.

My hands and feet clapped the wood as I scrambled fast as a spider, keeping my attention on the descent rather than the neighbors, knowing if I took my eyes off even for a moment then—

My foot found nothing. I fell.

Breath whooshed from my lungs as air ripped past my ears and my stomach hardly had time to enter my throat before I slapped the grass. I gasped, back arched, and a punch of pain consumed me.

Can't breathe...I can't breathe...

I scurried to my feet and hobbled across the lawn as Kit thumped to the grass. In my peripheral, someone broke away from the crowd, moving fast. We'd been spotted.

"Shit!"

Kit zipped by and shot for the bushes separating Lee's house from Rodgers'. I followed suit, moving much like Lee's father who intersected me, now joined by Nate and Richardson. I tried yelling for Kit to help but no words came, just a hushed gasp as my stomach muscles cramped. Kit disappeared through the greenery and into Lee's backyard, leaving me with the trio racing from the side. My heart kicked my ribs like a panicked prisoner.

The freaks moaned and dragged their bodies, heads lolled back to give me a clear view of gnarled teeth ready for flesh. Their outstretched hands squeezed in hunger, desperate to catch me, same as Paul Osmond the night before. Behind them, the mob crashed through Rodgers' back door and spilled inside the house, thankfully unaware of my presence. I chanced a glance at my mother's window, some primal calling wanting her help, but although light spilled from the room, the window stood empty. Hot tears stung my eyes and blurred my vision as I reached the bushes and crashed through, the prickles biting my arms and face.

I winced and raced across Lee's perfectly maintained yard as Kit braced in the empty home's doorway, his legs apart. He wheeled his arm, signaling me to hurry. "Goddamnit, Tony, *move it!*"

"Help me," I managed, and my raspy voice barely escaped an intake of air. Behind me came a noise like television static as the trio plowed through the bushes, their groans peaking as they caught sight of their target. Kit swayed like a runner waiting for the gun, one hand on the door, his conscience weighing options.

"Goddamnit, *Kit*, help me!"

He sprinted to my side, flinging an arm around my shoulders with a grunt, pulling me toward the house. My legs buckled and I almost went over, one knee skidding the grass before I regained control. At Lee's house, he unwrapped his arm and rushed inside, pulling me by my shirt and throwing me to the linoleum before slamming the door. Nate and the others smacked against it a second later, banging the wood much like Jack. My breath returned and I pushed to my feet, panting and wiping my hair from my forehead. Kit bolted the lock and faced me, his eyes wide.

Apple air freshener ghosted in the room, a remnant of normal days, and a mahogany clock ticked above the table. Framed photos dotted the wall near the fireplace: Lee at ten with a brand new bike, Lee with his parents at a showing of *Jurassic Park*, and a final one depicting a child all of four, grinning from behind a protective plastic bubble.

"Front door, check it," Kit said.

"Right."

I barged across the hallway, only then realizing I hadn't checked for Lee's mother or...I paused at the living room. I imagined Lee's brother through the wood, probably clawing against the plastic of his bubble, eyes rolled back to whites while an all-consuming compulsion blared: *Food. Food. Food.* If infected could the parasite overwrite his immune system? Could the Bubble Boy escape?

I jogged further and breathed a sigh of relief when I found the front door closed. I double-checked the lock, just to be safe.

"Tony, what's going on?"

"It's locked," I called, and my feet froze as my eyes returned to the living room door again. I wondered. Behind lay a child, possibly frightened and alone, with no means of escape. He needed food, he needed water, same as us. Or, of course, he needed to sink a fresh tooth into our throats and drain us of all life.

A crimson stain dotted the carpet, but whether from a scuffle with Lee or his younger brother, I couldn't tell. Muddy footprints had mushed it into the fabric.

If he's normal, I thought, *it's only right to know...I can't leave him alone.*

My fingers wrapped the cold metal of the handle, and I gulped. Slowly, I turned my wrist.

"Tony, what the hell is going on out there? They're banging this fuckin' thing down, we gotta move."

"Right."

Fuck it. I threw the door wide.

And Lee's mother collapsed on top of me.

I yelled as saliva rained across my face, my hands working into the—*wet!*—moss of her face and wrenching her head back. She made a sound like a clogged drain as I blinked my eyes clear, arms shaking with force. The red-tipped, spindly tooth hovered inches from my nose, a strand of spit connecting it to my cheek. An organic stench attacked my nose.

"*Kit!*"

I kept her head wrenched back, the green mess sloshing in my palms as that tooth jittered closer and closer. A stench of dog shit wafted from her throat and I gagged, coughing but maintaining my hold. One gnarled hand found my ribs, crawled up my side—and sunk in deep. I screamed as hot blood stained my shirt and my vision danced with blindspots.

"Offa him!"

Lee's mother shot off me with some force, and I gulped fresh air. As my vision adjusted, I watched Kit pant, a metal cooking pot swinging from his fist. A fucking cooking pot. I accepted his help to my feet and fell against the wall, my shaking fingers finding my wound. Pain pulsed in my side but I dared not look.

"She's getting up," Kit said, more to himself, and raised the pot like a baseball bat. He spread his legs and braced for a swing as the woman slapped both hands to the carpet and pushed upright, wobbling on stiff legs. Her head fell back as if her neck contained no bones.

"Fucking bitch!"

Kit swung a savage arc and a pot connected with a crack. Crimson streaked the wall. Lee's mother toppled, splaying across the carpet like a discarded doll. She convulsed, her limbs rattling, and a wet halo spread from beneath her skull. Then, slowly, she fell still.

"Jesus..." I wiped my palms on my jeans, leaving glistening black streaks.

Adrenaline tightened Kit's face as he pulled his gaze long enough from the woman to nod at my jeans. "The hell is that stuff?"

"Spit," I said. "At least I think it is. It's just *gunk*. Was all over her face, in her hair."

Kit grimaced. "Spit? The hell she wiping spit all over herself for?"

"I've no idea but we need to get out of here, man. They'll get inside the house sooner or later."

"Right." Kit let out a breath. "What were you *doing* down here?"

"I was..." I pushed from the wall and overstepped the woman's body, the light of the living room drawing me. I pressed my palm to the wood and eased the door open. And then I heaved.

Brown splatters soiled the walls, whether blood or shit, didn't matter. The TV lay face-down on the carpet, screen smashed to twinkling shards. A painting of a sailboat, held by a single nail, hung sideways and diamond-shaped. In the corner squatted a boy inside a bubble.

"Ah, Jesus..." Kit ran a hand through his hair, his eyes turning red and wet. I was reminded of his sister and knew to stay quiet.

It was the first time I'd ever seen him cry.

I cleared my throat, my mouth parched. "Poor kid," I managed. It's all I could say. "Nothing we can do."

The boy thrashed against his transparent cell, fingers crunching the plastic and leaving red splotches. Through all the smears and stains, the moss-covered mutant moaned, desperate for freedom the outdoors provided. The backside of the bubble sat in shredded pieces, torn wide by Lee's mother or father, but the kid seemed not to notice, and instead pressed forward—*toward us.* A green bud, some plant or other, jutted from his right cheek. Sooner or later, he'd find his way free, I assumed, and he'd see grass and blue skies for the first time in his life...if any semblance of life shimmered inside him to begin with.

"Let's get out of here."

I led the way back to the kitchen, avoiding the smiling family portraits on the wall. Kit exhaled and followed close behind, still clutching the pot. "They're at the back door," he said, "but if we take the front and circle around the far side of the house we can run past them just like from the tree house."

"Good idea," I said, trying not to point out that our hands would be full of bottled water and whatever food we managed. In the kitchen, Richardson smacked against the window, silhouetted in gloomy darkness. That damned tooth cut through the black like a glow-bug. His greasy hands left smears, and a dull thump came each time he pressed the glass. As soon as his eyes found me, he whined, leaving a circle of condensation.

"Fuck 'em," Kit said, and scooped the six-pack of water. The bottles looked to be about sixteen ounces each, enough to last us a while. I pulled open a cupboard and rummaged past bags of dry pasta, salt, and herbs, ignoring the commotion at the window. I found five cans of tuna and one of peaches. "Get me a bag, would you? Check the drawer by the oven."

Kit returned with a grocery bag and I took it with thanks, dropping the cans and a jar of jam. I went to the drawer and found a can-opener, a moment of relief when I remembered to even check for one. At the table I pulled a lone box of cereal and dropped it in, too, not bothering to check the type. I found six apples on the countertop, ripe but still good. They'd be good for Rodgers.

"Nate and another one are with Richardson," Kit said. "They'll break it soon."

"Two seconds."

I raced to the bathroom and plucked Lee's toothbrush and a half-roll of paste. If Rodgers balked at the idea of using Lee's brush, I'd pull his damn tooth myself. Hell, come two days' time, we might all be using the same brush. With that thought, I grabbed the other three brushes by the sink. I raced back to the kitchen, and as soon as I opened my mouth, the window crashed. Richardson's arms shot inside, grasping at thin air while glass teeth shredded flesh. He worked his arms back and forth, groaning as he sawed his limb to ribbons, unflinching. Dark liquid oozed down the inner wall.

"Let's go."

I secured the bag around my fist before following Kit back through the hallway. We leaped across Lee's mother and ignored the kettle-like cries from the living room. That kid would get out sooner or later, but right now I couldn't think about such matters. I unbolted the front door and spilled into the night, my breath shooting away in a cloud.

"Go right," Kit ordered, and sped past. I pumped my legs and grimaced as my back throbbed from earlier injuries. Something told me I'd damaged a rib or two but I pushed the worry away and raced on, taking the corner too fast and almost going down. The grocery bag crashed against my leg with each lunge.

We rounded the corner and into the backyard as the idiotic trio wobbled in our direction, drawn to us like metal to magnets. Their stiff limbs quickened but we moved like frightened foxes, smashing through the shrubs and back into Rodgers' garden in seconds. My breath caught as two more neighbors spilled from Rodgers' house and joined the chase. The smaller one moved fast, and it took everything for me not to scream. Jacob drooled as his arms shot up, and his head fell back on the stalk of his neck.

"Don't look!" Kit called, reaching the tree with the bottles clutched to his chest. He started up, using his left hand and chin to keep the water in place as his good arm made short work of the rungs. When I reached the base I looked up, and cried out as dirt and splints rained into my eyes. I spat and blinked, my vision blurry, and scrambled up after. Halfway to the hatch, someone slammed the tree, and a thump rang through my body. I grasped a rung as the grocery bag swayed, the plastic ripping into the crook of my forearm. With a grunt, I pulled myself the rest of the way and accepted Lee's outstretched hand. He winced as he pulled me inside. Then the hatch slammed shut, and the freaks' moans were mercifully dampened.

Lee wiped his palms on his pants, eyes glued to me. "The hell is on your hands, man?"

"Spit," I said, and my breath slowly returned. For a moment I thought something was wrong with my vision, the darkness making me think I was about to pass out, but then I noted the covering around the window.

Lee followed my line of sight. "Garbage bag," he said. "Five nails left over in Mr. Rodgers' toolbox. Needed to make myself useful while you guys were gone."

"Good idea," I said, and stood. Rodgers still lay curled in his sleeping bag, letting out the occasional sniffle. With all the ruckus, I imagined my friend would be panicked trying to help. Yet here he lay. "Rodgers, you all right? We got what we wanted...even cereal."

Rodgers grunted and shifted. I wondered how he could remain asleep in such a time. Probably due to overwhelming stress, but the human body was as much a mystery to me then as it is now. I forgot our age a lot that day, and reminded myself that despite it all, we did need our energy. I only then realized I could've grabbed painkillers for his tooth.

"Here," I said, and rooted out the tuna. I took the opener and began to work its teeth across the aluminum. My stomach growled in response. Then my fingers slipped and the opener clattered to the floor. "Jesus, guys. Can we get any light here?"

"Sure." Lee plucked a tea candle from the table and fished about for his lighter. After the wick caught, he dropped the candle inside a mason jar, throwing dancing shadows across the walls. The warm orange glow made me feel a little better, safer, and I finished opening the can as a slosh of brine spilled onto my jeans.

"Shit...never thought about the smell. Guess we're gonna have to make do and stink of fish."

"Better than tonight, when we stink this place up with farts," Lee said, and Kit honked a laugh.

I held the can into the light, disappointed by the small portion swimming in the brine. My stomach cramped at the sight of the pink meat. "Five cans...not very much here."

"Half a can each?" Lee offered, sounding as if the proposition pained to announce.

"Sure." Kit let out a long exhale and eased himself down beside me. "We didn't go through hell just to scoff it all tonight. Lee, you can stop looking at me like I have two heads. You all might hate me, but I'm not an asshole or an idiot."

"I don't hate you," I said, then fell silent.

I *did* hate Kit.

I hated how he teased us, how he made our lives hell, once even leaving a bruise big as a plum on Jacob's stomach. I hated how he called Lee names but never pushed beyond his limit, knowing full well he'd get his ass kicked. A coward in every sense. My teeth gritted remembering his eraser flicking at my skull in class, or his dead arms in the hallway. Yet, after the day we'd had, the kid before me was not that same bully.

This kid saved my life.

"I know how you all look at me," Kit mumbled. He flicked a speck of dirt from his knee. "Don't think I don't."

He deserved the right to speak this after such a brave act, but right then I didn't want to hear it. Neither did Lee, apparently.

"Dude, not now, okay? This has been hard on us all, and I—I mean *we*—really appreciate what you did, okay? And I mean that. Don't go and ruin it."

Kit nodded, his cheeks glistening in the darkness, unseen by the others, but I didn't say a word. Instead, I offered him tuna, and he took it with soft thanks. Pinching the fish between shaking fingers, he wolfed half the can in seconds and passed it back to me with a sniffle. I finished the can without a word, and the salty meat flooded my mouth with saliva. I wanted more but ignored my stomach and dropped the spent container into the trash. My gut bit with hunger but I pushed the urge from my mind. We needed to be smart with food. I wondered how the smell would fill up such a tiny quarter throughout the night, recalling Rodgers' farts on other occasions, and made a mental note to toss the trash from the window come morning. If I hit one of our neighbors—*one of the freaks*—on the head, so be it. Hell, I'd aim for Paul Osmond if I could.

If I had my guitar I could pass the time, and the urge to play crept to the forefront of my mind as regularly as Lee's nicotine cravings. My fingers tapped out an unheard tune on my leg.

Lee opened a fresh can of tuna, and when done, prodded Rodgers. "Always hated fish. Surprised there wasn't more tucked away in the cupboard. Hey, wake up."

The boy stirred and stretched, his mouth wide open. "No," he mumbled, and rolled back on his side. "Ten more minutes, Dad...please..."

My heart ached.

And outside, a storm rolled closer.

CHAPTER SIX

THE INSIDES OF my eyelids flashed red as light flooded the room. Alarm bells rang as the hard floor kneaded my spine and for a second, I thought I'd fallen out of bed. I opened my eyes to the cold, damp tree house, and sadness flooded my system as my memory fizzled back. I stretched and threw off the sleeping bag and scrambled to my feet.

Rodgers lay with his mouth open, snoring softly in the corner as Kit twitched beside him, eyeballs rolling beneath their lids. All but Kit's head was covered by Jacob's sleeping bag, and his hair jutted out in blonde clumps.

"Morning," Lee whispered. He peered out the open window, the garbage bag crumpled in his hands, freshly ripped from its nails. The crinkling had woke me, and light spilled across Lee's face, highlighting dark splotches under his eyes. If I didn't know better, he hadn't slept a wink. I myself had two hours here and there but always jolted alive with the sharp sense of danger. My heart still struggled to relax.

"What are you doing up?"

"Couldn't sleep." Lee continued peering out over the lawn, his face a mask of sadness. "Wanted to see them in the dawn, you know? See who's out there, how they act...what they are."

"And?" I crossed to my friend and shook out my limbs, my lower ribs still throbbing from my encounter with his mother and my palms sticky with spit and grime. I considered my water bottle, but decided not to use it—we'd need all the resources we could. "What's going on out there?"

He let out a breath. "They're quieter than yesterday, that's for sure. Just...bumping around with their heads thrown back, as if they know we're here, but...at the same time, don't know...y'know? I can't explain it."

"Braindead?" I suggested.

Lee winced. "Pretty much, actually. And then there's this...look."

He nodded to the ruined homes and the gardens where the sun threw long shadows across the dew-soaked lawns. Our neighbors milled about with their arms swinging, involuntary sounds escaping their parted lips. Then something caught my eye other than the usual freaks, and my throat caught. "No way," I said, my breath escaping. "Seriously?"

"Quite a sight, isn't it?" Lee gave me a sad smile. I couldn't imagine what he was thinking.

His brother fell through the bushes in the dawn, thick hair smearing his youthful face. Brown stains adorned his shredded clothes: a plain white tee and clown pajamas. His voice peppered the air, fighting for sonic real estate against the others, short bursts that creeped me out but also made me confusedly happy. Here was his brother, outside for the very first time.

"Bizarre, isn't it?" Lee said, his voice quivering. "There he is. Immune system be damned, he says. Play around in the dirt and the trees, soaking up the dew, and who cares? At the same time, probably no mind to enjoy a single moment of it, it's...tragic."

"Tragic," I repeated, and watched as the young boy plodded around the side of Rodgers' home. His legs thumped one after the other, tiny muscles unused to such exercise. Like the others, he faced skyward, and, just for a second, I pretended he was studying the birds and the clouds, the wonders of the world fascinating his developing brain instead of a virus wracking his system.

"Where do you think he's going?" I asked.

Lee sniffed back a tear and wiped his face. "Ah, wherever he wants. He's a free boy now, isn't he? He can go wherever he damn well pleases."

The boy disappeared from sight, and let out a burst of sound as if in goodbye. A sad, small voice.

Lee turned to me, his shoulders slack, and without a word, I embraced him. He broke then, sobbing into my shoulder as his shaking fingers dug into my shirt. I said nothing, knowing, even at that age, *it's all right* held no weight when our world had grown fangs. Instead, I shushed him and patted his shoulder, waiting for the spell to pass and all the built-up tension to spill. Warm tears heated my shoulder.

In the corner, Kit stirred, and I slapped Lee's shoulder softly, bringing him back to arms-length.

"He's waking. Don't think you want him seeing you like this." A stupid statement in retrospect, but we were only boys.

Lee nodded and wiped his face. It was the first time I'd seen him with his guard down. "Thanks, Tony...I needed that."

"Of course."

I peered out the window, the daylight hurting my eyes but leaving me unafraid of neighbors catching sight. Morning air chilled my skin and I shivered. My mom's bedroom light still glowed, soft in the dawn, but the window stayed clear. My chest thumped as I pushed back inside.

"What is it?" Lee asked.

"My mom...I'm just...I haven't *seen* her yet, you know? Makes me wonder."

"Schrödinger's cat."

I cocked my head.

"Schrödinger's cat," he repeated. "She's both normal and one of those things until you confirm it."

"Right," I said, not knowing what he meant but too tired for a complex explanation. "I'm worried about her. She cast me out, kinda, when Jack came along, y'know? But she's still my *mom*...I need to know if she's all right."

He folded his arms and watched as Kit rolled to his side, still not fully awake. "We need any hope we can get right now," he said.

"How do you mean?"

"I mean that waiting is just going to eat away at us. We will go crazy up here, Tony. You noticed Rodgers' behavior? Caught him checkin' his arms for growths last night while you guys were out as if he thinks he'll warp into one of those things any second. Double-checked his neck, he's got nothing, he's clean, but he's slipping, man. Could be his tooth infection. We gotta have distractions while we wait for...someone...I don't know, but, do you think help's coming, Tony?"

I stuttered. "Don't say that, man. Don't say that. Of course help's coming. It has to, right?"

"Does it?" He crossed to the table and eased himself down, picking at the splinted corner. "We always expect 'adults' to make it all better, because that's what they always do, but they're all gone. We're alone up here. And beyond the folks who live here, I've never seen a single car make its way up Riverside Mountain. You ever see one?"

"German packers, stopped by for directions," I said, quick as a flash. "Right to my house."

"*Two years ago*," Lee corrected. "That was *two years ago*, man. And we all talked about that for a week." He sighed and tapped the tabletop. "No one's coming, Tony...And we gotta get out of here."

I agreed but worried for Rodgers. The few times I'd woken throughout the night, I'd caught him checking down his sleeping bag with wide eyes, as if he expected to morph into a freak any second.

"You saw how Kit and I did last night. And we're fast. Rodgers...Rodgers wouldn't stand a chance. Not with them chasing full speed. Hell, myself and Kit barely made it back here, and we're quick."

"Well, we've got to do something." His eyes fell to my hands. "What *is* all that?"

"It's spit, I think," I said, and sat across from him, displaying my palms. Floor dust and wood bark darkened the now dry liquid. "All over their faces."

"You had a run in with one?"

"Yes," I said, and my stomach cramped. "Your mom."

It felt like a bad punchline, and in a way, I supposed it was.

"I see." Lee's lips twitched, but his gaze remained. "What do we know so far about them, man? What can we piece together? If we're not leaving anytime soon, we gotta make progress one way or another."

I eyed the other two a moment, making sure Rodgers wouldn't wake. I knew Lee's constitution mirrored my own, but I feared for Rodgers' mindset hearing such talk. I kept my voice low. "That thing in their mouths may or may not be a parasite, trying to spread itself."

"Right."

"Excessive growths, all across their bodies. Clumps of hair, some mossy shit."

"*Entire* body, you're sure?"

"Up close and personal last night, Lee. It's all over them. And their skin is all fucked up. Like blue cheese."

"The thyroid gland. That's what I'm thinking. Hyperthyroidism, gets the body covered in hair, messes the hormone balance. Links to the pituitary, like having access to our HQ. Then..." He grimaced before adding, "*lathers* the body in saliva."

"You've been reading up, huh?"

"Couldn't sleep."

"Why the saliva?"

"Something in the spit, I don't know. An antioxidant? I'll read more today, keep my mind active. Maybe watering the damn greens on them. Noticed that? Like they're sprouting plants."

I shivered and said that I had.

"A spore," Lee said. "Something like that. But I'll keep reading today. Gives me a purpose at least. Because fuck, do I need one."

"I know what you mean," I said, already feeling out of sorts with no plan of action. At least knowing Lee would possibly give us some answers, some understanding of what was happening, gave me hope. "And what about the rest of us?"

He took a moment, then looked me in the eye. "What do you think you should do?"

The question jarred me, bringing the realization that I'd always expected his direction, forever looking up to the older kid. The burden of being in charge upset my stomach and left me a ball of nerves. "I don't know...What if my mom is still there in her room?"

"If she is," Lee said, "then we'd have to take her here with us. She'd know more than we do about what to do. But it's not worth the risk going out there again. I don't mean to sound cruel. You said it yourself, you hardly made it back last night."

"But if she *is* there," I added, "it *would* be worth it, right? We'd be out of this mess. We could move to my house. Have cement walls around us, five of us to keep an eye on the doors, food, water, everything. We'd stand a chance. I know I don't have a phone, but we'd be able to form a plan to get to Allie and Nate's and use theirs in time."

"And what if she's...changed, Tony?"

"Then I'll know," I said. I forced a hard edge, but my voice slipped. "We wait here, we run out of food, we're...you know. We don't stand a chance. At least with her, it's some hope, right?"

"I suppose," he said, and, for a moment, I contemplated Lee's intentions. His eyes held a faraway look I chalked up to lack of sleep, but for the briefest instant, I caught something else. Was he jealous I might still have a mom? That my life had a sliver of hope at still being normal? Could Lee be planting the idea of risk in my mind as payback?

He'd never do it. Not Lee.

I hated myself for the thought, but couldn't deny my judgement. I remembered an old movie where locked-up characters slowly turned on each other and wondered how long such a thing took in real life.

"You think I should do it?" I asked.

"You do what you feel you need to do," he said. "And I'll do the same."

"I need my guitar." The shock on Lee's face matched my own. I hadn't expected the words to come, but there it was.

He cocked his head. "You *need* it? Or you *want* it?"

"I need it..." I said, and despite everything, a smile twitched my lips at the realization. "You know, when Jack was sick and Mom was taking care of him, I locked myself in the living room and played until the sun went down. Wrote the start of a song, got blisters. Didn't even notice time slipping."

"It's, like, an escape, right?" Lee asked. "I get the same thing from books sometimes. Games, too."

"Right." I made a mental note to scoop my Game Boy if I *did* make it to my house. If a freak greeted me in mom's form, at least I might get back with minor escapisms, a meagre comfort, but a comfort nonetheless. And if Lee's intentions soured, then the good gesture might snap some sense back. We all needed to be batting for the same team, friends or not. The idea that we might not be friends twisted my gut. "Let's see what the others think about heading back outside when they wake up."

"You really don't have a phone in your place?" Lee asked.

I shook my head. We'd never had a phone, not for as long as I could remember. Mom always trekked to Allie and Nate's had she needed use, a good ten minutes across the mountain at best. Rodgers' dad didn't have one, either, and if Lee asked then neither did he. Kit was out of the question, too, his dad hardly had food half the time. His one-way line to God seemed to be the only communicator needed.

"If your mom isn't there," Lee said, "you know we'll need to go to Allie and Nate's, that's the only option left. We'll need to try and get to that phone. Call the police, someone."

"And if my mom *is* home?"

"We'll have to bring her here—unless she's got the house safe. Then, like you said, we move down there."

I liked the idea of moving home, but after seeing Lee's and the Rodgers' place, the slim chance dampened my mood. Our neighbors' lack of sense left them at a disadvantage, but their mob mentality meant imminent damage. They'd get inside sooner or later, but having my mom at least gave us a leg up. She'd know how to get to Allie and Nate's and to use the phone safely. At times she might not have been the most attentive parent in the world, but she'd never put me in danger. I'd feel safer by her side.

I studied my friend. "We *have* to get to my place, don't we?"

"We do," he said, and nodded as Kit stirred. "He's waking. If you need to go, convince him to cover you."

"You wouldn't?"

"I smoke like a train, man. Speaking of which, I've got about fifteen left in this pack and afterward I'm gonna be a devil to you all. Fair warning."

I leaned across the table. "You think he's changed? Last night he really did help me, man. I mean it. He could've bolted, could've made for the mountain trail, but he stuck around."

Lee arched an eyebrow. "Don't think he would've made it far down the mountain. That's not all our neighbors down below, remember, a heap of 'em are still stalking the woods from the cabins. And with that sized crowd following behind, he'd be floored in seconds. I saw how they chased you last night. That said...I do think people change. So, yes."

I'd watched Jack remain a monster in all the time I'd known him. And, in a way, what he'd now become, at least physically, suited him. I wouldn't call Kit a *monster*, but I certainly wondered if he, or anyone else, could change. For the better.

"He's up."

Kit stretched and eased upright, scratching his scalp as he smacked his lips. At his back, Rodgers slept on.

"What's goin' on?" he asked.

Lee relayed our conversation, and Kit listened without interjecting. Afterwards, he simply said, "well, all right," and stuffed his hand inside the grocery bag, coming up with an apple. "You mind?"

"Go ahead," I said. "And pass a couple our way."

Kit threw us two at once and I rolled the waxy fruit in my palm before sinking my teeth in. The skin broke with a satisfying crunch and sweet juiced flooded my mouth. I chewed for a moment and, like magic, my energy increased.

"Wake him," I said over a mouthful. Kit held his apple between his teeth and prodded the boy. Rodgers stirred, but only snored in response.

Kit palmed his fruit and cleared his throat. "Fat boy, up and at 'em!"

"Hey!" Anger boiled in the pit of my stomach and my face flushed. "Man, seriously?"

"What?" Kit took another bite of fruit and stifled his grin. How he could act as if things were back normal dumbfounded me. Like he awoke to a sleepover and the past day's events were only a bad dream. Maybe, I thought, Kit hadn't changed, after all.

Rodgers awoke with a sharp intake of air, bolting upright with wide eyes. The three of us froze. His face matched that of a corpse. "No," he said, to himself or to us, I still have no idea. "I'm not awake yet."

"You're awake, Rodgers," Lee said. "Sorry to say."

"It can't be right..." the boy's voice trailed into sobs as he squeezed his eyes shut, a trail of tears cascading the slope of his welted cheek. "Come on, let me wake up."

"Rodgers." I scooted across to my friend and grabbed another apple from the bag. "Eat something, okay? Have this."

Rodgers took the food with a slow nod, his mouth open and emitting a noise like a wounded dog. His breath hitched as he crunched slowly, a trail of saliva linking to the skin.

"Fucking tooth hurts," he said as his voice slowly stabilized. "What's going on? They still out there?"

"They're still out there," I said, cocking my thumb to the window. "Took the bag off to get some air in the room. Still all around the yard."

"*My* yard," Rodgers corrected, eyes half-closed as he chomped another bite. The fruit wasn't much, but at least my friend had *something* in his stomach. I tried patting his shoulder, uttering *something* of assurance, but Rodgers stiffened and dropped his apple. "Gonna barf," he managed, before scrambling across the floor on all floors. Lee and Kit barely made it out of the way as he hung from the window and a jet of liquid shot from his lips. Vomit hissed down the side of the tree and I grimaced as he pushed himself back inside, wiping his mouth on his sleeve. He plodded back to the corner, easing himself down slowly. He scooped the apple.

"Got Paul Osmond," he said. "Not directly, just, like, a splash. But got him."

"Atta boy," I said, and slapped his shoulder.

As Rodgers tried again with his breakfast, I warned him to brush his teeth and told him the day's plan. He nodded at all the right places, but I doubt much of the news retained. Every so often he wiped some mucus and tears from his face and continued staring at his feet. Again I worried about his mental state, but his lack of outbursts, and even the small-talk served to calm my fears.

"So that's what's gonna happen?" he asked.

"If my mom *is* there," I said, "we stand a good chance of getting to Allie and Nate's and using the phone, okay? She'll think of something, I'm sure of it. And if not..." my chest thumped with dread, the image too much. "If she's *not* there, then I'll get something from my house, all right? Food, hell, maybe even my Game Boy."

"Your Game Boy?" Rodgers eyes finally found me, *really* found me, and I returned his smile.

"If I can manage it, I will, okay? Promise. But we need to check for my mom first."

"Right," he said, and shook his head. "I hope she's there. I really do hope she's okay."

"Me, too, man," I said, and finished off my apple. With breakfast over, I hauled the trashcan and waddled to the open window. The tang of vomit stung at my nose and I grimaced, chucking the contents without a look. Apple cores slapped off the branches, accompanied by the tapping of some other debris that had been hiding inside. The agitated moans of the freaks answered me and I dipped back inside, placing the bin back in the corner.

"What a way to start the day," I said. "Puke and garbage on their heads. We gotta be sending a clear message, right?"

"Right." I got a quiet chuckle as Kit pushed to his feet, unbuckling his pants. "Piss, too," he added. "I'll aim for Richardson. Ten bucks says I get his mouth. Anyone need to poop?"

CHAPTER SEVEN

"**G** O, GO, GO!"

I scrambled down the tree with a clear sense of déjà vu, the only difference being that this time, Kit had smashed Rodgers' dad's window. The freaks took to the sound quicker now, some part of the routine retaining in their muscle memory. They spilled into the house like wind-up toys, crashing off walls and each other, leaving slick brown streaks on the stonework. I fell to the grass with a grunt, and Kit landed beside me.

"Come on, hurry."

We'd waited for the cloak of sundown, keeping low as my heart slapped and I eyed the horde. We'd planned to skirt the house, move out to the main road and make a break for it, discussing our route for hours while our anxiety rose throughout the day. Unless, of course, one of the group caught sight of us, in which case we'd break for the field separating Rodgers' place from mine. A garden-length of overgrown grass, but with a nasty fence to either side. A backup plan. Scrambling over that fence meant time and noise, both of which we could not afford.

The freaks funneled into Rodgers' home sounding like a brain-damaged choir from Hell. At the back, Jacob fell away as the larger freaks blocked his entrance. He stumbled ninety-degrees. And faced us.

"Shit. Plan two, plan two," Kit said, and bee-lined for the fence. My stomach flipped.

Jacob's head fell back, that nub now a sharp arc the size of my middle finger. His arms straightened like water-dowsers pulling him to us, and his short legs smacked the grass. Browned blood stained his favorite shirt, one corner untucked and wet. The sight drew a scream I just about kept down.

"Move it, Tony," Kit said, and his eyes flashed to the tree house. "Unless back there is better for now."

"Only five pellets left, man, it's now or never, we can't afford the ammo. Come on."

We raced to the fence, working our fingers into the dew-soaked links, and hoisted ourselves up. The fence bowed from weight, arcing at an angle. Water dripped from the metal.

"Shit!" Kit leaped off, rubbing his red hands on his jeans. "One at a time, then. Can you make it?"

I pulled myself up another inch but the angle fought me. With a grunt, I managed to grab the sharp top and use it to heave my body over. I landed with a thump, my already damaged back cursing. After scrambling to my feet, I watched the fence posts wobble, droplets dripping from the links. Rodgers' dad had put the guard up before any of us were born, keeping out foxes or any other woodland critter interested in our garbage. I wondered the age of those posts, and how they'd hold.

Behind Kit, Jacob led a troupe, their lifeless eyes widening in their splotchy green flesh. They passed the tree house, just meters away now.

"Kit, you gotta move, man."

"I'm coming, I'm coming."

He leaped and crashed against the fence, left leg slipping a couple of times before finally finding purchase.

He blew out a breath. "The fucking wet, slippin' all over the damn—"

Kit fell with a yelp, the troupe collectively moaning and quickening. Almost upon him now.

"Get up!"

My body moved of its own accord, pulling me deeper inside the field and away from the group, tall grass soaking my jeans and shirt. Kit hurried to his feet and jumped again, his whole body swinging as he wrenched himself higher. The fence lulled backward at a dangerous angle. Then the post creaked and snapped. And the entire structure collapsed.

"Kit!"

The fence hissed to the grass and Kit landed with a gasp. He scrambled from beneath the metal net, a high whine drawing the attention of more freaks. I made to help him but fear glued me to the spot. On his feet, he stumbled into the field, wet blades swishing around him. I held my ground until he closed the distance, just enough time for Jacob and the others to reach the fence.

"They're close," Kit yelled, no longer fearful of being heard. All bets were off.

"Another fence at the far side," I said, tears stinging my eyes. I'd never seen our fence so much as slant—and with that, we were caged. "We're not getting over it."

Instead, we ran, not speaking, the cold grass licking our skin. The freaks followed in earnest, the bumpy terrain slowing them some, but not by much. To scramble over that second fence was a death sentence, and my brain struggled for a solution. Pulling ourselves up put us on the spot, and with a single slip-up, the *tiniest* miss-move? We were goners. I imagined Jacob tackling me, that nightmarish mock of his face wrenching back before plunging into my neck as hot liquid soaked my skin before the convulsions. Perhaps I deserved it for what had happened, for not taking him to the arcade that night. God, why had I been such an asshole? If I'd done that, then maybe something else would've changed, some minor detail that meant none of this ever would have—

"Ah!"

Kit disappeared into the grass and I instinctively dropped, too, reaching for him through the blades.

"My leg," he cried, his voice tight. "Godfuckingdamnit, my leg! I hit—I hit a hole, I think it's broken, it twisted and—"

"Sssssssh!"

I slapped a hand across his mouth as his cheeked puffed and warm tears collected on my skin. I pressed against him to keep him still, fighting to contain my own shakes. He whined, the sound muffled beneath my palm. Our wide eyes locked, and I held his gaze, trying to wordlessly warn him: *Do not make a damn fucking sound.*

The freaks moved clumsily. Grass parted like the sound of TV static. I prayed their lack of logic left our trail invisible to their hunting eyes—the trekked path bright green without dew, weaving right to our current spot. If they struggled with a door handle, we might just get a little time. Enough to figure out what to do.

"Kit, keep still, buddy."

A moan echoed across the field, sounding like a mute in pain. More movement through the grass, pauses, movement, pauses. Closer now, enough so that I felt each step vibrate through the dirt. Kit's breathing slowed, his eyes shaking beneath their lids, but I dared not move my hand from his lips. In fact, I pressed harder.

A high whine escaped him. I shook my head frantically, nerves tight as stretched elastic, my bladder threatening to let loose. I increased my grasp on his face, willing him to *shut the hell up*, mouthing, "no, no, no," again and again. But Kit whipped his head sideways and let out a cry that drained all hope, and his hitching shoulders left me cold.

It doesn't end like this.

I steeled my nerves and slapped my hand back in place, this time catching his eye.

Shut. The. Fuck. Up, I mouthed. *We are dead if you don't, Kit. Do you understand?*

I punctuated each silent syllable by shaking his head. Had my younger self known I'd have complete control over Kit's life right now, he'd have said to leave him. But I couldn't. I'd seen another side to the boy, and he had not left me.

I froze as Jacob's tiny feet worked through the field— coming straight for us.

I pictured my friend's deformed features now, never to smile my way again, and some part of me wished I'd remembered our last goodbye. All I recalled was a lie about the arcade.

Kit let out another screech of pain, muffled by my palm, and alarm bells blared in my brain. I thought of running. I *could* leave Kit and make a break for it, sure, I could haul ass to the fence and at least stand *some* chance of survival. Hell, I could scramble back up the tree house, supplies and Mom be damned.

Then something whizzed through the air, and a sharp *crash* rang out.

Kit and I stopped dead.

A warbling of groans came from Rodgers' yard over the high grass, and our pursuers shuffled towards the sound, moving with purpose from the field. Their cries made me shiver and raised the little hairs on my arm. I removed my hand from Kit's mouth as we sat in silence and amazement, eyes locked.

"He used your slingshot," I whispered, and as the realization hit me, hope flooded my system. "He hit a fucking window!"

I chanced poking my head from the grass like a gopher. The field stood empty. I ducked back down. "They're heading next door. Come on, while we got a chance."

I made to run but Kit grabbed my arm. "*My leg*, fucker! I can't get up!"

"Shit."

Fear seized my guts as I prayed our extra time wasn't extinguished. I wrapped my arm around his shoulder and hoisted him upright, his weight more than expected. Across the fallen fence, the black mass of bodies fell through the shrub division and into Lee's yard, joined by shadowy figures now coming from the main road. More people, more neighbors we had not yet seen. I wondered who'd joined the party, and decided I'd find out sooner or later.

"To the road," Kit said, his voice strained. "No...no chain-link. Just wood. We can get over that easy, come on."

I doubted Kit could scale anything with ease right now but decided better to find out than refuse. We shuffled parallel to my garden, parting the soggy grass until we reached the fence. Three fat timber rows lay held by the occasional post, the red paint in need of another coat that it'd never get. I scrambled over in no time and scanned the dark road for any signs of movement. Not even the wind blew, but my breath ghosted subtly from my lips as the temperature plummeted by the hour. All our neighbors seemed to have chased the crash.

"Can you do it?" I asked. "I can help if..."

"I got this."

He hopped on the fence and clutched the top plank. With a deep breath, he nodded before leaping onto the bottom plank with one foot, the other left dangling and useless. His eyes found mine, shaking with pain, and he gave a curt nod before simply throwing himself over, struggle be damned. He landed with a smack, back arching on impact. I rushed to his side and pulled him afoot, brushing off the back of his shirt as he let loose a string of cusses to make even the drunkest sailor blush.

"You all right?" I asked.

"No, but I'll make it to your house." He blew out a breath and raised his head, taking a moment. "Let's hope your mom's home. Because I don't know how I'm getting back up that tree house, Tony."

The words hit like a cheap punch. Kit had come through for me and the group, and the fact he'd found us at all now left me grateful. Why in the world couldn't he have shown this side of himself to us before this mess? I liked the kid, and not only that, now I trusted him. I *needed* to get him back up the tree house if my mom wasn't okay. That thought added to my nausea, but I pressed on, the task demanding I *move*.

"I'm sorry," Kit blurted, each hobble pulling my shoulder. "You know that, don't you?"

Words failed me. A tightness constricted my throat but I took a breath and managed to reply. "I know. Come on. My mom's home and she'll fix up your leg, okay? We'll get out of this. To a city. Get the police up here and we'll be safe, all of us. Right?"

"Right," he said, and his genuine optimism gave me hope. I tightened my grasp on him and we made it to my drive, the house jarring for a moment, its contents either the end of everything or the start of new hope. I took no time and made my way up the gravel, Kit's injured foot slowing us some.

"Think it's broken?" I asked.

"No idea. We'll check when we're inside but it feels like glass. Killing me."

At the door, I couldn't deny the false sense of safety. This had been the only sanctuary I'd ever known from the world, no matter how tough a day I'd had. Here stood walls capable of locking out the bad, sheltering me from dead arms and gut-punches and names like 'faggot' and 'pussy'...Hiding me from folks like Kit, actually. Now what lay inside was anyone's guess.

"Here." I unwrapped my arm from his shoulders and fished out my key with shaking fingers. I pressed my face to the glass and squinted into the dark hall, but the lack of light only returned a clear reflection of myself. I took a deep breath before sliding the key home, and the door fell open.

Through the hallway, my HAPPY BIRTHDAY banner hung limp, two balloons half deflated above that unopened present. I imagined my mom setting the table for when I got home two nights earlier, nervous if she'd done enough. The image made my heart slam, needing to find her okay, and I helped Kit over the threshold as I eased the door shut behind us.

We sat in silence a moment, soaking in the atmosphere. I never noticed it before, but my house smelled subtly of coffee, Mom's "battery drink", as she liked to joke. My art award, a printed and framed A4 from three years ago, sat at the foot of the stairs like a floor-mat.

"Mom?" I called, more a hiss than a yell. I waited. No response. "Mom?"

I crept further up the hall and paused by the living room. Using my index, I poked open the door and held my breath. No one inside. The tension in my body softened. On the couch lay my acoustic and Game Boy, both untouched.

"Here," I said, I helped Kit inside. "Going up the stairs is out of the question. Wait and be quiet, okay? I'll be back down in a minute."

Kit nodded and hobbled to our single armchair, easing himself into position. "Never been here before," he said. "Nice TV."

I flashed a smile before making my way to the kitchen, my entire body pulsing to my heartbeat. I strained my ears for any sign of movement but heard none, the hum of the fridge the only noise. Something creaked, the house settling I presumed, but my stomach still spasmed in response.

Get it over with. Sooner it's done, sooner you're safe.

I held my breath as I entered the kitchen, trying my hardest not to get upset by the birthday getup. I crossed to the sink and pulled a steak-knife from the counter, blocking all thoughts of my mom using it in the past to prepare dinner. The surreal fact I might need to use it actually made taking the weapon easier, more dream-like than reality. Hell, everything felt like a dream now. That, or a nightmare.

"Mom?" I tried again, but still no response.

I poked my head back in the living room and gave Kit a thumbs up before tiptoeing to the bottom of the stairs. Using the banister for support, I kept the weight off my feet, the knife hilt slippery in my hand. On the fifth step, I paused, a shaking breath in my throat, and gathered my nerves.

Part of me wanted to make my way to my room, to lock the door and pretend the world hadn't gone to shit. I could curl up in bed and wait it out, bring my Game Boy and whatever canned goods hid in our drawers. If any of the freaks came and scratched the door they'd eventually wander off because I sure as shit wouldn't leave. And if help never arrived? Hell, I could just sleep and never wake up. Pretend there were no starving friends in the tree house next door...

Something moved.

"Mom?"

The scent of her perfume ghosted down the stairs to greet me, pinging back the notion that everything was fine. I was in *my house*, for Christ's sake. My mom was in her room, reading or watching TV. A nightmare, that's all. I must've caught the flu from Rodgers again. Or had my first lucid dream.

A groan snapped me back, and my grip on the knife tightened. Maybe she didn't sound like the others—she could've been hurt and unable to move. Jack probably did a number on her, finally flooring her out cold like he always wanted. Like we all expected.

"Mom, where are you? Are you hurt?"

I pushed to the landing and crossed to her room with surprising confidence, some maternal connection falsifying everything as safe. I eased her door open, and mouthed something my ears refused to hear as a dull ringing filling my head. And terror flooded my system.

My chin trembled, alarms blaring in my skull, the very fabric of existence untangling before curling around me and locking me to the spot like a wild snake. My grip on the knife loosened.

She stood by the bed, back to me. She swayed ever so slightly.

My mother turned with all the grace of a rusted toy, and a glistening, deformed face fell back to reveal a single jagged tooth. One red at the tip. An organic rot mixed with her perfume.

I walked backward, unable to turn from the monstrosity wearing a mockery of my mother, instinctively taking the landing to my room instead of the stairs as some lying part of my mind told all would be okay in there—nothing could reach me in my bedroom. Could it?

When Kit yelled, 'the hell's going on?' my trance broke and I rushed inside and slammed the door—just as two outstretched arms slipped from my mother's room, casting elongated shadows on the wall. I turned the key and collapsed, the knife clattering to the carpet. I cupped my face.

My mother let out a sound identical to the other freaks and stomped to my door, hitting face-first. The force shook me and I cried, fear spilling out like a sprung tap. Tears gushed down my face and dotted my jeans, my strength popped like one of my birthday balloons. I mouthed the word 'no' over and over, and the fact my room sat in total normality somehow made the situation that much worse. My action figures sat lined on a shelf above my bed, not a single one out of place. My game console lay before the TV, two controllers still connected from the last time Mom and I tackled *Mario Kart*. Hell, a stuffed dinosaur, owned since childhood, sat sideways on the windowsill with its head cocked sideways as if to ask, 'everything okay?'. All *looked* fine, safe, just like home, but the smacks against the door destroyed my illusion. As Kit yelled again and my mother turned in the direction of the stairs, I pulled to my feet and swiped the knife, knowing I'd been forced into this corner—and no amount of wishing could take it back. I'd entered hell.

Second-thoughts had no chance as I whipped the door open and gritted my teeth, the knife tight in my fist. My mother spun, arms outright as she came for me, and her head fell back once more.

Not my mom, I told myself. *A monster in her skin, that's what this is. It's not Mom.*

She moved faster than expected, feet clomping the hardwood as I raised the blade and an aggravated yell boiled in my gut. I screamed as I planted my feet, and slashed a vicious arc.

And I sliced her throat.

Her head snapped sideways and jetted hot liquid across my face. I ducked as she went, thumping on the threshold, crashing on her stomach. From here, she almost looked normal, her face obscured by her brunette hair, and I froze for a second. Then she rolled over and gave me another clear view of the mockery. Her dull eyes showed no signs of love, no recognition at all, and I stared at only basic compulsion from a parasite—the need to *spread.*

While more crimson spilled across her blouse (a navy blue top, always worn indoors), my hands fell to my side, knowing the fight was over. Her energy was zapped by the nano-second as she struggled to regain footing, but the lack of blood said no. She collapsed in the spreading puddle, lips moving soundlessly around the protruding needle in her mouth. I noted a sapling jutting from her left ear. This new world, the one with teeth and claws and no room for innocence, had claimed her. Just like it would us kids, I imagined.

I made for the stairs on shaking feet, blood drying on my hands and face like cold cement. I wondered if she'd get up soon, and decided we wouldn't be around to find out.

I didn't so much as walk the stairs as fall down them, my body refusing to cooperate, overloaded by the sights and implications of what'd happened. At the foot of the stairs, Kit clutched the banister with his face scrunched in confusion. He took the knife from me as I fell to the landing and cried. He shushed me—but not too loudly—we still needed to be mindful of the lurking dead around the house I no longer called home. For the first time in my life, I had no one to care for me.

Chapter Eight

"**T**his it?" **Kit** asked, seated in the armchair usually reserved for my mom and her newspaper. I squatted on the floor with our loot splayed out before me: four cans of fish, three of plum (Rodgers would be delighted), a loaf of still fine bread, and, of course, my guitar and Game Boy. I flicked out a grocery bag and gathered up everything minus the instrument.

"You all right?" Kit asked with caution. I gave a grunt, testing the weight of the bag—not bad at all, although my shaking hands made accurate judgement impossible. "Here," he said, and took the goods. "I'll carry it. You take the guitar, if it's really necessary. I don't think you should, though, we've been here a good hour, already. Freaks are sure to be back out around the place by now. We're gonna need speed, and I'm already slowing us down."

His use of 'freaks' no longer bothered me, in fact, I welcomed the term. My mother's dried blood splattered all across my face and hands made me want to never call them by name again. A certain numbness had settled inside me that I couldn't quite place, dulling my thoughts and actions, leaving me capable of only finishing whatever needed doing.

"Let's go," I said, and stood. A blood-rush almost smacked me on my ass but I shook my head and took a breath. Kit eyed me nervously, but he didn't say a word. His fear was almost tangible, and I wanted to punch his fucking face, tell him to get the hell up and move because that's what we do. I'd just knifed my own mother and *I* was moving, why the hell couldn't he? Damaged leg? One, two, soldier, get the fuck up.

"You're staring at me, man," he said. "Maybe we should talk before...?"

"I'm fine." I'd never heard my voice so sharp, never felt like a backseat driver in my own mind. "If you're not carrying the bag then give it to me and I'll take it. I'll take the guitar and you, too, if you're not going to fuckin' help."

The rant came before I had time to cork it, and I winced same time as Kit.

"Sorry," I added, and reached to give him a hand up. My mother's blood made him recoil, but I didn't withdraw my offer. After a moment, as if gauging if it were a trick, Kit accepted my offer and eased himself up, left leg still limp.

"How bad is it?" I asked.

"Hurts, but I don't think it's broken. Just feels...weird."

"Can you put weight on it?"

Selfishly, I'd asked because I needed to carry my guitar. Right then and there, I needed to strum out a melody, no matter how quiet. My thoughts screamed to be collected in a way I could make sense of them, in a song, and process the night in my own way. I *needed* that instrument back in the tree house—without my mom, we'd be there a while. Without family, I needed music.

"Lee might know what to do," I offered, and it was true. I'd watched Lee pop Rodgers' arm back into place after a rough game of basketball two summers back, and even though two adults had rushed to his side, they stood back and watched Lee do his thing. The nearest hospital lay twenty miles away, and Rodgers' screaming made that ride a trip from hell. Lee sounded confident, so Mr. Rodgers let him try. And it worked, even though Rodgers passed out pale as a ghost and soaked in his own urine.

Kit tested his foot, pressing gently. "It'll get me to the tree house, I think. If I take it easy. It'll have to."

"It will."

He held my gaze. "Tony, I never left you last night. I want you to remember that now, okay?"

I nodded, distant as could be. For what reason, I didn't know. Perhaps I enjoyed having power over the bully for once—or maybe (and this seemed more likely), my brain raised an emotional dam to stop me experiencing what had just happened with my mom, clogging empathy by proxy. Clogging everything, for that matter, because, right then, I felt nothing.

"Your head's not right at the moment, Tony, I understand, okay? I've watched my dad do things to me and my sister that I've never told no one and..." his chin trembled. "At least you had a good mom for the time you did, all right?"

I kept quiet, even in my dulled state knowing that such an explanation from Kit was rare. He held my gaze.

"I lived with a monster, Tony. A goddamn fucking monster. Wake up to an alarm clock for school? Imagine hearing an alarm clock in the morning, when lunch came around, when dinner was ready, when it was time to go to bed, alarm clocks, alarm clocks, *alarm clocks*! The man was a maniac. And the worst...the worst was the alarm clock for cleansing."

Here it was, I thought. The secret of the Peters family, told by one of the victims. Not that the information mattered much now.

"After my mom left, he took to the 'good book' in a way that'd scare a pastor. Know how you get fundamentalists readin' the book all wrong? Takin' metaphors as literal and stuff? It...it was like that." He cleared his throat. "*No one can enter the kingdom of God unless he is born of water and the Spirit...To make her holy, cleansing her by the washing with water through the word...I will sprinkle clean water on you, and you will be clean; I will cleanse you from all your impurities and from all your idols...*on and on and fucking on. And then... splash. Our heads went under. He'd hold us there for a good ten, sometimes fifteen seconds. Taking away the sins of our school day. Could he keep us home, he would have, but he knew I'd have ruined everything for him. That's how sneaky he was. He gave me just enough wiggle room that I'd be okay with it. I was allowed to see friends from time to time. Allowed to go to school. Allowed to even play video games once in a while. But I always needed to be cleansed of it. That was the deal. And my sister...*godfuckingdamn it*, my sister. I wanted a better life for her. I think he knew I was going to leave."

"You were?"

He sniffled. "Not that it matters a lick now, huh? Who cares. But you were shocked I woke up happy this morning. I woke up happy, Tony, because I didn't hear a goddamn alarm clock."

My senses flooded back, and a slab of guilt slopped into my gut as my mouth fell open. "I'm sorry," I said, and my eyes refused to meet his now. "Guess I was being an asshole...I didn't mean to, man, it's just..." I motioned to the stairway, unable to finish.

"I get it, man. You don't need to explain. Let's just get back to the tree house, all right? I thought of moving us here, but they'd smash the windows out soon as they caught wind of us. Upstairs might work for a while, but it's just steps. They'd get up eventually. Not worth the risk when we have a ladder they definitely can't climb."

Kit's planning surprised me, to be honest. I still expected him to buck first chance, but here he was, looking out for the group's best interests. A true friend. I gave him a nod before scooping the guitar, some small sliver of happiness pulsing for the briefest moment, and held the instrument to my side, comforted by the reunion and its weight. Then I pocketed the Game Boy as Kit took the grocery bag.

"Got a free hand," he said. "Can I take the knife?"

"Sure." I passed him the weapon, glad to be rid of it, and then a thought struck. "We should grab another few from the kitchen. Just in case. Put them in the bag and have 'em with us up there."

Something crashed in the back garden. We froze.

"My back door doesn't close properly," I whispered, voice quivering. "That'll have to do, come on."

I checked the window—all clear—and we made our way to the hallway, myself in the lead but staying slow enough for

Kit. I unlatched the lock with a steady hand and pulled open the door, the cold night air prickling my skin. I would never enter that house again, my real home, and a flood of denial overwhelmed me. An involuntary sound escaped my lips as I caught sight of the lulling banner and floating balloons up in the kitchen. Then a shadow passed on the wall and Kit slapped my arm.

"Someone's in there, man. Let's get moving."

I stepped across the threshold, leaving behind the scent of coffee and childhood memories.

We speed-walked the drive, pausing at the bottom. To the left, the dark forest stretched out into total nothingness, pine branches swaying in the slightest breeze. The subtle rush of the Riverside namesake ghosted on the night in a soft hiss.

"Could make it down there..." Kit offered. "If we hurry."

"Dude, the others."

"We'd be helping them, man. Soon as we reached the highway we'd get others up here and rescue them. I'm not saying we *bail*."

A good point, but I still felt uncomfortable. "What about your leg?"

"Then *you* could make it. If you hurried."

I thought of the other houses down that way, a good dozen peppering the winding path. Paul Osmond would've passed each and every one on his way back, and I can't imagine a single home was left untouched. There'd be plenty of those things shambling amongst the trees. Still, could be worth a shot. Not like we had many more options, besides making a break for Nate and Allie's house and using the phone. But that lay on the other side of the mountain...

"I suppose, if I was quick..."

I imagined myself racing down the mountainside by the starless night as the guitar banged my hip. A comical idea. But if I *did* reach the highway...

A rustle in the bushes voided our idea, and a voice like gravel echoed through the trees. Another answered, someplace further down, like a pair of mutated morning birds. The Lacey guy, I imagined, an eighteen-year-old into black metal with a nice dog living in one of the cabins. A shame if true.

"No use. They're crawling all over the place. Best chance is getting you healed and making for Nate and Allie's to use the phone. Mom or no mom, it's still a solid plan. Only one we've got."

A figure rushed from the thicket and stumbled onto the moonlit road, hunched over with swinging arms. Something stuck from its head like the rotted hand of a corpse. A sapling, I realized. A tattered rock band teeshirt confirmed its identity.

"Patrick," Kit said, already hobbling towards the Rodgers' place. "Always hated the prick. Come on."

I jogged after as Patrick gave chase, but his stiff limbs leveled his speed with Kit. If we didn't pause, didn't have any barriers, we were golden. At Rodgers', we crossed the lawn to round the house while keeping a close eye on Lee's yard. Beyond the bushes, the freaks slapped Lee's home as if at a bizarre garden party gone wrong.

Kit muttered for me to move, and we did. We picked up speed and raced toward the tree house, the hatch popping and throwing a suggestion of light. Someone in Lee's garden let out a howl that reminded me of dentist's surgery and we broke for the ladder. Another trio of ghouls broke into chase from the direction of the downed fence, and the horde now followed in an inverted 'V'. I yelled for Kit to climb first, and he worked the grocery bag far up his right arm before scrambling the rungs. Once his legs passed the height of my face, I held the guitar with one hand and wormed up to the best of my ability. As the freaks reached the trunk, I considered dropping the instrument and bashing someone's face, freeing up my hands to climb safely. I squashed the idea when I remembered just how much I'd gone through in order to get the damn thing, and thoughts of losing that guitar again gave me a jolt. I needed this instrument.

Kit hissed each time he strained his damaged leg, and I opened my mouth to tell him to keep moving when a sharp crack boomed as he slipped two rungs, right leg inches from my face. Debris rained and I blinked frantically, heart slamming my ribs.

"You okay?" I shouted. Dust and bark stung my eyes.

"Slipped. Holy—*holy shit.*"

Lee yelled from above, glaring from the opening. "Move it, for fuck sake! Come on!"

Kit scrambled and reached the hatch in record time as Lee and Rodgers pulled him out of sight. I struggled with each plank, grunting as I swung the guitar alongside me. The body smacked the tree and let out a hollow discord, and as I reached the hatch, Lee mercifully took the instrument, freeing my hand.

"Thanks, man."

I accepted Rodgers' help and he pulled me to safety, just as Lee slammed the hatch and bolted the lock, rocking the structure. A soft orange glow danced from three lit candles, the garbage-bag back in place to hide the light from the outdoors.

"Cozy, huh?" Lee joked, and I shuffled to what I now thought of as 'my' corner, placing the guitar upright. I smiled a shaking smile, proud I'd gotten the instrument back, and sat against the wall.

Lee's face fell as he studied me. "Blood," he said.

I licked my lips and gave a curt nod, unable to answer, but he understood. I sniffled and wiped the fresh tears from my face, drawing my knees to my chest. Blindspots danced in my vision.

"I'm so sorry, Tony," he offered, and took a seat at the table. No one spoke then, afraid to react. Afraid to make it real. The muted moaning continued below us, our personal hell adding to our wounds.

"Your mom's one of 'em?" Rodgers asked, and it took everything in my power not to bust his lip. I glared at him.

"Jesus, Rodgers," Kit said. "Obviously, for god's...what the hell's *wrong* with you?"

"Sorry, I just..."

Silence elapsed, and in it, the loss of my mom felt about as real as a Saturday morning cartoon violence. Reality tried shoehorning into my brain but some psychological barrier refused it entry like a stern bouncer checking for identification. I looked at Lee.

"We got some supplies. Bread. More fish. Fruit."

"Bread?" Rodgers asked.

"Yes. But I'm serious when I say if you eat too much candy and shit, I'm not putting up with your crying."

Rodgers shrugged. "It's bread, man. Just bread."

Lee nodded. "That's a good haul, Tony. And the guitar, too, I see."

"Yeah." The awkward conversation stagnated, but with the ceaseless sounds below, I had to speak. "We still go ahead with the plan, Lee. Nothing's changed. We make it to Allie and Nate's house."

Lee tapped the table. "I know, man, I just...Okay. Tomorrow, maybe. When we have a little light. I saw what happened to you, by the way, Kit."

Kit lay atop his (*Jacob's*) sleeping bag and let out a breath, hands beneath his head. "Thanks for doing what you did. They almost had us."

"I used up two pellets. I'm not a good a shot as you. Cracked a brick on my first try, but got my kitchen window second shot." He smiled. "Have to admit, felt kinda good to smash the damn thing. Wanted to do another."

"How many pellets we got?" I asked.

"Three now," Lee said, and pushed from the table. "Hey, let me see your leg. Up."

He eased beside Kit and rolled the boy's jeans to his kneecap. The reddened skin already looked plump and sore. "Hurt when I do this?" Lee maneuverer the ankle slowly, left to right, feeling along the bone. Kit sucked a breath and clenched his teeth. "Fucking yes it does."

"Hmm...Doesn't *feel* broken, and I don't see anything out of place. Looks like you got a bad sprain. Luckily."

"Luckily," Kit repeated with sarcasm, placing a palm on his forehead. "How long you think it'll take to heal?"

"Could be weeks, depending on how bad a twist you got. Ligaments stretched, you'll need to stay off it."

"Shit."

"Shit's right," Lee repeated, and stood. "Meaning you're off limits for an outing tomorrow." He placed his hands on his hips and blew a breath. "So who goes?"

"Me," I said, almost too quickly.

My friend clicked his tongue, took a beat. "I'll go with you, then. Rodgers, you think you can make the trip?"

His eyes widened. "Hell no. I mean, Tony and Kit could do it, just about, but me? I'd take a tumble the minute I stepped foot on the ladder. I've done it before. At least a dozen times."

He had, too, I remembered a fall just a month before.

"Plus my fucking *tooth*, Lee. I'm in agony here."

"Then it's me and you, Tony." Lee made his way back to the table. "I think we should eat now. My stomach's cramping pretty bad."

"We took shits," Rodgers blurted, and it took everything in my power not to slap my palm to my face. "We flung 'em out the window just after, like, don't worry, just sayin' that if you need to go...we've been goin'."

"Thanks for that, man." Lee scooped the bag, opening it on the table. He arched an eyebrow. "Looks like you got something more than food here, too." He plucked the blood-soaked knife by the hilt (my mother's blood...), and the sight flipped my stomach. "That'll do wonders tomorrow," he said. "Good work, guys."

"Thanks." I pushed to my feet and shuffled to the bag. The bread and fish inside worked a gurgle from my gut and I winced. "Let's have something *proper* to eat. I'm shaking."

My worries I'd upchuck whatever I scoffed disappeared the moment the sandwich passed my lips. My mouth flooded with saliva and a good pain, the bread soft and the salmon salty. We munched in silence, savoring the respite and taking our time, low light dancing across the walls. When finished, my mood stabilized some, and the flashbacks at my house felt more like a TV show I'd once watched rather than something I'd actually witnessed.

Lee popped the final corner of his sandwich in his mouth, chewed, swallowed. "While you were gone..." he cleared his throat. "I needed to keep my mind busy, so I've been reading a little more."

"Anything useful?"

"Saliva," he said.

"Sorry."

"No, I mean *their* saliva. All over their hair."

"What about it?"

He scooped a notebook from the table, pieces he'd scribbled from the evening. Once tilted into the light, he worked his index across the page. "I know this sounds crazy...but I think the saliva could be used to kill strains of bacteria, some mutation of neutrophils. Keep the body in some manageable condition, y'know, just enough to move...like a shield against the elements. And replace it with something else, something that can take the weather. And thrive from it."

"Like the green shit?"

"Vegetation."

The entire time Lee spoke, Rodgers occupied himself with a spec of dirt on the floor. I imagined my friend had heard enough already, and could only imagine what the pain in his mouth had flared to.

"So, by that measure," Lee said, "I think that yes...they're all dead."

The room spun slightly, and I pressed my back against the wall for balance. I uttered a cuss that barely penetrated the high-pitched ringing in my head. Hearing Lee speak my fears aloud somehow made it real, and my nerves jolted to life. "So this parasite, that thing that's like...what's the name?"

"I think it could be some form of *cordyceps*."

"Right, like *that*. So, it grows like a tooth, what, in disguise, and takes control of their bodies? And why the tufts of hair?"

Lee shrugged. "Like I said, hair and saliva to preserve the host long as possible. Avoid decomposition. Until they grow into something new. Something easier to manage. Parasites controlling a dead host body is nothing new,

I've seen documentaries about caterpillars, ants, all types succumbing to it."

"But now people."

"But now people," Lee agreed.

"They're like vegetable werewolves," Rodgers added, no trace of humor despite the odd statement. "Braindead vegetable werewolves."

"Except without the lunar part. So they're not werewolves. Plus, werewolves don't have little saplings sprouting from their heads. This is a fungal parasite. I'm pretty certain of that at least."

A snore from Kit gave us a jolt and my hand shot to my chest. A slight smile crept onto our lips.

"Jumpy," I said.

"Right." Rodgers sat upright, keeping his voice low. In the soft light, I imagined we'd simply decided to camp out like old times, making up apocalyptic stories to scare ourselves silly with the addition of Kit as some kind of glitch in the matrix. The hardened blood on my hands said otherwise.

A thought occurred to me then, and I fished about inside my pocket. "Hey..." I passed the console to Rodgers, feeling like a good dad on Christmas.

My friend's face lit up. "Holy shit, you serious? You got the Game Boy!"

He swiped the device and scuttled to the nearest light, a robotic ping ringing out as he snapped the console to life. The bags beneath his eyes deepened in the electric glow, but beyond that, in that moment, he looked like an average and happy kid. The digitized theme of a game began to lull, and Lee and I watched our friend enjoy his escape, a downtime that was more than welcome.

Kit smacked his lips and woke, easing from his sleeping bag like a mummy. He scratched his head and blinked, attention on Rodgers. "Whatsat?"

"Game Boy," Rodgers muttered, eyes glued to the screen.

"I know that game." Kit scooted to my friend, sleeping bag still wrapped around him and his sleepy face glowing in the light of the screen next to Rodgers. Their smiles mirrored.

"No, you gotta go down there," Kit said, pointing. "There's a secret."

"There is?" Rodgers jabbed a few buttons, igniting a *bleep*, and his face lit up. "Hey, I never knew about that."

"Yeah, found it months ago. Thought everyone knew that one."

"Not me...didn't even know you played."

"Yeah..."

Lee and I shared a look, our smirks identical to our thoughts, I imagined. Because there sat two boys free from the mess our lives had become. No longer bully and victim, at least for a brief moment. They both laughed and sighed in unison, each accompanied by an appropriate sound-bite. Both whooped when things went their way, passing the device back and forth.

I shook my head and scooted to my corner, the guitar calling me all night like an overeager lover. With a soft hand, I pulled the instrument across my lap and took a moment. The heaviness of the wood drew a blanket of safety across my body. With this in my hands, I felt complete—an amputee finally gifted a prosthetic. My blood-stained fingers found the strings and fell into position, the pressure on the pads of my digits nothing short of wonderful.

I strummed a chord, a D, and a smile forced its way onto my lips.

Only Lee paid me any mind, and he watched with folded arms. "You're good," he said. "Been practicing."

"Every day," I replied, and plucked out a scale. "Think I've got a couple of *Deep Purple* tunes down if you wanna hear."

Lee chuckled. "That'd be great."

My fingers discovered an off-note, something dissonant, and my skin prickled in response. I looked up.

"What was that?" Lee asked.

"Dunno...but I like it."

I repeated the phrase, this time with more confidence, and the monotonous moaning below us melted away, replaced by a melody. Minor key, of course.

"Hey," I said, and pointed to the table. "Rip me a page and pass me a pen?"

"Sure." Lee worked the paper free from his book and tossed me a pen. I stopped playing just enough to flatten the page before me and then played a little more. I took a moment as my imagination geared to life and burst with possibilities. On top the page, I hastily scribbled a song title: *From Up Here.*

CHAPTER NINE

"Y OU SONOFABITCH!"

I jolted upright, my hair a bird's nest, and gasped as Kit shoved Rodgers. Soft light glowed from the corners of the garbage-bag, illuminating the scene. Kit grabbed Rodgers by his shirt as my friend sniffled back tears, his eyes wide.

"You know what we went through to get that? Do you? *Do you have any idea?*"

Kit's fist connected with Rodgers' cheek to the sound of slapped steak. I imagined the pain coursing through his infected mouth and sprung to my feet alongside Lee. We raced to them—two boys once again bully and victim. I grabbed Kit by the shoulders and wrenched him back. He slapped the ground in a splay of limbs and clamored to his feet. With an adjustment of his shirt, his feverish eyes found mine.

"Little cunt snuck a can of fruit." He jabbed a finger in Rodgers' direction as Lee kneeled next to him, turning the boy's head sideways for a better view of his reddening cheek.

"I'm sorry," Rodgers muttered, his mouth already swollen. "I...I got hungry and didn't know what to do."

"Well you sure as shit don't steal food I risked my damn life for, fat ass!"

"My fucking *tooth!*"

I stretched my arms to keep Kit at bay like the attack dog he'd become. "Calm the fuck down. Rodgers, the hell happened?"

"I couldn't sleep," he whined, batting Lee's hand away. With a grunt, he wormed into the far corner and sobbed. "The pain kept me up, man. I got hungry, didn't want to wake anyone. Thought I'd have my breakfast during the night, that's all, I swear. I didn't *steal* anything."

Kit scoffed. "Bull-fucking-shit. You were halfway through stuffing the can through the window, I woke 'cause I heard the bag rustling. You were tryin' to get away with it, you greedy fuck."

"I said calm it," I warned, and my attention never left my friend. As a tear slipped down his cheek, skin the color of plum, I couldn't deny I felt more loyal to him than Kit. The sight and situation was all too familiar from our days at school. "It can be mine," I said at last. "We don't need this shit."

"Yours?" Kit sounded deflated. "Seriously, Tony, you risked your *life* for that food. You're going out there again today, you need to fuckin' eat. This sonofabitch would go a full week trapped up here without any food. *You* need it. *Not* him."

"I said I'm sorry," Rodgers repeated, and his voice cracked. "*Please.*"

"It's all right." I looked to Lee for help. "Right?"

"Yeah," Lee said, still muddled with sleep. "Yeah, we're all good."

"Right?" This time I spoke to Kit.

The boy took a moment, a snarl curling his lips, and finally, he huffed a laugh. "Right. Whatever. But this shit happens again and I won't stop, hear me? My leg is fucking useless because we needed that food. I didn't do it for fatty's comfort. I did it to keep him *alive*. Hear that, you thick bastard? I did it to save your damn life. And you're here trying to kill us."

Harsh as it seemed, Kit did have a point. I didn't want our efforts to mean nothing any more than he did, but I also didn't want my friend smacked and abused like old times. With all that'd happened, we could not afford to devolve to that. Not now.

"We have three cans left," I said, rubbing at the tension in my forehead. "I assume it was the plums, Rodge?"

Rodgers nodded, eyes to the floor. We'd already scoffed the loaf of bread last night, a victory supper I forced down despite my mood. With the jam from Lee's, we at least had something substantial in our stomachs.

"Right." I crossed to the window and plucked the empty can on my way. He'd drained every drop of juice, too, not that I could blame him. I took the bag from the window, careful to not rip any of the plastic off the nails, and stuffed the can outside, gaining the attention of some shufflers below, thinking we'd become neighbors in a whole new way. Their heads fell back at once and a discord sound bubbled from their throats. At the trunk lurked Jacob and Allie, Nate and Richardson further out. Jack wobbled alongside the damaged fence.

There you are, you sonofabitch.

He shuffled at the sight of me, crashing against Jacob and smacking to the tree, head tilted back. I watched him a moment, waited until he crossed right beneath me, and undid my fly. The cold air made my nose run and I sniffled as I positioned myself just right—then I pissed on the bastard's face.

Jack didn't move as urine splashed across his molded face, but even that didn't lift my mood. The weight of the previous two days refused to let up, like waterlogged clothes on a cold evening. Finished, I ducked back inside and handed out the fruit. Lee and Kit thanked me. I seated myself by Rodgers.

"How's your tooth?" I asked, chewing.

"I didn't sleep a wink with the pain. Feels like its rotted completely." He sniffled before placing the back of his palm to his cheek. "I think *he* knocked it loose."

Kit glared at him. "Good. We can pluck the fucking thing out. Sick of hearing about it."

"You know, we might have to," Lee said.

Rodgers paled. His breathing hitched. "Can we not talk about that please? When it's too much, *I'll* say so. Don't get any ideas."

"Fine," Lee said, and thew up his arms in defeat. I decided to change the subject, and spotted something by Rodgers' sleeping bag. "What's that?" I asked.

He plucked the object and held it my way. "It's my polaroid, remember? Found it while you guys were out last night. Dusted it off to keep myself busy. Still works."

"Nice."

"Yeah. Dad always wanted me to use it. Think I will."

With our breakfast finished (a tastier snack than I cared to admit), I tossed the cans and waited for Lee to take a whizz. Then we prepared for the day.

"Blade each," Lee said, and passed me a steak knife I'd cut a thousand dinners with. I tucked the knife into my belt and adjusted my shirt as he did the same.

"Kit, you wanna shoot out my bedroom window? Think you can do it?"

"Oh, I think I can do that." He hobbled to the table and took his slingshot, positioning one of the final ball bearings into place. He tested the balloon, flexing it to full length and back. Then he sidled up to the window.

"We gotta move fast," I said. "They're not quick, but once they catch sight of you they'll make like the elderly after medication."

"Gotcha."

"Allie and Nate's is further than we've been before, though. So we need to stick together. Find the phone, make the call, and then..." I was stumped. We hadn't thought that far ahead. At least, I hadn't.

"Then we lock ourselves in the upstairs until help arrives."

"You're not coming back?" Rodgers said, alarmed.

"Too dangerous, man. We can't risk rushing through them again. We get to the phone, call for help, police and all sorts will be here before long. Hell, maybe even the army."

"You think?"

"I do."

"Right." Lee shook out his limbs and positioned himself by the hatch. He nodded to Kit. "You two going to be okay together while we're gone?"

Kit chewed his cheek, looked at the floor.

"Dude. Come on."

"We'll be fine."

"Right."

Lee looked to Rodgers. "You? All good?"

"All good, long as he doesn't beat the shit out of me again. And if my tooth doesn't kill me."

"Right, okay." Lee motioned for me to join him and I knelt by the hatch, hand on the lock.

Lee wiped back his hair, greasy from our time in the tree house, and blew out a breath. "Gotta say, I'll be happy to stretch my legs at least. Feels like a prison up here."

I knew what he meant, but at the same time, I couldn't help but think: we'd want this tree house more than ever if something went wrong. Being surrounded by the freaks at Nate and Allie's would make our little quarters in the trees Heaven on Earth. I took in the room, and my friends, hoping it wouldn't be the last time I'd see either.

"Good luck out there," Rodgers said. "I mean that."

"I know."

A sharp crack rang out as Kit let the ball bearing fly, and seconds later came the familiar crash. Kit waited by the window.

"Going," he called. "Give it a second...Hold on...all right, go, go, go!"

I slammed the lock and lifted the door, the drop below squeezing my stomach. Without a thought, I scrambled out, making it to the bottom in no time. Lee followed shortly after, and we raced across the dew-soaked grass, drawing the attention of the few stragglers left in Rodgers' yard. Dark shapes drifted by the shattered windows downstairs as we sped around the corner, hopping Jacob's blood stains on the concrete.

At the front of the house stood Rodgers' father. He turned like a frozen robot, all jerks and lurches, and his baseball cap toppled from his head as his dead eyes found us. A tuft of weeds grew from his left eye cheek, and his mottled skin looked as if it could slop away with one wrong move. His head collapsed back then, and that gnarled tooth pointed right for us. We broke for the road, making it to the tarmac before he got moving. After all that man did for us to make our childhoods what they were, this was what he'd become. Tears stung my eyes.

Our feet slapped the pavement, breath streaming from our lips like cigarette smoke, and for the briefest moment, without the freaks, the world appeared completely normal. The illusion shattered the moment a man tumbled from the woodlands to our left, slapping the pavement clumsily before forcing himself back upright. Drool slithered from his rotted face, and he wobbled just a moment, enough time for us to race by, as his hands grasped thin air.

Lee's chest wheezed, those few years of smoking catching up to him. He chanced a look behind us and let out an involuntary sound. "Five of 'em, at least," he said. "Maybe more. Fuck, they're fast when they wanna be."

"Yup!"

Allie and Nate's roof peeled into view, chimney top and shingles cutting through the pines. We veered left, taking their driveway, and past the green-painted letterbox to the gravel, our shoes spitting small stones. At the porch, we skidded to a stop.

Lee pressed his hands to his knees, coughing violently, face red and sweaty. "A...a key anywhere you know of?"

"No damn idea." I kicked over two flower pots by the door, revealing nothing but earthworms and a couple of pissed off spiders that scuttled into the drive. "Nope. Fuck it, window it is. Don't touch the door, the less chance they have of getting in, the better."

"Look." Lee pointed to an open window and my heart fluttered in hope.

"I can squeeze through there," I said, and crossed to the glass. "Hold on."

As I pulled the window open, something caught my eye. I froze and squinted into the woods, something by the trunk of an old pine out of place. A man. I turned my head sideways, like a dog who'd heard a strange noise, but didn't see growths.

The longer I looked, the more my vision blurred, and I started wondering if I was seeing things.

"Tony, fucking move!"

"Right."

I plucked a flower pot and planted it by the window for leverage. With its help, I pulled myself onto the sill and whipped back the drawn curtains, revealing the empty and dark living room. Dust danced in the fresh sunbeam.

"We're good," I said, and hopped inside. I landed with a dull thump and took a moment, gauging the house. A grandfather clock ticked somewhere in the hall, and all else stood in silence. I wondered about the man in the woods, if I'd seen him at all, but the panic in Lee's voice kept the notion at bay.

"Come on," he hissed. "Get the fuckin' door open."

"Coming."

I crept across the room, lilac air freshener still ghosting from the fabrics, and eased open the door to the hall. Three photos dotted the stairway, and my brow creased in confusion. A young boy, perhaps twenty years old, stood alongside a much younger Allie and Nate. His nose matched Nate's, a little too long and almost bird-like, while his eyes matched his mother's, soft and warm. They had a son.

Lee appeared distorted through the frosted glass on the other side of the door, hopping from foot to foot, his voice muffled. "Shit, seriously. Dude, hurry!"

I undid the latch and Lee pushed inside, the door catching on a pile of unopened letters. Lee closed the door with one shoulder before turning and re-doing the lock, still panting from the run. The redness of his face had drained, replaced by a tight fear that set my nerves on end. His eyes found mine.

"We've been spotted," he said.

"What?"

I expected him to mention the dweller in the forest, but instead, he said, "at least five of 'em starting down the drive."

"Shit."

"Come on, the phone. We've made it, at least. Those depressing old farts will come in handy for something."

We pushed through into the kitchen as morning light glared from the slide-doors to a well-kept garden with a ladder propped against the house. A breakfast island separated the cooking area from the table and two simple chairs. An armchair sat in the corner, an unplugged electric heater by its feet. A simple and cozy setup, yet there hung another photo, once again with three people, not two.

"They had a son," I said, pointing the picture out. "You know that?"

"No." Lee studied it a moment, his face mirroring my confusion. "Never heard anyone mention it. Mom said they had to 'go away' last month, remember that? Never thought anything of it, just...Always thought they pottered about around here. They were always stern as shit, but in the last month especially, I mean, I didn't think...It sounds stupid, but I didn't think they had a *life*, you know?"

"Exactly." Something I didn't quite understand caused a pang of guilt in my stomach, and not until years later would I learn its meaning. I'd judged them on face value, just a couple of old folk with a mean attitude, never knowing they could've gone through something I didn't get. When my eyes landed on the urn, I did understand.

"Shit."

"I never knew," Lee said, the words just a breath. "That's awful."

"Yeah." I shook my head. "There was a man in the trees."

"A normal man?"

"I think so. I didn't see anything *weird* about him, he was just...standing. Wasn't their son, that's for sure, but someone's out there. At least, I don't think my eyes were playing tricks on me."

The few breaks in the storm allowed glaring light passage through the fat clouds, messing with my sight. I wondered if I could've imagined such a thing, perhaps *hoped* for such a thing, but decided now was no time to ponder. We had a job to do.

"Come on, before they get here."

I pushed aside the remorse and crossed to the phone, one set above a calendar on the wrong date. My eyes happened upon the only penned in square, April 19th: Benny's cremation. They'd never turned a page since. With a shake of my head, I lifted the receiver from its cradle.

No dial tone.

"Lee." My voice came from somewhere far away as a familiar ringing filled my brain. "Lee, there's no dial."

"What?" He rushed to my side and snatched the receiver, chest pumping with adrenaline. "No...no, no, *no!*"

He slapped the cradle pin with his index over and over. "*Godfuckingdamnit!*"

With a yell, he smashed the receiver off the wall, plastic and mechanics raining to the floor. The bottom half swung back and forth from its curled chord. I collapsed against the wall, burying my face in my hands. We were finished, with no options left, and the tears came hot and fast.

"It's not possible," I said through a sniffle. "Not fair. Just give us a damn break."

The look in Lee's eyes dimmed, and his arms went limp by his side. Any trace of color dissipated from his complexion. "It's over," he said, his voice a monotone. "That was it, Tony. We're done for. No phone. No way out. We're completely fucked."

I wanted to say otherwise, wanted to fight him, but my mouth refused. Instead, I emitted a noise similar to a boiling tea-kettle as thoughts of what my mom had become, what our *homes* had become, kicked into top gear. The wall of numbness protecting my will finally broke. I fell sideways, cradling my knees to my chest, and yelled. Lee spilled down the wall beside me.

"They'll be here soon," he said, voice just as flat. "And the only place left for us is back at that tree house. No use going upstairs. There's nobody coming."

"The tree house? For how long?"

"Until the food runs out. Until they get us. One or the other."

The front door rattled. A moan echoed through the hall.

"They're here," he said. And I didn't even bother moving.

Someone slapped the side glass, and another dull thump followed. I hadn't even closed the window.

"I never kissed a girl," Lee said suddenly, speaking almost to himself. "One time, nearly, but it never happened." He chuckled then, soft and humorless. "Jenny from school, remember her?"

I sat up, wiped my face with the back of my hand, the sight of the dried blood across my palm re-building my numb barrier once more. "Blonde?" I asked.

"Yeah, that's her."

"Saw you guys talking in the courtyard a couple of times, thought maybe that's what was happening."

"Yeah, almost. She liked *Deep Purple* and *Sabbath*, wouldn't think it to look at her, huh? Then Eddy came along and ruined it all."

"I hate Eddy."

"Yeah, me, too." Lee studied his jacket, the leather creaking with movement. "Think this thing might've piqued her interest to begin with. I'd just be another loser without it."

"*Another* loser?"

"Sorry. You know what I mean." He sighed. "I should've hung out with people my own age. They were all assholes in class, though. Never shared any interests."

"I get you. But you liked us, right?"

"Of course. But without this jacket, I was just another nerd. Smoking always turned off Jenny, too. Had to stash my pack until she left every time. In movies all the 'cool' kids smoke, but any girl I've talked to hates it."

"When did you start? I've never asked you before. Just always remember you doing it far back as I can think."

Someone smacked the door, and I winced.

"Thirteen," he said. "Same year I got the jacket. Found it in a charity shop in the city, bought it with my own pocket money. Two sizes too big but I've grown into it nicely, I think."

"Why did you start?"

"Smoking?" Lee slapped a hand down. "Dunno. I guess I just hated my folks not paying attention to me."

"Because of..."

"Michael, yeah. Felt invisible. Not that it was his fault, I didn't blame him. Poor bastard didn't ask to be born with SCID. Thought if they thought something was wrong with me, too, then they'd listen. But they only got angry every time I tried help by reading up on immunodeficiency. Mom used to snatch my damn books. At least they were safe in the tree house. But, I hated her for it." His eyes failed to find mine. "That make me a bad person?"

"No." I squeezed his shoulder, the act making me feel a little foolish. Lee was three years older than me, after all. "Just makes you a kid, I guess. Wanting your parents to notice you."

Hell, I could relate.

"I mean, I get it, y'know? Wanting to make sure Michael was safe. Shit, *I* tried doing that. But it always meant *I* slipped from their radar. Somedays...somedays I wished he never existed. And now..."

His shoulders hitched as he sucked a breath, then let out a raspy sigh in frustration. "Know what their smell reminds me of? Remember when my dad got all environment conscious and had the compost bin?" He sniffled. "About a year ago he had me carry a bag full of stuff out back. Height of the summer. Flies all over the place. And when I unscrewed that lid, man, the *smell* of *rot*. Vegetables, mainly, just this overpowering *green* stench. That's what this makes me think of."

I said nothing, just nodded.

"What do we fucking do, Tony?"

The fact he'd asked me turned my stomach. Lee led the group, not me. So many changes in two days, this just another.

"What else have you never done?" I asked, trying to get his mind back to a better place as another thump came from the door. "I've never smoked," I added.

"Good. You don't want to. I hardly made it here I was wheezing so bad."

"So why do *you* do it?"

"I dunno, man...I...I wanted to stand out? Make myself different from Jimmy or Pete, the other 'nerds' my age. Give myself an edge, not feel so...dorky. Always seemed to work. Phil or Tommy, hell, even Kit, never came near me. Like I had a shield against 'em."

"Can I have one?" I asked, the reason coming all too clear as I said it—our odds of getting out of here slipped by the second.

"A cigarette?"

"Yeah."

Lee took a moment, said, "not like it'll do much harm at this stage. Shit, I'd choose cancer over being shredded apart by freaks."

Another neighbor slapped the front window and my chest lurched. My breath quivered as a sloppy moan followed, sounding like a clogged sewer pipe.

"Left my smokes back at the tree house," he said. Then his eyes lit up. "I have an idea."

My heart slammed. "Seriously? Can we get out of here?"

"Of Riverside? No."

I felt like I'd been kicked in the balls.

"But," he said, "we can make the most of what we've got."

"How do you mean?"

"I never drank. Have you?"

"No."

"I've never been to a proper party. Have you?"

"No?"

"Then, let's get some booze. Let's get some cigarettes."

Years later I'd think back on this, a perfect example of childhood logic distilled into a single moment: with the world on fire, we'd do everything we never did. Had I been an adult, I'd have rationalized we should stockpile more food, get more weapons, try armor our necks to avoid a bite...But we weren't adults. We were children, and we were seeing the nasty underbelly of the world for the first time, thrown from the nests with no lessons on how to fly. And we acted accordingly.

"I'll get a bag," Lee said, and climbed to his feet.

CHAPTER TEN

BOOZE?" **RODGERS' SKIN** paled as he peered inside the bag, sweat glistening on his forehead. He slurred worse than ever. "So we're done for? That's what you're telling me?"

I picked grass blades from my jeans, having taken a tumble in the woods. Lee and I, after ransacking Nate and Allie's, took a detour through the forest back to the tree house, giving the freaks the slip. I'd hoped to catch another glimpse of the stranger in the woods (if I'd seen him at all) as seven neighbors stalked us. I spotted Jack and Jacob amongst them.

Lee rubbed his hands before pulling a bottle from the bag, his eyes red from lack of sleep. "Got a full vodka here, unopened." He slammed the booze on the table and the clear liquid sloshed. Rodgers whined.

"Can we get back to what the hell we're going to do here? I'm being serious."

"So are we." I waited for my friend to stop pacing, my patience at an end. "Rodge, Lee and I were talking. The booze isn't only for a party. The vodka will work as a disinfectant, too."

Rodgers froze. "What are you talking about?"

"Dude, your tooth needed to be out days ago. And Kit knocked the damn thing loose. You know what we have to do. You're burning up, you're sweating...It's time, man."

A high tension filled the room. Rodgers looked to each of us like a feral animal, his breathing intensified. His hands worked in and out of fists.

"It'll fall out by itself," he said in a small voice.

Lee sighed. "Dude, it's...come on. It's time."

Rodgers opened his mouth but no words came. And when he involuntarily winced, Lee stood.

"Kit, Tony, grab him."

"No!"

Rodgers bucked and yelled as Kit and I slammed him to the floor. His elbow connected with my stomach and I gasped. As Kit grabbed his shoulders and slammed him down, memories of *The Exorcist* came to mind.

"You cocksucking assholes, let me *go!*"

"Shut it!"

I grabbed hold of his shins and kept his legs down but Rodgers' knee shot free and cracked me in the cheek. My head snapped back and I tasted blood. Rage exploded through me. I snatched his legs and slammed them down as Lee raced over and sat on his chest. Rodgers let out a winded gasp.

"Now," Lee said, swaying as Rodgers' thrashed beneath him. "You gonna stop? It's for your own good, man. You'll be thanking us."

"Fuck you, you four-eyed freak!"

Lee threw me a look over his shoulder. Then he returned his attention to Rodgers and pressed one finger to the outside of Rodgers' cheek. Rodgers' screamed.

"See? That's only gonna get worse, man. We can make it go away. It won't be pretty, I'm not gonna lie, but we can make the pain stop. Look, another reminder."

Repeating the process, Lee pressed his finger to the boy's swollen cheek as Rodgers' roared his throat raw. Tears cascaded down his face. "Stop, stop, okay!"

The strength in his legs dissipated as he surrendered. I eased my hands off his shins, ready to go again if he attempted anything stupid. He didn't.

"How are you going to do it?" Rodgers cried. "You don't know anything about it."

Lee clicked his tongue. "When all my baby teeth were coming out, my mom tied a string around one and gave it a hard yank." His voice cracked, and I imagined the memory caused as much heartache for him as it was for me. I forced myself not to think of my own mom. "We got any string around here?"

Knowing the tree house inside and out, Rodgers said we didn't.

"Right. Then we do it old-school."

"You're sixteen," Rodgers said. "You don't have an *old-school*."

"And we don't have string, but we do have fingers."

"You're not putting your filthy hands inside my mouth, Lee."

"Want to do it yourself?"

"I'd pass out."

Kit looked to me then, a slight grin creeping onto his face. "Another job for Tony, huh?"

My chest tightened. "No way, man. I'm not putting my hand inside your mouth."

"*Tony*," Rodgers whined.

"Shit, no, man. Not happening."

"Look," Lee said. "We have to do this, man. You want Rodgers getting worse? Come on."

I suddenly wanted to punch each of their annoying little faces. Then again, I knew we had no other choice. Rodgers could not go on with the pain, and soon enough, he'd attract too much attention with his screams. Especially at night when the inflammation kicked up.

"Right," I said. "How do we do this? We've got no string."

Lee pushed from Rodgers' chest and shook out his legs. "You still got your baby teeth, Rodge?"

Rodgers propped himself upright. "I dunno, how am I supposed to know?"

"I don't know, but I think it makes a difference in how painful this will be."

"I'm twelve," Rodgers said. "Almost thirteen. Think that counts?"

Lee made a face. "Well, we'll find out, won't we?"

"Oh, fuck."

As Rodgers pressed his palm to his face, I grabbed a bottle of water and popped the cap.

"Whoa," Kit said. "What are you doing? Can't waste water, man."

"Well I can't exactly put my filthy fingers into Rodgers' mouth and make the infection worse, can I? I need to clean them."

I poured water over my hands and scrubbed, rinsing off the dried blood and dirt and spit. Lee unscrewed the vodka and took a sniff. He grimaced. "Smells like shit, but it'll disinfect your fingers. Here."

He gingerly spilled the cold alcohol across my hands and I worked it into my skin. I winced as some grazed a cut. A smell like thick gasoline hit my nose.

"Jesus. Okay, I think this is good."

"Let me see," Rodgers said, and inspected my hands. "Turn them."

I did as instructed and Rodgers nodded. "Okay, that looks good."

"Can I just do it?" Kit asked. Rodgers threw him a middle-fingered salute.

"Okay," Lee said. "Rodgers, open wide and close your eyes—"

"—And you'll get a *big* surprise!" Kit finished.

"Dude." Lee took a breath, then faced Rodgers. "You ready?"

"No."

"Well, you're going to have to be. Tony, when you're ready."

I stood before Rodgers as he closed his eyes. His lids shook. He took deep, slow breaths, and then his mouth creaked open. His rank breath almost made me balk but I reminded myself that all our mouths faired the same. We'd need to share Lee's toothbrush come nightfall. I placed one hand on Rodgers' cheeks—*warm from infection,* I noted—and slipped my index past his lips.

"Ugh!" Rodgers whipped his head back and spat, his eyes wide. "The *fuck* is that taste?"

"Your mom," Kit shouted. "Jesus, it's just vodka, Rodge, relax."

Rodgers clawed at his tongue as his face scrunched. "As if you know what vodka tastes like, asshole."

"He has a point," Lee said. "Come on, Rodge. Try and relax now."

I noted Lee's amusement at the situation but decided not to call him out. Rodgers needed no distractions. As his eyes fell shut and his mouth opened, I returned to my task.

"Sick."

I pulled his cheek out with my finger, revealing the crooked and infected molar. A white lump jutted from his gum at the root, and I sucked a breath at the sight of it.

"Man, this is bad. You ready?"

Rodgers grunted and saliva drubbed from his lips.

"Okay. Here we go."

My fingers trembled as I pinched the tooth between my index and my thumb. Rodgers shuffled foot to foot. He whined.

"Okay…"

I yanked.

Rodgers screamed and whipped his head back, smacking against the tree house. My hand was empty.

"Shit, grab him!"

"No, stop, no!"

Kit leaped onto Rodgers' back and wrapped his hands around his neck. Rodgers yelled and punched him in the face but Kit ignored the hit and gripped him around the sides, pinning his arms against his chest.

"Hold still, Rodgers, I need to finish this," I said.

"You put your fingers back in my mouth and I'll *bite* them the fuck *off!*" Pink spittle dribbled from his lips and I took a deep breath before stalking forward and forcing his mouth open. His jaw trembled in my grasp.

"We're nearly there, man. Nearly there."

Reluctantly, he opened his mouth. I grabbed the tooth once again as crimson gushed across my fingers and Rodgers screamed. He whipped his head back and my fingers slipped free.

"Goddamn it, Rodgers, this is happening!"

"Fuck this," Kit said, and whipped Rodgers around to face him. Then the boy jammed his hand inside Rodgers mouth and yanked. He pulled his fist free just as Rodgers' jaws snapped shut. In his palm lay a white, bloody lump the size of a pebble.

"Fuck," was all Rodgers managed before he crashed to the floor.

We raced to his side and Lee squatted beside him, then rolled him over. He gently slapped Rodgers' cheek. "Shit. He's *out*."

"Roll him on his side," I said. "Don't want him choking on his own blood."

"Right."

Lee grunted as he hoisted Rodgers sideways, and the boy let out a groan. Red spit oozed from his lips.

"Gnarly," Kit said, and rolled the rotten tooth about in his palm. Pinkish gunk caked the four long roots, and trails of pure white lined the yellowed tooth like tiger stripes. A ring of calcium circled the lower portion from where the tooth met the gum.

"This is fucking disgusting," Kit said. "I'm keeping it."

As he pocketed his reward, Lee clapped his shoulder. "Good job, man. I mean it. I couldn't have done that."

"Ah, took my mind off my leg for a bit. It's all good."

"At least it's over now. Tony, you okay?"

"I'm fine."

A little shaken, I thought, but fine.

"Think we could all use a drink after that, huh?"

The joke fell flat, and I squatted by Rodgers, making sure he was okay. I pressed my palm to his neck and felt a solid pulse. He'd be all right, though I worried about his gum bleeding. We weren't exactly equipped to deal with medical recoveries.

"What now?" I asked.

"We wait for Rodgers to wake up, and then we get on with our plan. We're getting drunk."

I had no objection, both from exhaustion and lack of my own scheme. I shuffled to my sleeping bag and waited for

Rodgers to come around. And as silence settled in the tree house, the cries from beneath the floorboards increased.

CHAPTER ELEVEN

RODGERS CAME IN and out for the next twenty-four hours. At six in the evening, he sat up and puked. Then he cried and clutched his swollen cheek. I'd seen Rodgers in dire situations before, even pitied him, but this was something entirely different. One part of me wanted to comfort the boy, couldn't imagine his pain, but a new part of me wanted to tell him to suck it up and stop wasting time. He wasn't unique in his pain. The new world had taken everything from all of us.

We convinced him to eat a can of plums, and he slowly sucked the fruit as he sniffled. We each ate a portion in silence, and with dinner finished, I stood and cleared my throat.

"Don't want to say this, but I snagged these from Lee's place the other day."

I pulled the three tooth brushes.

"Now you can balk and cry and joke and be assholes, but if we're stuck here for god-knows-how-long, then we need to look after ourselves a bit. That includes brushing our teeth. Not going through what just happened again. Okay?"

Lee nodded his approval, and I caught a look of pride. "Sounds good, man. The blue one is mine. And it's staying mine. The red is—*was*—my dad's, so you can fight among yourselves for that. The pink was my mom's."

"I should have my own," Rodgers said. "Not being a dick, I just don't want any of you getting an infection if I have something, y'know, contagious."

Kit grinned. "Tony and myself will share mommy's brush, then. Dirty."

Lee closed his eyes and took a deep breath. I imagined he counted to ten. "Fine. Whatever. Pass it here."

We each took a brush and Kit was kind enough to let me use the pink one first. His constitution impressed me—I couldn't imagine putting such a thing in my mouth after watching someone else use it. Then again, Kit was built from something different.

With that out of the way, Rodgers curled back up in his sleeping bag as Kit busied himself with the gameboy. At the table, Lee lit a candle in a jar, and the orange glow danced across his troubled face. I joined him.

"Hey."

"Hey yourself." He ran a hand across his head and squeezed his eyes for a moment. Dark circles hung beneath his eyes.

"Sure you don't wanna go sleep, man?" I asked.

He gave a slight smile. "Nah. Better stay awake to take care of Rodgers if he needs something. He wakes Kit in the middle of the night and we have another fight on our hands."

He pulled his packet of cigarettes, stuck one in the corner of his mouth and lit up. The smoke curled towards the ceiling and a not unpleasant aroma tickled my nose.

"Can I have one?" I asked.

He blew smoke from his nose. "When we have our party, man. It's not time."

"Still going ahead with that?"

"Yes," he said, and flicked ash. "Yes, we are. We need the distraction. Especially these two. Look, I'm not giving up, man. I just need the break, y'know? Come at it from a fresh perspective. And if we gotta run, which we most likely will have to—I don't know if we'll all get that far."

A sickness washed through me at the idea of any one of us getting caught by those things. Like how I imagined playing Russian roulette might feel. Could be any one of us.

"So," Lee continued, "we count this as our last hurrah before shit hits the fan. You dig?"

"Okay. You've got a point."

A snore from Kit drew my attention. His mouth fell open as the Game Boy dropped from his open hand. Out for the count.

I couldn't imagine losing him or Rodgers now, but, then again, I couldn't have imagined losing *anyone* before my dad. Lee yawned and inhaled another lungful of smoke.

"Not just Rodgers keeping you up, is it?" I asked.

He chuckled and rolled the cigarette about in his hand. "You're perceptive, Tony. Always have been. You been getting them too? Nightmares?"

In truth, I hadn't been. Sleep brought a nothingness I didn't know was better or worse than our reality now. Part of me wanted that empty void to stretch out forever, but then again, the waking hours promised a sliver of hope. A *maybe*.

Still, I lied and said, "yeah. Every night."

"I just can't stop thinking about them," he said. "What they've become. It's like they're turning into the environment, if that makes sense? Buds and plants sprouting from their skin...I had a nightmare of this guy, like, half-tree, just lunging through the trapdoor and grabbing me in my sleep. It's disgusting."

"It is," I said, and then decided to pick his brain to get his mind off the fear. My own, too. "Any more ideas what's causing it all?"

"Fungal parasite, like I said. That's my *numero uno*. Some spore that's embedded in their flesh, growing to protect the parasite itself. Found out mosses reproduce by spore, believe that? So, yeah, I'm sticking to my guns with my theory."

The idea my mother had been turned into a optimal environment for a fungus to thrive was too much. I remembered the shroom patch where Oswald took down Jack, and decided I agreed with Lee's assumptions. I'd never seen this *cordyceps* Lee mentioned before, but I didn't want to either. It wouldn't bring anyone back.

"It's like they're becoming the earth itself," Lee said, and actually laughed. "I sound like a pompous dickhead, don't I?"

"No more than usual."

"Funny, man." He inhaled, and the cherry of his cigarette glowed and crackled. Then he spoke as if in a dream, his eyes far away. "It's taken them all, man. The world took it all. No more safety. No more love. No more *fun*."

"We can still have fun," I said.

"Exactly," he said, and jabbed the cigarette toward me. "Not gonna let it win, are we? We're goin' out swinging, one more night of damn good fun, even if it is our last. Nothing else, Tony, those are *our* terms. Shit, that counts for something."

I grinned at that, admiring my friend's constitution. Like a battle-weary General leading his troupes to war. A war against everything they'd ever known or loved. Because those were the cards we'd been tossed. For Lee, time might've made a monster of some—but it would *not* do that to us. Not if he had something to say about it.

Our late-night chat, despite the morbid subjects, gave me comfort. Reminded me of simpler days. Then Lee asked, "think you really saw someone out at Nate and Allie's place?"

"I don't know," I said. "Thought I did, but the more time that passes, the more I'm doubting myself. I just can't think of why someone would be out there with *them* and not help us."

Lee nodded, and a silence overcame us. I didn't want to go to bed just yet. The simple chat felt as good as a warm fire.

"You think he'll be okay?" I asked, and nodded to Rodgers.

Lee took a moment, stubbed out his smoke on the table. "I don't know, man. Felt his forehead after dinner, he's burning up. But at least that damn thing is out of his mouth. It's all the more reason we're to have our little party, y'know? Just in case."

Tears stung my eyes and a lump lodged in my throat. "Yeah. Yeah, I hear you."

"Will you break it to him in the morning?" Lee asked, and stood. He stretched. "Rodge isn't fond of the idea, but I think he'll listen to you. And we do need the break, Tony."

I blew a breath. "Okay. I'll talk to him."

"Still can't believe Kit did that," Lee said with a chuckle. "Just reached on in and *pop*. Fucking *sick*."

"Saved me the trouble, at least."

"True. He's an asshole, but at least he's our asshole."

"I've grown to trust him. Even if he is a dick. It's Rodgers I'm worried about now. He's really slipping, Lee. I've seen him sad before, y'know, locking himself in his room and not coming out for a day, stuff like that. But this is something else. I mean, I understand where he's coming from, I feel the need to curl up and cry myself, but I think there's a time and a place and right now isn't it."

"Get some sleep, Tony. Go on. No use sitting up worrying about him all night."

"But isn't that your plan?"

"Yeah," he said, "but I'm the oldest and that means I can do what I want. Do what monkey says, not what monkey does. Now go on, you need your rest."

I stood and yawned, my fear for my friend struggling against my weariness. "I'm just worried he's slipping. He's not himself."

Lee shook his head. "Shit, man, none of us are any more. But at least the four of us are more ourselves than anyone else for miles and miles. Now get some sleep."

CHAPTER TWELVE

"**D**UDE, WE'RE NOT getting out of here. I hate to say this, but with my mom, with the phone, with everything that's happened, we've got nothing. God knows how long the food will last."

"Especially if fatty tries taking any more," Kit added. He leaned against the far wall, arms folded, watching the booze with a skeptical eye.

"Thought you wouldn't say that anymore."

"Rodge, when I thought we were getting the hell outta here I was in a much better mood, man."

"Well fuck you, too, asshole."

I noted the Game Boy by the vodka bottle and guessed the guys reconnected while I slept late. That bond, however, was stuck together with nothing more than spit and bubblegum, and dissolved the moment I turned conversation towards the party.

"And we got whiskey," Lee added, placing the bottle by its sibling. The brown liquid piqued my interest more than the clear, though both filled me with dread. I'd watched what drink did to Jack, and to Fred, an elderly alcoholic who'd died in his home on the hill when I was ten. I didn't want to end up like either, but with no escape, a little fun could at least give me something to look forward to, some escapism.

"What time is it?" I asked.

Lee squinted at the gunmetal sky. "Guessing about ten. Eleven, maybe. That storm's gonna break soon."

_____

The roiling sky had spat droplets against the tree house throughout the night, the temperature lower than ever, and I imagined the real storm would hit soon.

"Should we eat before?"

"Probably."

"Here." I pulled the cereal box from our first haul, a bland but 'high in fibre' knock-off called *Hoopi-ohs*. The box looked almost full and I worried they'd gone stale, but as I grabbed a handful and shoved them into my mouth, my teeth came down with a satisfying crunch. I swallowed the mush dry, saving a gulp of water for last. After repeating two more handfuls, I passed the box to Rodgers who did the same. His swollen cheek looked a little better, but the sweat beading his forehead still worried me. I needed to keep a close eye on him.

After we'd eaten, Lee sat at the table and scooped the Vodka, turning the bottle over in his hands.

"Meant to spill a drop for the dead," he muttered, scanning the label. "That's what my dad did after he lost a friend couple of years back. Filled a capful and emptied it onto our backyard with tears in his eyes. Said it's the right thing to do."

"You want to waste what we got on that?" Kit asked.

Lee arched an eyebrow. "They *are* trying to kill us. Suppose that voids any ceremonies."

"Damn right."

My mouth watered at the drink, thirsty from the dry cereal. I imagined the clear spirit to be sweet, almost like candy, and the whiskey to be like chocolate. Then I recalled the sharp stench when Lee had poured the drink over my hands. Still, I nodded to my bottle of choice.

"Mind passing that here?"

"Sure." Lee pushed the bottle along the table and I took it with thanks, the glass heavier than expected. I ignored the guttural sounds outside as I scanned the label over myself, my chest fluttering in excitement. If my mother caught me, she'd have slapped me sideways and I'd be locked in my room for the better half of a year. All things considered, I'd take that over what cards I'd been handed, but Mom was dead. And my house was no longer a home.

The label told me the percentage, but at the time it could've told me the booze had come from unicorn farts and made about as much sense.

"Is this safe?" Rodgers asked, genuine fear lifting his voice. "Shouldn't we be getting proper rest, eating right, go back to making plans for an escape?"

The logical part of me agreed, but at thirteen, my rational voice slept on like a grouchy teenager. Had I been Lee's age, perhaps I'd have voiced my concern and put a stop to the party, but right then, an older kid *had* suggested this. And the mask of hopelessness he wore as he unscrewed the vodka cap drained my own enthusiasm. He *was* right though, I thought, we did need the break.

I pushed to my feet and crossed to the window, peering down on the swaying heads of our neighbors. Amongst them, I spotted my mother with moss scaling her arm and neck. If ever there was a time I needed to cloud my brain, this was it.

"Fuck..."

My fingers bit into the sill and the wood creaked. As her head tilted toward me, a hand grabbed my shoulder, squeezed.

"Spotted her while you were out." Rodgers' voice drew a tightness from my stomach. "I'm sorry, Tony."

She staggered in a beeline for the trunk with legs like a badly controlled puppet. Dry splatters (my own knife's doing) stained her favorite blouse, her bare feet slogging through the glistening grass as her cold eyes drifted up.

"Get away from the window," Lee called. "It's pointless, Tony. Come on. Back inside. Fucking celebrate being alive."

"Pointless?" Rodgers slapped his arms down. "What we're doing *here* is pointless. We should be studying the road, waiting for a clear break to make a run for it."

"Easy for you to say," Kit mocked, and slapped his thigh. "Dude, my leg's off limits for at *least* a week."

"*A week.*" Rodgers slogged to his sleeping bag and thumped down. "We don't have enough *food* for a week.

And, Kit, don't you *dare* say anything. I've already said I'm sorry about that."

Kit raised his palms in mock surrender. "Wasn't sayin' a word, man. Not a word."

At the table, Lee sniffed the bottle and his brow creased. He rolled the glass over in his hands. "Gotta wait until Kit's leg is at least a little better, Rodge. Three days, minimum. We've got enough food to last us that. Then we chance a run down the hill. I agree with you, okay? But for now, it's going to be a long, long three days. And I'll be damned if when I risk my life I've not done some things I've always wanted. You want to die never having had a drink? Never smoking a cigarette?"

Rodgers' lips tightened. "I...I don't know. I just want to get out of here."

"We will. Soon. But right now we're living it up, just in case...Just in case, Rodge."

Rodgers mulled it over with his eyes to the floor. "I suppose."

"Atta boy." As Lee pulled his stool across the floor, shuffling like a crab, we formed a tight square. A subtle grin lifted his cheek. "And what else?"

"What else what?" I asked. The bottles made my stomach giddy with butterflies—I'd never imagined I'd try a drop of alcohol before high-school.

"What else have any of us never done? What do you wanna do before we die?"

"Hey." The word flew like a bullet, stunning Lee. "We are not *dying*, Lee. Watch how you speak."

His smile faded and he nodded. "You're right. I'm sorry. *Just in case.* That's what I meant. I'm just damn tired."

"Right."

"...So?"

Kit shifted, pressing his back against the wall. He studied the ceiling. "I've never sung."

Lee glared at me, waiting for an outburst of laughter, some bubble of the joke to pop. But it never came.

"What?" he asked. "That such a shocker?"

"No, man. Not at all." I hoped Lee or Rodgers wouldn't ruin this. I could only imagine the courage it took to say that out loud with us here. Yet my friends remained silent. "Well, hey, I've got my guitar," I offered. "That can happen. Not like the noise will give us away when the freaks already know we're up here."

Up here, I thought, and my mind turned to my song, the monster I called a muse growling to life and itching my fingers.

"That's true," Lee said. "Rodgers, anything?"

Rodgers picked the dirt beneath his nails. "Never... kissed a girl."

Now we all laughed. We laughed so hard that Kit farted. Then we laughed some more.

After wiping my eyes clear, I got my shoulders under control. Perhaps this wasn't the worst idea. I threw my head back and drew a breath. "Well, 'fraid to say that ain't happening here, man."

"I know!" His lips drew tight. "He asked, so I'm just fuckin' sayin'."

"Yeah, yeah. Tony?"

All eyes fell to me, and my heart jacked. "I...I don't know, man. I've never smoked, like I said."

Lee's lower lip jutted and he nodded along. "Well, I've already said that can happen. Made a promise. I got seven left in the box, so yeah, willing to share, seeing that this is the end times."

"It's not the end times, but thanks." I'd said it without thinking. I needed to rekindle the hope he no longer provided, especially for Rodgers' sake. The stubborn bags under Lee's eyes gave me a prick of fear.

"We drink," Lee said, "and we smoke. And that's what we do. For now."

Rodgers grimaced. "Some plan, guys."

I raised a finger. "And *then* we leave. Okay?"

"Scout's honor. In three days, when Kit's good, we leave."

Kit threw a mock salute. "I'll drink to that."

The monotonous wailing outside the walls melded to a white noise, no longer as threatening as it had been the day previous. The altitude comforted me enough to relax, and I watched Lee unscrew the bottle with fresh excitement. I chanced a glance at Kit and Rodgers and recognized my own thrill mirrored there. Lee looked to each of us before saying a quick cheers and then eased the bottle to his lips. Our heads tilted along with the liquid. A bubble gurgled and fell to the underside of the tipped glass, and Lee's throat clicked as the clear liquid meandered its way to his stomach.

"Oh, fucking hell!"

He coughed and brought the back of his palm to his mouth, face red and eyes watering. He sucked air between his teeth, drooling slightly. "Shit, that's disgusting." He spluttered and handed the bottle to the right, to Rodgers.

Rodgers took the offering with a sigh, but took it all the same. "That bad?"

"Like barbecued gasoline but worse. At least it'll help disinfect your mouth."

Rodgers eyed the booze as if it were a dangerous animal with raised hackles. "Smells rank."

"Tastes just as bad. But I drank it. Now you gotta."

"Where have I heard that one before?"

Rodgers upturned the bottle without pause, perhaps needing the ordeal finished, and took a gulp. Then he spat a spray of vodka. His hand shot to his mouth as booze dribbled from the neck onto his jeans. He corrected the bottle, and looked to Lee as if our friend had just made him eat poop. "You serious?" he spat. "Why the hell would people drink this stuff? Burns and stings like shit."

"Here, here, pass it over." Kit grabbed the bottle and Rodgers let it go all too gladly. Kit rolled it about in his palms before studying the label like Rodgers with a new video game. "Russians did something right, eh?"

I didn't know if the Russians invented vodka or not, but I watched as Kit took the bottle to his lips with fevered curiosity. He swallowed and lowered the booze as his face warped into a grimace. *"Mmmmm,"* he said with a chuckle, sarcasm as subtle as an elephant on the highway. "Delicious, Tony. Here. Take it. Just like candy."

Only me left. I took the bottle and my body fizzled with the pressure. I felt like telling them to all look away, but if Rodgers had done it, I had to. Hell, I'd just taken out my mom, and my friend got murdered by my other friend's father—I could take a damn drink.

"Here's to us," I said, and brought the bottle forward. I pursed my lips and sucked as little as possible. My tongue prickled, a flavor I'd never tasted before sending a shiver across my skin. I gulped, and my mouth flooded with saliva in preparation for vomit. My eyes slammed shut as they watered, stomach fighting to keep that shit down. Fireworks went off behind my lids, and each breath was like sucking petroleum.

"Mother of God that's foul," I managed, and passed the bottle back to Lee. They all laughed and I chuckled along, bringing a hand to my gut as the burning liquor snaked ever lower. The heat, I had to admit, felt all right.

Lee brought the bottle to his mouth and squeezed the bridge of his nose, his lids shaking. He took three liberal gulps before sighing and slamming the back of his forearm against his mouth. His voice came with a wheeze. "Not so bad if you block your nose, it's...actually, I think I'm regretting that."

He rushed to the window, and I gagged as vomit hissed down the trunk, drawing a unified groan from all of us. Lee belched and dry heaved, his back jerking as another stream shot from his lips. When finished, he dipped back inside and wiped his face clean, complexion drained.

"Okay," he said, "one gulp at a time. Schientifically proven and..." his eyes widened.

"Say that again," I said, and laughed.

"Schien...scien...*sssscientifically.* There. Scientifically."

"You're slurring!" I clapped my hands as my own head began to swim, a pleasant numbness matching my emotional barrier. I pointed to the whiskey. "Pass that one my way? Looks more appetizing than the piss-water."

"Sure, if you think shit-water looks delicious." He threw me the bottle and I snatched it mid-air, surprised by my reflexes and a little less fearful now that I'd tried devil's spit. "Here's to our friends and family," I said, and drank deeply.

The whiskey burned my mouth and throat, but after using the word 'family', the pain seemed fitting. I fought the vile booze and managed to keep it down as tears slipped along my cheeks. If ever I imagined drinking wood smoke, this was it.

After we'd had our fill (a quarter of each bottle gone and two more vomiting bouts from all), we sat red-faced in a circle, swaying ever so slightly. We'd lit a candle (stupidly enough), and for a moment, I actually felt cozy. Rodgers shifted forward. His swollen cheek looked a little better, but his skin had taken on an ashen hue. The shine of his eyes told me he had something to say.

"Kit. Why do you hate me?"

Tension filled the room and Kit's face dropped. "I...I don't hate you, Rodge."

The first time I heard Kit call him by his name, and it took the end of the world to drag it out.

"You made my life hell."

"I know."

"So why'd you do that? To me, and to Tony? Not just yanking my tooth out, I mean *all the time*."

I cringed being brought into the fight, but the alcohol seemed to demand answers as much as Rodgers. I stayed silent.

"You *know* what I *hate*?" Kit asked. "I hate having my head dunked in a tub of ice water every second night by a fuckin' maniac. I hate not being able to help my sister, even when she turns blue and screams for nights on end. I hate when she got head cold after head cold and I couldn't help her because he'd throw me to a fuckin' wall before I reached her room, man. I hated alarm clocks blaring ten times a fucking day. I hated *my* life. I hated it, hated it, hated it...Is that so hard to understand?"

"Why take it out on me?"

"Rodgers," Lee warned. "Come on, man."

"Legitimate question, Lee."

Kit sighed, finished toying with the zipper. "Because you had a good dad, okay, Rodge? Because Tony had a mom who acted like moms are supposed to. That what you wanna hear?"

Tears glistened his face then, and my chest tightened in response.

"Jesus, man. Try understand it from my point of view for a second."

"I'm sorry," Rodgers said, almost a whisper, and I believed him. "Sincerely, Kit. You helped me out yesterday, even if it hurt like a bitch. I'm...I'm sorry."

"Yeah...yeah, me, too."

I wanted to know something, too, and the alcohol backed me up like a good friend. "Kit," I said, "so what about Lee, huh? Why didn't you ever pick on him?"

Kit motioned his way. "Scared of the fucker."

Surprisingly, Lee's drunken smile melted to confusion. "Really?"

"That fuckin'...jacket. And the smokes, and the lone wolf shit at school. I dunno."

"Hey," Lee said, "let's drop this, okay? It's meant to be a break from all the bullshit. A bit of fun. We're all in this together."

And my friend had a point. Today we were no longer nerds, dorks, or bullies. Right then we were four kids having a first experience. And drinking to forget the end of the world. Another song idea struck, and the sense of purpose filled me with joy.

Lee's fingers moved like the work of a crap puppeteer as he pulled his cigarettes.

"Time for a smoke," he slurred, and popped the butt of a Marlboro into his mouth. Kit busied himself with his sleeping bag zipper again as the older kid's lighter swayed past the tip of his cigarette.

"Kit, you all right?" My swollen tongue mushed the words.

"Yeah...yeah, fine."

The lighter found its destination and the cherry of Lee's cigarette glowed, a soft crackle of tobacco following. A stream of smoke danced to the ceiling, and he took a deep drag before passing the cigarette my way with an unsteady hand. "*Now* it's time."

"Cheers," I said, and reminded myself that no trouble could come of this. Not when every adult in our lives had become a moss-covered abomination. I studied the cigarette a moment, and a finger of smoke tickled my eye, making it water.

Fuck it, I thought, and popped the thing in my mouth. Orange light swelled as I drew a breath, and a thick, harsh cloud whooshed down my throat. I coughed, a grey pillar puffing from my lips, which only made me cough again. Booze and cigarettes seemed to want to make my eyes water as much as possible that day, and my stomach roiled with nausea. Seconds later, blindspots danced before my eyes as nicotine zapped my brain for the first time in my life. The first of many. The room spun slightly, aided by the booze, and as I passed the cigarette to Kit, I struggled not to upchuck what little food remained in my gut.

Easy now. Don't get sick again. Do not puke.

Miraculously, my body complied, and with enough deep breaths, the room no longer felt like a wind-swept boat. Kit passed the cigarette Rodgers' way without taking a drag, and suddenly his zipper fixation no longer seemed like a mere distraction.

"Kit, you sure you're all right?"

"I'm good, man." He forced a smile, twirled the metal piece some more.

"All right, then."

Rodgers pinched the cigarette like royalty, three unused fingers splayed like peacock feathers. His eyes crossed the closer the cigarette came to his pursed lips, and then he sucked a sharp breath. His eyes shot wide and smoke blew out in a cloud as he coughed and spluttered, jabbing the smoke in Lee's direction. Lee took the cough-inducer with a laugh and popped it back in his mouth, inhaling as cool as any adult I'd ever seen. He twirled the butt in his fingers.

"Almost gone, Kit, you sure you don't want a pull?"

Something felt 'off' then, an obvious point my drunken brain struggled to make. But Kit forced a smile. "Sure."

As he motioned for a pass, he took the cigarette gently between his thumb and index. He twirled it a moment.

"Well look at that," Rodgers said, slurring more than any of us. "Big, tough bastard can't handle a smoke."

"*Rodge.*"

Rodgers chuckled, watching the bully like an animal at the zoo. He spat a wad of pink spit as, with a deep breath, Kit inhaled. He allowed smoke to drift from his lips in a controlled stream. Then he took a second, as if to prove a point, and passed the cigarette back to Lee.

"Had to do it better than any of us, huh?" Rodgers sulked.

"Enough, man."

Lee finished the smoke before putting it out on the table, snuffing the flame. Grey curls danced in the light from the window, and my head continued to swim, morphing to a pleasant sensation I'd never felt. My arms tingled as giddiness danced in my chest.

Then Kit coughed, fist to his mouth, and a wheeze followed. He coughed again, with another wheeze, and his free hand shot to the ground for stabilization.

"Hey, man, you all right?" My voice trailed with a chuckle out of fear rather than anything funny.

Kit nodded, but his cough continued.

Rodgers laughed. "See, not so fuckin' cool now, are ye?"

"Rodgers, shut the fuck up. Kit...Kit, you all right?"

Lee stood, his brain overriding the booze better than mine, and knelt beside Kit.

"Hey, hey, look at me, look at me."

The kid continued to wheeze, and as his color changed, Lee cursed.

"Guys, he's asthmatic. He's having an attack."

CHAPTER THIRTEEN

THE WINDOW SMASHED—my starter gun—and I lifted the hatch to an empty tree trunk doubling in my vision. The streaks of puke on the bark roiled my stomach as my cold metal knife pressed into the small of my back.

"Go, go, go!" Lee yelled, and I shuffled out, heart jackhammering while the booze struggled to steel my nerves. Lee'd wasted a pellet before finally shattering his own bedroom window, leaving us with our last projectile—one final outing.

My hand missed a rung and my chest leaped before my fingers curled around another and I continued descending, whispering a string of curse words I hardly noticed.

I'm drunk. Goddamnit, I'm gonna die for this bastard.

At the bottom, my foot missed its mark and my gut tightened as I plunged. I slapped the ground and wobbled, the impact shooting through my legs before I landed with a gasp on my back, the handle of my knife punching my spine. The yard swayed as I struggled back to my feet, drawing the attention of two monstrosities that neared the bushes at Lee's yard. The duo detached from the group and stumbled in my direction.

Fuck!

Survival instinct kicked and I forced my eyes and limbs to work in unison. I jogged out on the road in a zig-zag, throwing my trail, and then passed Rodgers' house as my stomach sloshed, the whiskey leaping to the back of my throat like acid. A guttural call sent a scurry of fear across my skin. After a quick glance back, I saw the source: at least three had spotted me, and I'd have to lose them quick.

Why in the world Kit had never told us about his asthma, I'd never know. I suspected he had his image to upkeep, and seeing myself and Rodgers smoke just wouldn't do. But for god's sake, life wasn't like in the movies—we didn't think he'd be cool if he smoked crack, let alone a goddamn cigarette. Somewhere in his house lay that inhaler, the filler to the latest hole in our boat. I remembered what they looked like from my cousin William always having one on hand, and if Kit treated his condition anything like him then it'd be within reach by his bed. Upstairs for starters, whichever room belonged to him.

A cry like a sludge-filled blender made me scream and I narrowly avoided the swinging arms of a green and deformed man in an I Visited Dream Woods shirt. He lumbered after and our movements mirrored as the alcohol refused to release my limbs. A rock tripped me and I went down hard, skidding on my stomach and whacking my chin. I scrambled to my feet while my skin burned as if I'd been raked across needles. I chanced a look back, breathing in short gasps, and another freak had joined my pursuers, giving me a needed adrenaline jolt. I wondered if the mystery man watched from the trees, if he'd intervene should I fall. I didn't plan on finding out.

At Kit's, I barged through the rusted gate and down the drive, stopping only long enough to smack down the handle and spill inside. I slammed the door behind me. As my eyes adjusted to the gloom, a stained staircase bloomed into focus while the scent of something rotten swam in the air. I pulled my knife and crept to the stairs, my chest fluttering with each breath.

Enough horror movies taught me not to ask if anyone was home. So instead, I controlled my pacing and treaded lightly up the steps, cringing each time I drew a creak. Halfway there, gravel shifted outside as my chasers shambled along the drive. Moments later the door bucked, but held. I released a long, quivering breath.

Get the inhaler, get down the tree Kit used. Simple. Get it done, and get back.

Another noise caught my attention, a slow shuffle accompanied by a sound like a rusted hinge, coming from the upper landing. Kit's sister. My mouth fell open.

She shambled from her room with both arms stretched forward, cracking against the doorframe like a drunk in the middle of the night. Her blue nightgown was stained with her own blood. A thick matting of moss obscured her features, her trademark missing tooth replaced by that gnarled appendage I'd grown to loathe. As her head fell back, I imagined a believer slapped by the palm of a charismatic preacher. Then she wobbled to the stairs.

"Stay where you are," I hissed, knowing the words were meaningless, but nonetheless needing to try. Thoughts of stabbing a young girl, infected or not, made my knees weak. "Please, Josie. *Please.*"

Her foot hovered above the top step for the briefest moment, a few seconds that, for me, felt like an eternity. She leaned forward. And then she fell.

I balked as she barreled down, clattering from wall to banister, wall to banister. I jumped but my foot caught in her gown and I yelled as the room turned like the inside of a washing machine. A steady *thump-thump-thump* filled my head as I smacked each step, but the pain only bloomed when my head cracked the hardwood of the landing. Fireworks exploded behind my eyes, and I gasped as she collapsed on my chest. With a grunt, I threw her sideways and snatched the knife currently digging into my spine. My skull pulsed in agony.

"*Get back!*"

She rose like the living dead, each mechanical motion completely unnatural and jerky. She reached again, and her left arm fell at an unnatural angle. Then she shuffled forward.

"Goddamnit!"

I jabbed, wincing as my blade parted her neck all too easy, like cutting hot butter. The stench of rotted vegetables filled my nose. A gurgled cry emanated from her torn throat as her tiny hands snatched thin air. I stayed just out of reach.

I pressed harder on the hilt and then slashed sideways as the blade popped free in a spray of crimson. She toppled and cracked her head by my feet.

"Jesus...Jesus fucking Christ."

I backed to the stairs and a red halo reached my way, all the while eating up dust and dirt. The freaks outside smacked the window by the door, distorted silhouettes throwing shadows across the young girl's corpse. I recalled Josie waving and smiling every day of the week, and a strange lump settled in the pit of my stomach. If an omnipresent deity did indeed watch over us, he damn sure had a skewed sense of fairness. Six years old, dead on the floor.

The glass cracked.

I bound upstairs, gritting my teeth the closer I came to the impenetrable darkness of the second floor. I prayed Kit had enough time, I'd never experienced an attack before, had no idea how long they lasted.

At the top of the stairs, the open door ahead revealed a grimy bathroom with track marks leading both in and out. I wondered if Kit's house looked this state before the nightmare hit. A painting of Jesus Christ hung crooked on the wall, eyes staring at something I'd never see. At the next door, I gagged as a wave of spoilt meat assaulted my nostrils. That little girl must've been inside all along, smacking off pink walls like a moth at a bright light. I sped past to the next door, praying it to be Kit's room, and peered inside.

A king-sized bed sat in the centre with a plush rug by its feet. A collection of faded Mary statues peppered a vanity table to the left, and although Kit's mother was out of the picture a long time, his father's room remained unchanged, life frozen at that very day. Dusty curtains masked the window, a sliver of light at its edges. And alone in the corner stood a man.

My breath caught.

"Hello?" I wheezed.

He didn't turn.

I backed away, feet pulling me to the left, toward the final room. I hadn't seen clearly, the space too gloomy and my feet moving before I had time to think, but even though his back was to me, I swore he wore a butcher's apron. Something dangled from his right fist, something my brain interpreted as a very large knife. My thoughts turned to the Lacey kid's ornamental machete.

My fingers found the handle and I pushed into the final room, no time to look around as my eyes remained glued to Kit's father's bedroom. I looked down only long enough to find the lock and twist it shut, securing me inside.

My mind reeled at the possibility an adult stood next door. If it was a freak, the scuffle with Kit's sister would have drawn its attention. I imagined it toppling down the stairs to get me, a misshapen tooth slicing into my skin.

Then a floorboard creaked. And another, this time slow and deliberate.

I called against my will, needing a reply. "Hello?"

No answer. My stomach and bladder tightened like an over-tuned violin string.

"If you're out there, you gotta help me! Hello? *Hello?*"

Something happened then that made my skin crawl: The man laughed.

A low and wheezy chuckle trickled around the doorframe, as if the lunatic grappled to hide such glee. I stayed quiet.

Another step, this time in the hallway, a boot, not so quiet now, something dragging behind. And getting closer. A shadow fattened at the foot of the door. I felt his presence, right there on the other side, mere inches away. I held my breath, eyes wide, heart pounding, and listened. I listened for that laugh, for a word, for *anything*. Anything at all...All I got was heavy breathing, and only a slab of wood for protection.

I backed up a step, and another, passing a heap of dirty clothes and a splayed magazine. When a dresser pressed against the back of my thigh, I felt around and thanked the heavens when my fingers closed around something plastic and cold. I brought the item around and squeezed my eyes in thanks as I saw the inhaler in my palm.

Go, go, go, go.

"Little pig," said the man, changing his voice to an almost comical degree. "Little pig, let me in."

I raced to the window, no longer caring for noise, and pushed open the frame as cold air hit my skin.

"Saw you and another boy outsmart a pack of 'em yesterday," he said. "Impressive. Got out of that pickle right n' slippery, didn't you?"

I shuddered as I lifted my leg across the sill and slipped outside, my panicked state lying that the fall wouldn't be so bad, *just jump and go. Jump and go!* I almost did, too, had it not been for the solid branch to my left. I stuffed the inhaler into my pocket and hoisted myself onto the tree. The thick limb promised to hold, and I clutched my legs around it, using my weight to shimmy to the trunk like a caterpillar.

"Run all you like, little boy. My time is here, and I intend to soak it all in."

He slammed against Kit's bedroom door—*whack!*—slammed again—*whack!*—and a crash followed from downstairs. The freaks were in. Using the distraction, I reached the trunk and carefully meandered my way down to the lawn. After brushing off the bark, I took in the area, spotting two more monstrosities stumbling to Kit's open door around the side of the house. Soon, more would follow, and the maniac would be forced to fight his way out.

The adrenaline in my body overrode the alcohol, and I pushed for home on the double, keeping to the bushes and trees. The bloated sky promised a night of rain, and I only paused once to piss as I neared Lee's home. The freaks sounded like a down-pitched beehive from out of sight, and, surprisingly, I found myself unafraid. I'd dealt with our neighbors, learned their pattern, knew how to handle them to some degree. They were familiar. A human, on the other hand, was unpredictable. He lingered in town, after all, never calling for help, only observing. He had a laugh like a hyena on coke, and a mind sick enough to make me taste a new flavor of fear. One tasting of copper and spoilt meat.

He also had a butcher's apron.

As Lee pulled me inside the tree house, I cried with relief. The trip had taken its toll, and my body ached for rest and fuel. I needed safety, some food, and the pounding headache behind my eyes threw an unwanted blanket of gloom over the already dire situation. That was my first hangover.

"Here." I fished the inhaler from my pocket as Kit pushed from the corner, quiet and sulking, but he took the inhaler with thanks. He slid the device inside his mouth and pressed the top. Medicine hissed from the cylindrical container. After three long pulls, he took a deep breath, now seemingly calm.

"Passed about ten minutes after you left, but thanks, man. I really needed this."

"Of course."

"It happens again, I might not be so lucky. Shouldn't have been so cocky."

"It's all right."

The room smelt of cigarettes and booze despite the open window's efforts. A sharp tang of vomit lingered, too, and I imagined unless it rained, we'd be dealing with that stench for a long time. Rodgers sat slumped in the opposite corner, Game Boy clutched to his face, blips and bloops coming each time he thumbed a button.

"Everyone all right?" I asked.

"We're good," Lee said. "Despite the hangovers. And that was an awesome thing to do, Tony."

"Yeah, well..." I went to Rodgers' side, the mental distance from my friend bothering me more and more, and watched him play a level of *Super Mario Land*. "We might be in more trouble than we think."

The *Game Over* melody danced from the device as Rodgers' attention, like the others, shot to me. With a gulp, I told them of my run-in with the stranger. I made sure I included the finer details, like, oh, a fucking butcher's apron. A man who didn't call for help and dressed as such was no man I wanted to get acquainted with.

"You think he knows where we are?" Kit asked.

"I'm pretty sure he's figured it out. And I think we need to block off the window at night. The freaks mask sound pretty well, but we can't be too careful, just in case."

"Who've we got in town that'd do something like this?" Lee asked. The puffiness of his eyes worried me again (I'd still yet to see him sleep), but I needed one problem at a time here.

"There's that Lacey guy down the street," he said, "used to have a goddamn machete he bought as an 'ornament'. All kindsa horror stuff lying around his house. But it's not him. You've seen him changed...What about his buddy Ford? The long-haired dude. They hang out. Lives closer to the river. He creeps me out just as much."

I shook my head. "Not him. He was one of the freaks with Jacob. Recognized his shorts and sandals."

"Can't believe it..." Kit avoided eye contact as he spoke. "Some bastard hanging out in *my* house. Why my dad's room?"

"Religious?" I posed the question carefully, not wanting Kit upset any more than necessary. "Could be all the, y'know, statues and stuff 'round the room. Makes him feel safe?"

"A religious nut with a butcher's apron at the end of the world," Lee said. "Well fuck me."

I caught Kit's panicked expression but said nothing. He'd seen his father turned already, after all.

As we sat in silence, we digested the situation. I noticed Rodgers' lack of input and gave him a nudge. His mental absence since we'd gotten drunk bothered me, and I wanted to keep him involved, not have him retract again. I worried for his fever.

"Huh?"

"What do you think?" I said.

Rodgers shrugged and sighed, holding up the game console. "Game Boy's dead. Batteries. Think we can get some more?"

Kit slapped a hand to his forehead. "Rodgers, you fuckin' serious? Get your head out of your ass, man. This is serious."

Rodgers' shoulders slumped as he toyed with the buttons on the silent Game Boy, the screen now just a black mirror. As Lee and Kit discussed the possibilities of the newcomer, their voices faded to the background and I tapped Rodgers.

"Hey, you okay?"

"I'm good, Tony."

"You promise?"

"I promise." He smiled then, and a chuckle escaped his lips. "Polly didn't want to come here, you know."

A thousand imaginary ants skittered across my skin, and although I wanted to speak, I just slowly nodded. Polly, we all knew, was Rodgers' dog, two years dead. Run over by Richardson while making a round to Nate and Allie's during a blizzard. Rodgers had wailed like a mother who'd lost their baby, even taking the collar from the dog's broken neck and wearing it around his wrist until his dad talked him out of it. We'd buried Polly out in the field between our homes, same field Kit and I had hidden in the tall grass. Probably right around that very spot, too. Gorgeous Labrador, five years old, and a coat as shiny as gold.

I licked my lips. They'd dried fast. "Polly, Rodgers?"

"Huh?" He looked at me with genuine confusion as another cold fist of fright constricted my gut. "What did you say?"

"Nothing," I said, and tuned back into Lee and Kit's conversation, allowing Rodgers to return to his dead console.

"Any conclusions?" I asked.

Lee shook his head. "Only one I can think of is Kit's dad."

"And I saw him," Kit blurted. "Came out of my sister's room after turning her, too. Green all over the place, just like the others, covered in that *shit*. Shredded Josie's neck to ribbons, man, I saw it all." His own throat bobbed in response and he sniffled, wiping his face with the back of his hand. I decided not to tell him about his sister.

"The butcher's apron is a clue," Lee mumbled. "Nearest place is, what, two towns over? Can't be sure, but I remember my mom picking up chops there a couple of times. Never seen it myself."

"Yeah," I said. "Just past the school on the east side. Think that's the nearest place."

"So, you think this is an outsider?"

"I know just as much as you, man."

"Right."

The groans outside peaked and Rodgers finally dropped the useless device, face to the ceiling. "Will they ever just *shut the fuck up*?"

"Don't think that's gonna happen, buddy," I said. "Try occupy yourself. Keep your mind busy."

Before you lose it completely, I almost added.

Lee pushed to his feet and crossed to the window, studying the neighbors below. "There's more of 'em out there now. At least five or six that I'm seeing." His eyes narrowed to slits as the cogs in his mind began to whirl. "Which means we could get a good estimate of how many are left out in the woods...We know everyone in town."

"What are you thinking?"

"Well, if we write down everyone's names who's down there, we'll know who's left lurking in the surrounding area. And if we know a path's clear, we can risk a run for it. It's, what, a mile and a bit to cross the river out to the highway? If there's only a handful in the forest, we'd get around them. But Tony, the transport trail from the mill is on the other side of the mountain, very few homes out there. Except, that entire section is fenced off with razor wire. We'd have to go through the grounds themselves."

An anvil of emotion clapped me on the head. "Lee, I can't..."

"Look, we get through the mill's fence, we're on the other side in no time. Don't even gotta go inside the building. We race around to the truck road and it's a free shot to the highway."

Flashing blue and red, blue and red...Richardson at the door...the wood chipper...

The transportation trail closed along with the mill, no longer needed. I hadn't seen it for some time, but last I checked, weeds choked the once concrete road through that damned fence. Taking that trail meant getting through the freaks, giving them the slip, but like Lee said, if we saw everyone from that side of the mountain gathered in the yard, it could be possible.

"I'll do it," I said. "I will."

"After my leg heals," Kit added.

"Of course. After your leg heals."

I clicked my tongue. "And we've only got one ball bearing left. We'd have to make it count. It'd be our last trip out there. Plus, we're running out of windows."

I knew my friends were thinking the same: risk smashing one final window and making a break for it, or smash the final window for a food-run, leave our fate in the hands of the world. But the world had already proven to be unfair and heartless. And both options looked equally uncertain. I decided I'd write another song and distract myself, needing the purpose and escape. I'd come to think of the instrument like a psychologist, healing my mind and helping me process what I'd been through. I pulled my pen and got to work. I ignored the tears.

As moonlight slithered into the tree house, it brought yet more shadows, and a taste of rain.

CHAPTER FOURTEEN

MY **BLISTERS SCREAMED** as I pressed a chord and strummed, the note ringing while I scribbled a new verse into the copybook—my third song of the night. After my run-in with the biblical butcher, my mind flooded with sonic possibilities. Each flashback to my mother dropping by my bedroom door, every mental glimpse of Jacob falling slack in Lee's father's arms, surfaced a melody that my hands frantically documented. Like speeding butterflies born of my own brain, my music became a waypoint for their existence. And I *had* to give them life.

"That's nice," Rodgers said, his eyes drooped from lack of sleep. He sat propped in his sleeping bag, while beside him, Kit snored softly. Lee had fallen asleep beneath the table after another bout of booze. At least he hadn't puked this time.

"Thanks." I set the guitar aside, knowing my friend needed a chat. Also, having Rodgers off to La-La Land put us all at a disadvantage, and I couldn't overlook that. The root of his far-off eyes could be from booze and nicotine, or could be from a damaged mind. I intended to find out which.

Polly didn't want to come here.

I closed the copybook, taking a moment to scan the scribbles my shaking hands managed to produce. Half an album's worth of material, all born of death and decay, and all within three days. Shit, at least the end of the world caused an overflow of musical fodder.

"Rodge," I said, "what did you mean earlier?"

"When?"

Genuine confusion crossed his face, and I waited for that look to break. It never did.

"You said, *'Polly didn't want to come here.'*"

His lips curled. "No, I didn't?"

"You did."

"Oh."

"You wanna talk about it?"

He looked to the covered window. his lids half-closed. The bottom corner of the plastic had ripped while Lee put it into place, probably due to alcohol distorting his hand-eye coordination. That left a sliver of insight to our hiding spot, and us seeing out meant the butcher, if he rounded the corner of one of the homes, could see in. We'd doused the candles soon as night fell.

"Earlier," Rodgers said, "what did *you* mean when you said my dad couldn't come up?"

"Rodge, I never said that."

"You didn't?" Here came that look again, genuine and fear-inducing. My mouth dried. "But I heard you? You said he wasn't allowed up here anymore."

"I never said that, Rodgers. And you're starting to scare the life out of me."

The past few days had broken through in dribs and drabs, my mind only allowing entry to a sliver of reality, just enough to keep me moving and get me through. I imagined the same went for Kit and Lee, judging by Lee's outburst at Allie and Nate's and his otherwise collected manner, and Kit's newfound harmony with us, but still lashing out at Rodgers. We were dealing as best we could. Except for him. My fears had come true. Rodgers had lost it.

I saw that now, in his distant gaze, his lack of expression. And...

Polly didn't want to come here.

I tapped the copybook, at least proud of the work I'd finished. Being in control counted for something. That work gave me purpose, an outlet, and I'd be lying if I hadn't dreamed of recording those tracks one day. More than that, it'd become my sole purpose in life. "Rodge, how about we get some sleep, huh? Your mouth still painful?"

Genuine confusion overcame him. "Painful?"

"Because we pulled your tooth, Rodge. R-remember?"

"Oh, yeah. Sure."

"Rodge, you do remember?"

He sighed. "Of course I do, Tony. How could I not?"

The tense moment passed, and he smiled. His cheeks lifted as it reached his eyes. I believed that smile. I'd seen it a thousand times before.

"Things might look better for us tomorrow, okay?" I said. "We've got this, man. We've got each other. It'll all change in the morning."

"It will?"

"I promise." I strained all the sincerity I could muster, like milking a sick cow. "Someone will find us. They have to. We'll be racing for the highway before you know it."

"And what about the man?"

I was happy to hear him ask a productive question. It proved his brain hadn't completely snapped. At least not yet. And, truth be told, I hadn't planned on actually sleeping because of that man. My stinging eyes demanded I dozed, but no way in hell could I actually drift away with him lurking. Also, I didn't want to worry Rodgers.

"That man won't stand a chance. We'll be outta here before he ever finds us."

I hope.

"All right." Rodgers scooped his polaroid and clutched it to his chest. After looking the device over, apparently satisfied, he rose and crept to the window.

"What are you doing?" I asked.

With a light hand, he brushed aside a torn section of plastic and raised the camera to his face and squinted down the lens. His mouth fell open absently as he tilted the device just right. "Getting a snap," he said. "See a break in the clouds, moonlight looks great. Wanna give you something to return the favor for the food."

As the flash blared and lit up the tree house, spotlights rained in my vision and I squeezed the bridge of my nose, waiting for my sight to clear. Rodgers had just captured something I'd be forever grateful for, something I never would've thought of due to my musical vortex, and something I'd keep for a very long time. I hoped the light hadn't woken our friends, but I needn't have worried, they continued sleeping like the dead.

Still, I hoped the biblical butcher hadn't noticed the flash.

Rodgers' sniffling woke me. I sat with a sigh and cleared the sleep from my eyes, the room swimming into focus. He sat on a chair by the window, back to me, framed in moonlight as his shoulders hitched.

"What's going on, Rodge?"

He jumped, startled, and my stomach tightened as his belt jangled, followed by the zip of his pants.

"The hell are you doing?"

I reached him just as he got to his feet and brushed away tears from his eyes, keeping his distance like a wary dog.

"Rodge, what's up, man?"

The bulge in his pants told me plenty, and the embarrassment that flooded my system matched his own right then and there.

"I'm sick," he said, the words through tears and snot. "Goddamnit, I'm *sick*, Tony."

"Were you...?"

He nodded and cleared his face with the back of his hand. "I couldn't help it. How fucked up is that? I'm a fucking monster."

I shushed him, bringing a finger to my lips. "Dude...you're not sick. I get it, all right? I get it."

And I did, too. Much as I didn't want to admit, the urge had taken me over the past six months at the worst times, too. On the school bus, *in* school, the goddamn garden, you name it. An extra birthday present from Mother Nature that no one warned me of. Though, I had to admit, beating one out to the symphonic cries of our infected neighbors was another level.

"I just...just wanted something to feel nice."

I nodded and my eyes found the whiskey bottle on the table, more empty than when I'd drifted. That explained a lot.

"How much did you have?" I asked, sounding as conversational as possible. "Hey, how much?"

"Few sips. Didn't even like it. Helps with the pain in my mouth."

Despite the drink, I noted his moment of clarity and decided to grab hold of it like bull horns. "You remember everything clearly, Rodge? You said some stuff yesterday that worried the hell out of me."

"About Polly? I was just joking around..."

I offered a laugh, trying to keep Rodgers calm. The Polly statement had been no joke. We both knew better. And if the others woke now, the embarrassment of being caught masturbating would drive him over the edge. I needed him to sleep as soon as possible. Hell, I needed us out of this claustrophobic trap as soon as possible. The slippery slope of Rodgers' mind couldn't hold much longer, and I remembered the tales of cabin fever, such a condition becoming more alarming by the second.

"Hey, I want you to have this. It came out nice."

He passed me the photo he'd snapped, and I took it, cautious of his unwashed hands. A glossy square showed the back of his house, windows shattered, walls splattered with gore, and the mountainside stretching out to blend with the storm. Only the freaks' heads were visible at the bottom like humanoid greenary.

"Thought you'd take a photo of them," I muttered, and placed the photograph within my copybook.

"It's a nice photo, Tony. I wanted something nice. We all need to enjoy ourselves...Before it's too late. I get what Lee meant when he offered the drink and the cigarettes now."

"And you added in another activity, too, huh?"

The joke flopped and I swallowed what little saliva I could, my throat parched. "Rodge, it's all going to be okay, all right? We'll get out of this."

"How can you say that, man? How can you say that so certainly?"

I shrugged. "Well...I can't. But we need to hold on to something, even if that something's a tiny bit of hope, right?"

"Right."

"It's not the end."

"It's not the end," he repeated, and peered through the hole in the garbage bag to the freak show. "You think any part of them knows what's happened? You think something, even in the back of their minds, is screaming out? Not wanting to do what the parasite, or whatever, is making them do?"

The thought turned my stomach, but with Lee's explanation, I doubted it very much to be true. "I don't think so," I said, and made to sit Rodgers back down. He flinched at my touch and I retreated. "Dude, look, it's okay. Nothing's wrong here."

His eyes darted to our sleeping friends and back again. "I need to show you somethin', Tony."

A pang of guilt hit as I shifted on one foot, making sure my knife was still tucked inside my belt. The cold blade pressed against my skin. I'd taken out my mom, after all. I'd take out my best friend, if needed. I realized that now. "What is it, man?"

Rodgers sighed before unzipping his pants.

"Rodge, seriously, what the fuck?"

"No, no, no, just wait. Please."

Oh, sweet holy shit in heaven...

He cupped his genitals to keep them from view and I gritted my teeth, squinting with one eye.

"Dude, please, look."

"Fuck," I muttered, but did as instructed. In the subtle moonlight, I fought not to laugh at what I saw. I got it now. At least part of Rodge's weird behavior made sense. "Rodge, you serious?"

A suggestion of hair dotted his pelvis, tiny strands barely visible above his palm, all-consuming shock still clear on his face.

"Dude, what?"

"Don't you see it?" he hissed. "Tony, look closely. *Look*. I've got whatever the freaks have. It's that shit growing on them. My tooth, now this shit? *It's got me.*"

"Dude, they're pubes."

The color drained from his face fast as buckshot, leaving him the hue of cottage cheese. Quick as he could, he buckled his belt and zipped his jeans. "You mean I'm not...?"

"No."

"Oh my god. But my tooth, my..."

I shook my head, momentarily speechless. "Jesus, man, this is what's been bothering you? You thought you were *infected*?"

I recalled Rodgers slunk in the corner each time I made a run. His lack of response to anything Lee or myself said. His escape into video games until the Game Boy died. His *off* comment about Polly and his dad.

Rodgers ran a hand across his head and paced the room, breathing heavy.

"Rodge, I can't believe it. *That's* what's been bothering you? Everything's fine!"

He spun, a fire burning in his eyes as he snarled at me, his body tense as a fresh spring. "You think it's funny?"

I couldn't help it. "It's fuckin' funny as hell, yeah."

He seated at the table, face still contorted in a grimace. "You're lucky, you know that?"

"I don't understand, Rodge. What's going on here?"

"My dad never talked to me about...that stuff, man. Never. He got flustered and left the room when I was eleven, I'd asked him what girls have...you know, down there."

I nodded but didn't respond, wanting Rodgers to get it out and flush his system clean. I eased myself down directly across from him and waited.

"He mumbled something under his breath and got a glass of water. Then he just left the room. Can you believe that? And...I still don't know what they've got. Down there."

Stop saying 'down there', stop saying 'down there'...

I winced, not knowing how to respond. My own mother, at least, had filled me in on basic sex ed and puberty a couple of years back, using the cringe-worthy *birds and bees* starter pack edition. The rest I'd figured out from friends while kicking around the playground. Rodgers, on the other hand, always grew red-faced and stalked away each time someone so much as mentioned jizz. Now I knew why.

"He was embarrassed," I offered. "Your dad. For himself. I can't say I wouldn't be either."

"But it was his *job*."

"I know, man, I know. But..."

My unformed point hung in the air. After finally getting somewhere for the first time with Rodge since shit smacked the fan, I didn't want this line to snap before getting the fish to the boat.

"He built us a damn tree house," Rodgers said. "Gave you that guitar. Read me Roald Dahl each night before bed. Always had breakfast, lunch and dinner ready, rain or shine. House clean as a whistle. Just...couldn't talk to me about sex."

An anger I'd never known simmered in my gut, one that bore rage at Rodgers for not knowing how good he had it. His father *had* done all those things, both for him, and for all of us, too. All the while, the likes of Kit got his head dunked in a tub by assholes such as his father each time the mood tickled his fancy. Hell, I'd grown invisible to my own mother after Jack sailed onto the scene, and I lost my dog and safety in the process. At some point, man, you had to learn to do for yourself.

"He's all I had," Rodgers blurted, and his chin quivered. "I just miss him so much."

I palmed his hand and squeezed. "I know, man, I know. I miss him, too. I miss all of 'em."

"What kind of god would do such a thing? Do that to them? What fucking world do we live in? We're only kids, Tony...only kids."

"A damn cruel one. That's for sure."

"One where...where an adult *knows* we're alone out here, scared, and *he doesn't call for help.* One where no one's here to rescue us...It's cruel, Tony. It's cruel and I don't like it."

"I don't, either, but we've got to make our own way now."

Like baby birds thrown from the nest, I repeated. *Either fly or splat, Rodge. We fly or splat.*

"I can't do anything right," he said, and my heart leaped at his volume. I looked to Lee and Kit, still sleeping.

"You're fine, man, we're all fine. Just adjusting. We're making do."

"You and Kit risked everything to get us food to keep us alive. Got water from Lee's place. Tried the phone at Allie and Nate's. Had to put down your own mother...how were you not scared?"

"I *was* scared, man. I was fucking petrified." I pointed to myself to hammer the statement home. "All I knew was I just had to do it, I'd been pushed into a corner. *That's* how I managed. Because if I didn't, Rodge, we'd be dead."

"And all the while, I just sat in the corner, waiting for food to arrive. Waiting for water and rescue, not getting off my ass and helping."

"You were scared. We all dealt differently. And you're okay now. You thought you were sick."

An image of Jacob, lax in Lee's father's grasp, flashed before my eyes. I winced.

"No, Tony, you don't get it, that's what I've *always* done. When Dad got the flu, all the while this shit was going down, I hardly checked in on him. Can you believe it? I didn't *want* to because that would make it real. It felt like too much responsibility, and what if I screwed up? I watched TV while he dragged himself out of bed and slumped to the kitchen for a sandwich, sneezing and coughing, and I just turned the TV up louder to block it all out. And you know what, man? He never even gave out to me...just gave me a sad smile, like that's about what he expected. Like he wasn't even disappointed. People don't expect anything from me. No one expects me to do anything important ever. Not even myself."

In class, Mrs. Blume even once forgot to grade his test last semester. He sat silently as she passed out each exam and then dismissed the class. No one invited him to play ball or sit with a group beyond myself and Lee. And for all of his whining, I even found myself zoning out a couple of times we'd been alone, much as I hated to admit. For all intents and purposes, Rodgers was *the invisible kid*. Much like myself at home. Much like Lee at home. Like Kit. Like all of us now, actually.

"You've got music," Rodgers said. "You can *do* something."

A new defensiveness rose inside me. "I didn't just get handed it, Rodge. I had to work on it. Day and night until blisters bled. Until I pulled my hair out and shook with rage, night after fucking night. Frustrating times, man. I just stayed with it. Why not try *something* for yourself?"

"I've never been able."

"You don't need permission."

Rodgers eyed my guitar, his lids half closed, and in that instance, I saw him retreat back down the dark corners of his mind, quick as water down the drain. He reached for the booze. "Want a sip?"

"I'm fine. Thanks."

"All right, then. I want to be with my dad, Tony. I miss him."

I patted his hand and pushed from the stool. My eyes stung with exhaustion. "We'll get through this, Rodge. We've done well for ourselves so far. We haven't given up."

"We'll never reach the mill."

I sighed. "We *will*. It's far, but Lee and I made it to Allie and Nate's, and that's halfway. We'll get there. I promise."

"Not with Kit's leg the way it is. Not with my fat ass dragging you all down."

"Rodge, I'm tired, okay? Let's talk about this in the morning."

"Okay." He tapped the whiskey bottle with his index, thinking, and as he spoke, he rolled his tongue around the missing gap in his gum. "Goodnight, Tony. You're a good friend."

"Goodnight, Rodge. Get some sleep."

I awoke to a thud.

CHAPTER FIFTEEN

MY BODY WAS moving before my brain booted, and I shot to the window, the source of the sound. I gripped the sill, my heart smacking, and ignored the white noise of Lee and Kit yelling as a familiar ringing now filled my ears. My stomach lurched, vomit rising, as below, Rodgers lay in a twisted heap, covered by the wriggling forms of freaks. Moans and smacking sounds forced me to back away on weak legs, and I collapsed, shaking the whole tree house.

"He didn't!" Lee yelled, his voice coming from far away as he paced the room and grabbed his hair in tight clumps. "Jesus fucking Christ!"

Visions of Rodgers' lifeless body burned into my mind, twisted and twitching, and—*red! So much red!*

My head fell back, cracking the floor, and the ceiling swam before my eyes, the slops and moans below overloading my brain. I drifted off to that sound, to the yelling, to the cussing and cries of my friends, and a memory of Rodgers at his last birthday, with just myself, Lee, and his father in attendance... Rodgers smiling like it was the greatest day the world had ever known.

The day passed in silence. I clutched my guitar in the corner of the room, doing my damnedest to keep my eyes from Rodgers' empty bag, all the while still fighting the sickening racket below with my music. Without effort, without being aware, my fingers clutched the pen and scribbled a page of shaky lyrics throughout the day. The one I landed on, the one I liked, was titled 'You Never Know'. I'd crossed out a dozen others.

The garbage bag had been shredded, Rodgers—*fucking hell...*—had jumped right through it. I snubbed the cinema of my mind as it tried double-featuring his fall and the impact over and over and over and over...music helped, but only just about.

A dull light filled the tree house as the sun set, the open window allowing in the cold and the darkness. And the sounds. Awful, awful sounds.

I stopped strumming and dropped the pen, squeezing the bridge of my nose as my puffed eyes ached from tears. In the far corner, Lee eyed the ceiling. It'd been seven hours.

"Guys," Kit said, almost a whisper. "We need to eat something."

They're eating Rodgers, my mind teased. *You saw it, Tony, you saw his bone white body covered red! So much red!*

"Not hungry," Lee answered in a monotone.

Kit nodded but shuffled to his feet all the same, careful of his bad leg. He hobbled to the table and rifled through the plastic bag, pulling three cans of fish. He dolled them out silently before returning to his corner and cracking a can. My stomach growled in response, my hunger indifferent to my feelings. The last thing I wanted was food, but I knew I needed sustenance. My guts bucked but I managed to keep a meagre meal down, unlike Lee, who vomited first bite. Luckily he reached the trash can in time. Afterward, he dumped the contents of the plastic bag and used the bag itself as covering for the bin, locking the smell as much as possible.

"I'll toss it tomorrow," he said. "I don't want to..." He threw a hand to the window, and Kit and I nodded, knowing without question what he meant.

Rodgers is dead. And there's so much red...

After keeping down a mouthful of water, I drifted off with the guitar still in my hands. A simple comfort, but a comfort nonetheless.

I jolted from a nightmare, consciousness swimming back and flinging my friend's death at me. I slapped my face, skin slick with sweat, and emitted a sound I wasn't aware of making. When the room came into focus, my chest tightened as the weight of death once again shackled my shoulders. By the window, Lee sat framed in moonlight.

"Hey," I said, and got to my feet. My soles tickled with pins and needles, my lower back sore from sleeping upright. Kit snored softly from his bag.

"Hey," Lee said, and stared outside, his eyes as red as I imagined my own. He sniffled and shifted his position, as if afraid of me seeing him in such a state.

"What time is it?" I asked.

"No idea. I imagine about four in the morning. You've been out a while."

"You sleep at all?"

"Nope. Too many nightmares. Woke in seconds."

"Sorry."

"Yeah...Yeah, me, too."

I didn't expect it, but Lee reached out and gave me a hug. I fell lax in his arms, flooded by emotions. My entire body hitched with another bout of tears and my arms found their way around him, returning the gesture.

"Fuck, man," I managed. "What the fuck."

"I know." He shushed me, keeping me held. "I just don't know what I can say."

We stayed like that for a long time, cold wind chilling us from the permanent window.

After some time, Lee brought me back to arm's length. "I like the song you wrote, man."

"You did?"

"Yeah. Good lyrics."

I hadn't even been aware of singing, only the beehive cries below and the knowledge my hands were scribbling *something*. Still, right now I only wanted to know one thing, one thing that bothered me like an ignored toothache. "Is he down there?" I asked.

Lee winced, but nodded. "Don't think you should look."

Part of me knew I shouldn't, but I needed closure, needed the truth, no matter how painful. And one thing I liked about Lee, he always gave the truth, no matter how harsh. I crossed to the window and he stepped aside, busying himself with something else. I took a deep breath and held it.

Rodgers' eyes locked me like radar, his mangled body somehow holding upright. Brown stains caked his clothes, his face already budding with patches of moss. I gasped as his mouth fell open to display the parasitic growth, a nub of white reaching past his lower lip. It would grow longer throughout the day, I knew, and that infection would eventually claim every inch of his pale flesh. Rodgers would be a freak come sunup.

Beside him swayed his father, eyes lifeless as a shark, the two reunited in abomination. I wondered if some sliver of Rodgers' brain, some part *way deep down*, felt comfort in being with his father once again. I doubted it, but I couldn't deny the sinister thought.

"Rodgers," I whispered. Tears spilled down my cheeks, and I pushed from the window as more of the freaks shambled to join my friend and his dad, my mother and Jack amongst them. I knew every ghoul by name.

"Hey, listen," Lee said, and picked a splinter of wood from the table. "I don't mean to sound crass, but with what happened, with us screaming and the thud and the…*noise* of the freaks… if that guy is out there, he heard us, for sure."

"Definitely."

I'd thought the same throughout the day, but hearing it aloud still got my heart speeding. I scooped my water and took a mouthful, washing away the acrid taste from a lack of food. "What do you think he'll do to us?"

"I have no idea. But if he didn't go to find help, and he toyed with you in Kit's house, it won't be good, whatever it is. Fucking psycho."

"That means we've gotta move."

"Right." Lee pulled a book across the table and opened to a page he'd dogeared. "I've been thinking about it all night. Our plan. My house is out of the question, for sure, the windows are completely gone, 'cept for my parent's room. And Kit'll need to hit that dead-on for us to get out. It's our last bullet. Now, Kit's house, I dunno, that psycho could still be in there. Hell, he could be anywhere, but I'm most nervous about Kit's. That leaves Allie and Nate's place as the closest and safest if Kit needs a stop on our way. I'm just covering all grounds. With his leg busted, he very well could need a break halfway, and that's our cover spot.

"Remember the kitchen? They've got good knives. Weapons we can use. If the freaks follow—most likely they will—we can rest upstairs, use the ladder outside as an escape to the backyard."

"But they'd follow us around the house?"

"We smash some plates, drop some pots and pans from an upstairs window around the *front* of the house, we'd get around and down the ladder before they know. We're faster than them, that's our only advantage. And, hell, being there, we're already halfway to the mill."

Kit snored softly, mouth falling open as he rolled sideways. I hadn't seen his leg in some time, but I imagined it couldn't be good. I found myself remembering all the times he'd given myself and Rodgers dead arms and kicks to the school bag across the years. Yet, here we were, bound by circumstance and survival.

"You'll need sleep before we set out," I said. "You haven't slept in over a day, man."

"Yeah, I'll be fine."

"Lee. No. You're getting some rest. This is our only chance and I'm not having you fuck it up for us. Not when Kit's leg is the way it is. I can't have you at half-mast, too."

"Okay, Sargent." A look of genuine pride came over him before quickly fizzing to exhaustion. "I'll get some sleep. You, too. But keep an ear out for anything. That psycho comes knocking, we've gotta be ready. Tired, busted leg, don't matter. Okay?"

"Okay."

As Lee hobbled to his corner and slipped inside his bag, I shivered in the cold light of dawn. Rodgers' high voice jutted from the others, unfortunately easy to identify. I heard him ask: *You think any part of them knows what's happened? You think something, even in the back of their minds, is screaming out?* I shivered. The memory stuck a knife of sorrow in my heart and twisted.

As I returned to my own sleeping bag, I ran over the plan one more time in my mind: Kit smashes the final window while we make a break from the tree house. First stop, Allie and Nate's, if Kit needed the rest. An open living room window was a godsend, and if we moved quickly, we'd get inside without a hitch. We'd give Kit some much-needed respite, snag some knives from the kitchen, and rest. The freaks would surround the house, sure, but only a handful if we gave 'em the slip. We'd distract them at the front of the property and scramble down the back ladder, bolting for the Mill—*the Mill, fuck...*—and out to the old forestry route. No homes that way, just a straight break for the highway through miles of pine. Once there, we were free.

I shimmied into my bag and sighed, folded my hands beneath my head. I stunk to high heaven but ignored the smell, thinking only of the freedom that the highway promised. I brought my knee forward, brushed off my guitar, and promised to take that, too. That battered sonofabitch had been my only constant since the world fell apart. Without it, I wondered how long before I crumbled, too, ending up much like my friend, my family, my neighbors.

Another bout of tears struck and, this time, I allowed them their escape. Hell, it was better than thinking about my cramping stomach and full bladder and aching bones. At some point, I drifted off.

"You're fucking kidding me."

Lee turned from the window with pure shock stretching his features. I cocked my head and crossed the room. "The hell is going on?"

"Tony, you're not gonna believe this. I don't even know what it means."

"What?"

"What's happening?" Kit asked, his voice groggy. His covers swished as he stirred.

At the window, my breath caught.

"Jesus H. Christ, Lee."

Five bodies lay strewn across the lawn.

Decapitated.

In a heap by the trunk lay Allie and Nate, headless in a pool of blackened blood, their heads close by. The parasitic tooth jutting from Nate's lips, his frozen eyes bulging. Beyond the couple, I noticed Jack's pajamas on another corpse, head nowhere to be found. Ribbons and chunks of intestines had been pulled from his initial wound, glistening from the open neck in a tangle. By Rodgers' house lay Richardson and my mom, their attacker having removed their heads with the precision of a surgeon. Vomit stirred in my stomach. I don't know if seeing her at peace was any better.

The world swayed as visions of her flashed before my eyes: past birthdays, watching late night TV while wrapped in a duvet, a glass of red in her hand. Our trip to the city two years prior, sharing headphones and listening to Deep Purple cassettes the whole way...And now there lay a headless monster that'd once been my mom.

The other freaks stumbled about the slaughter, oblivious, Rodgers amongst them.

"He's here."

By *he*, I knew Lee meant our biblical butcher. I recalled the glistening blade in his fist, dragging on the carpet—a blade as sharp as a sword. He'd found us. On the back of Rodgers' house, the man had left a message. One written with Jack's innards. Slathered across the bricks, I read: TRY IT NOW. GO ON.

Go on...

Kit pushed me aside and silently studied the carnage below. "You think he's actually helping us?"

"No," Lee said, the word like a punch. "He is not helping us, Kit. If he'd just written *'try it now'*, I'd maybe believe him, but *'go on'*? That's a dare. That's a tease."

"How do you know?"

"I know a tease when I see one," he said with a snarl, and Kit's face flooded with shame.

"I'm with Lee," I said. "He's a lunatic. Anyone in their right mind would've dropped 'em all and come get us. He only took down five. Just five. A sliver of hope, that's all. A dare, like Lee says. Plus he's nowhere to be found. He didn't go get help. He didn't kill them all and save us or wake us with a shout. He just...teased us."

"But it's a good thing?" Kit said. "Getting rid of them."

"No." Lee scanned the yard once more. "He's waiting out there. Waiting for us to come down, drawing us out, that's all. It's a trick."

"But what if we just stay up here?" Kit said. "What can he do then?"

"I guess we'll find out. But he sure as shit hasn't tricked me."

"We need to wait for your leg to heal more, too," I said. "We wouldn't have risked it anyway, even if he was a good guy."

"Which he's not," Lee added. "He's just chancing it."

"Why?" I asked, deflated. "Why the hell is he doing this?"

It'd be just another nasty nail in my innocence, I realized later, that the world didn't operate like I'd imagined only weeks before. Good guys didn't always win, Rodgers' dad had proved that. Kind-hearted kids didn't always grow up to have nice lives like they deserved, as I saw with Rodgers. Bastards got to wreck nice homes and lives. And some people wanted to hurt others, just because they could. The tunnel of adolescence was a dark and terrifying place.

"So we stay up here?" Kit asked. "Fuck it, hopefully he kills five more and then another five, problem solved." He shook his head. "Only proves he's an idiot. What else can he do?"

A voice froze us.

"You did not take my offering," it called, and my hair stood on end. Without thinking, I grabbed hold of Lee's arm. The freak-choir gurgled in reply. "I give you a way forth, and you do not accept. Is this true?"

A smell hit me then, no longer masked by the sharp tang of day-old vomit and cigarette smoke. A smell that forced my heart to punch and my palms to sweat. "Is that gasoline?" I asked.

"*Try it now*," he called, punctuating each word. "*Go. On.*"

My eyes bulged from yet more recognition. I knew that man's voice. Back in Kit's house, he'd tried to scare me by warping his tone, freaking me out like a real psycho. However, I'd heard him yell before, from the open windows of two very unlucky siblings. And one of them was standing right beside me.

"It's your dad," I said, and Kit's shoulders slacked.

He rushed to the window, scanned the yard, his knuckles white on the wood. The smell of gasoline grew harsher now, brown and terrifying. "Dad!" He yelled. "Are you out there? It's me!"

No response. Kit sniffled, crying for the second time I ever saw. He wiped his eyes, looking from us to the window, us to the window. "I-I saw him change, I saw him in the hallway, I did, I swear."

"It was dark," I offered. "They're covered in that *shit*."

"I swear...I saw you! Stop this!"

I wondered how many times Kit had yelled those very words in the past, and a brick of sorrow smacked my stomach. The boy leaned out the window, tears now streaming his face. "Leave us alone!"

Leave us alone, I imagined Kit screaming as his old man dragged him and his sister to the bathtub by the scruff of the necks for their 'cleansing'. *Dad, stop it!* His dad would pull them from the icy water at the last minute, responding, *you survived,* as the consequences of his actions froze him from murder. One final synapse of sense flaring. But he'd try it again the next week, and the next, never quite following through. Until now.

"I'll cleanse you, Kit," his father said. "I told you I would."

Kit pushed from the window, panting, and the three of us scanned the room as if help lurked in some corner. We found nothing but empty cans, candles, and booze.

"Where is he?" Lee hissed. "Hey, hey, Kit. Kit. I need you to calm down. Listen to me."

Never taking his eyes from Kit, Lee swiped the homemade slingshot from the table. He clenched his jaw. "One shot left, man. You hear me? *One shot.*"

Kit accepted the slingshot in shaking hands and blew a breath, crossing back to the window. He held out his palm and I snagged the last ball bearing, passing it to him and stepping back, my skin slick with sweat. Kit dropped the pellet inside the balloon and stretched the rubber a couple of times, testing durability. With a breath, he planted his feet and eyed the yard.

"I don't see him," he whispered.

"Kit, I offer you a chance to get free. Do you hear me?"

Kit's head turned, searching for the voice, the weapon quaking in his hands. The freaks grew agitated.

"You don't accept what I have given you. As always," his father yelled. "A cleansing, son. It's time. Time to pay for all your mistakes."

"Get fucked, you absolute creep!" Kit's foot came down hard, shaking the tree house. I gripped my guitar on instinct. "You wanna come up here and drag me out by my fucking neck again, go right ahead."

Silence from his dad, but the neighbors answered in earnest.

"Water isn't right this time," his father answered. "It's End Times now. Like I always knew would come."

Lee rushed to the window, grabbing the sill. "Get help! For god's sake, get help!"

The panic in my friend's voice matched my own. My nerves were alight and I wanted everything to be a dream. Here was a chance to get free, to be down on the highway with an adult, away and safe. Yet our savior was insane, and reasoning with a madman felt like the cruelest joke in all the world, rivaled only by my friend taking his own life.

"Please, Mr. Peters," Lee pleaded. "Please, get help. We're starving. We need to get out of here and get the police, the army, hell, get *anyone* up here. *Please.*"

His voice cracked and I cringed, knowing our final attempt would fall flat. I squeezed the bridge of my nose, took a breath.

"You're punished." His voice echoed, location untraceable, and the ceiling blurred as my eyes ran with tears. "It's a cleansing for all, Kit. And I say thankya, Lord."

"Well, I say fuck you, Dad."

A pause. "Exactly why this has been put upon us. You and your friends, ungrateful and ungodly. It's why I've survived and they did not. It's time to complete this."

"He's insane," I said. "He's batshit insane."

"*Everything that can stand the fire, you shall pass through the fire, and it shall be clean. Nevertheless, it shall also be purified with the water for impurity. And whatever cannot stand the fire, you shall pass through the water...A storm's coming, boys.*"

"There he is," Lee hissed, and I pushed to my feet and joined my friends at the window.

Lee's father strode with purpose from the Rodgers' home, stained machete limp by his side. He'd scrubbed his face black with ash, appearing as monstrous as any infected, except for his eyes, and they were much worse. Just as lifeless, yet burning with terrible intent. His gore-splattered robe billowed in the wind, and his right arm was red to the bicep. He hoisted the machete and cleaved a nearby freak's head with one swish. The body toppled and spurted jets of dark crimson, legs and arms twitching in the throes of death as the head rolled to a stop. The biblical butcher kept coming. And then pulled a lighter.

"Kit," I managed, "One shot. That's all we've got here."

"I know, asshole, I know." He brought the slingshot to eye-level and strained the rubber, squinting like a sniper. My throat seized as every drop of saliva disappeared from my mouth.

Kit's dad ignited a healthy flame with the flick of his thumb, fire licking around his fist. His eyes targeted us and refused to move, even as the dead shambled after him from around the corner of the Rodgers' place, their arms outstretched and heads lolled back.

"Kit, do it now!" I yelled.

Kit took a breath, held it, and let the bullet fly.

Chapter Sixteen

THE LEAD BALL zipped through the air—right past Kit's father's head.

When I was seven, I'd dropped my favorite toy car down the stairs. As the well-made vehicle cracked off each step, a sickness pulsed in my chest. The thumps seemed to stretch out for a lifetime. They say time stands still in those moments, and I comprehended that fact now more than ever. My hope flew with that projectile, and I mouthed 'no' repeatedly, unable to move, my friends silent beside me.

A flick of crimson shot from a freak's leg and the monster toppled forward, smacking the lawn face-first, the bullet having passed right through its calf. Our last ball-bearing, used to cripple a freak.

Kit's father tossed the lighter, and the whoosh made me gasp as heat billowed past my face. I stumbled to the centre of the room, hyperventilating and emitting involuntary sounds—I did not get stuck up here to die. In movies, Kit would have hit his father and left a dime-sized hole in his head, dropped him right there. The lighter should've sizzled out on the grass, the storm coming to our aid at the right time. We should've scrambled down to take the machete, behead the rest of the beasts and be heroes...That's how this was supposed to go... shoulda, coulda, woulda...

As the bark crackled and Lee screamed in shock, I crumpled to the floor.

"We're dead!" he yelled, hysterical beyond reason and tearing at his hair. "I don't want to burn!"

Kit swiped his inhaler and puffed two jets down his wheezing throat, his skin glistening in the now orange glow that pulsated from the trapdoor like the mouth of hell. The wailing outside crescendoed and my skin broke into gooseflesh.

A plume of smoke danced through the floorboards as the wood crackled and popped. The sharp scent of charred wood reached my nostrils and scratched my throat. I gagged.

"Wait," Kit screamed. "I have one more idea. Hold on."

His terror was as infectious as the parasite, yet he yanked Rodgers' tooth from his pocket. With a shaking voice, he said. "I gotta hit the bastard, I gotta."

"Kit, it's not going to help, man. We gotta move!"

Kit raced to the window and loaded up Rodgers' tooth. A high whine escaped his lips as tears cascaded down his face and he aimed the projectile. The balloon *slapped* as the tooth flew through the air. Kit punched the tree house wall. "I missed him! How could I miss him!"

"We need to get out of here," Lee screamed, bug-eyed. "Tony, move it."

"How could I *miss*?"

I scrambled to my feet, snatched what I could and stuffed it inside our remaining grocery bag: the last of our food, my copybook and pen, and then I reached for my guitar. If I didn't have it with me, I'd lose my mind. Music helped process everything, kept my mind clear and gave me purpose. With that gone, I imagined my senses snapping as easily as cheap porcelain. I'd end up like Rodgers, and that wasn't about to happen. I grabbed the guitar and swung it out the window, cringing at the thump that followed.

"Come on."

Lee hoisted the trapdoor as sweat dripped from his nose. Heat whooshed inside, accompanied by a flickering red light as the flames climbed higher. No freaks surrounded the tree now, and, at first, I thought some survival mechanism geared the infected away, the heat registering as a threat, but then I saw no sign of Kit's father. They'd chased the madman, unfazed by their headless brethren, brains overridden by a single purpose: to spread.

"Tony, get down there, go, go."

Lee grabbed my forearm and wrenched me to the trapdoor where the temperature scorched my skin. My eyes stung and watered from smoke and I blinked away tears, handing the grocery bag to Lee who flung it out of the window. Then I shimmied to the hole and slipped my legs outside.

The heat was unbearable.

As the trunk crackled and popped, tongues of flame crawled along its bark, eager to meet my legs and swallow me whole. Three rungs down, I yelled in shock as my skin oozed sweat, making my hands as useful as lathered bars of soap. My left hand fell away, stomach entering my throat, and I quickly found another rung, picturing my fall all too well: lungs popping, hair sizzling, skin blistering. Halfway down, the first flame flicked my sole and I sucked air thick as soup. I braced. Then shoved off from the tree.

The ground shot up to meet me and I landed outside the halo of fire by mere inches, kneecaps smacking the grass as I toppled and rolled. Nate's headless corpse was alight, the smell of seared flesh mingling with the burning wood. I quickly clambered to my feet and ignored the pulsating pain in my legs as Kit scrambled down behind me. Then the storm finally broke. I looked skyward as cool drops pelted my skin, dripped from my nose, soothed my heated flesh.

"Jump, Kit!"

I watched his left leg closely, imagining how he'd land. Around me, the freaks had vanished, seeking Kit's father instead. Wherever he'd slipped off to. I imagined we'd see the blood-soaked machete again.

Kit leaped, and I held my breath as he smacked the lawn to my right. He yelled and clutched his ankle and I fell to his side, helped him up with one arm around his shoulder.

"You okay?"

"Hurts like fuck but I did it. We're out..."

I pulled him away from the fire, giving Lee some room for his fall. I looked for something that could to help break his fall, a makeshift firefighter blanket, but we'd left our sleeping bags in the tree house.

Lee descended the trunk with his leather jacket glinting in the rain, the flames claiming two more rungs for fuel. A knot popped and sparks flew like fireworks. Lee, like us, scrambled as low as possible before shoving off. His arms cartwheeled as he plummeted before crashing sideways on the lawn, the air punched from his lungs as his head smacked the grass.

"Here," I said, and unwrapped my arm from Kit's shoulders before bolting to his side. Lee accepted my outstretched hands with one of his, the other holding his midsection. "Hurt myself," he wheezed.

"We're out, but we gotta move, man. Come on."

Another *crack* shot from the tree as flames tickled the underbelly of our hideaway. I raced to my guitar, and a pang of relief struck as I spotted only a small split on the bottom of the body. My instrument had made it intact. I clutched the neck and raced to the grocery bag, wrapping it around my free fist before hobbling back to my friends, my knees still thumping from the impact.

"Storm finally came," Lee said. "Took its damn time."

He stabilized Kit with one arm, and I nodded for them to follow before shuffling into the field separating Rodgers' place from mine, the same route Kit and I took on our first outing.

"Careful of holes," I warned. "Keep a close eye."

The freaks moaned from somewhere out of sight, masked by the gurgle and crack of the fire as it ate up our tree and our safety. The storm would put it out eventually, I imagined, but not soon enough. Our last sanctuary would be ash and embers come morning. We overstepped the downed fence.

Rain dripped from my hair and I used the back of my forearm to wipe my face, soggy waist-high grass soaking through my jeans and shirt. I kept watch for holes, knowing the last thing we needed was for myself or Lee to snap a leg, too, or for Kit to break another and leave himself in need of a damn wheelchair. I gasped as I slipped but quickly corrected my footing.

"Good, Tony?" Lee called.

"I'm good. Just keep moving."

At the wooden fence, I threw the guitar and bag across before climbing over, the wood soft with moisture. Lee and Kit followed, and on the main road, we kept side by side, maintaining an eye on the pines and shrubs. Rain hissed through the branches now, smaller ones bobbing and masking any noise a freak might make. A bird shot from the canopy and my heart kicked, nerves singing. Still, no sign of any freak.

"You see him?" Kit called. "I'm...I'm so sorry, I thought he was one of them. I should've checked closely, I should've."

"Kit, stop, we don't have time."

As Allie and Nate's home appeared in the distance, our pace quickened.

I chanced a glance back at Rodgers' house, where a thick pillar of smoke jutted from dancing flames, the tree house now fully alight. The deluge would douse the fire in time, but I hoped a passerby down on the highway had enough sense to phone the fire department and send for help. Though in Riverside, it wasn't uncommon to burn gorse around the farmlands this time of year, and controlled fires in the mountainside were as common as horseflies.

I slipped off the main road and onto Allie and Nate's drive, gravel crunching beneath my feet as I studied the gloom of the thicket to my left. A twig cracked, followed by a shuffle of feet, and I motioned with my bag-hand for my friends to hurry. We jogged to the house and caught our breath by the porch.

A small overhang kept the rain at bay, leaving a sizzling curtain before us. I shivered and handed Kit our loot before reaching inside the shattered window by the front door, the freaks having left nothing but jagged glass-teeth in the frame. My fingers found cold metal and I unlatched the lock, pulling my arm free with a shudder. I opened the door and stepped inside the bloodied hallway, followed closely by my friends. Brown footprints led to the kitchen, two dried trenches dragged from the feet of the dead. I noted two separate tracks, and placed my guitar by the living room door before easing my knife from my jeans.

"Quiet," I warned, and crept towards the open door at the far end of the hall. I wondered how many had gotten in from the time Lee and I had been here. If the tracks were anything to go by, we had two to deal with. Creeping proved useless when one of the attackers rambled from the kitchen, arms outstretched and head swinging on that rubber neck, tooth on display. Rotted mushrooms sprouted from its forehead. Thunder boomed from outside. I yelled as I slammed the blade home, slicing through decomposed flesh with little resistance. Crimson jetted from the throat, the wound opening in a sinister grin of gruel. The assailant toppled off-balance and crashed against the pink-papered wall, streaking it dark red. Lee moved fast and raised his boot, crashing the monster's skull in a violent stomp. A sickening crack accompanied spurting brain gristle beneath his heel as Lee worked his ankle back and forth for good measure.

"Tony, careful!"

I instinctively turned as Kit pointed behind me—at something right over my shoulder. I got halfway around before two moist and bristled hands clasped my forearms. I crashed with a grunt, wrestled my right arm free, and slammed the blade home—a moment of resistance before piercing the temple.

Like an egg cracking, I thought, then cried out as cold ichor drooled from the wound and coated my face. The sharp stench of rotted vegetation filled my nose. I pulled my left arm free and snatched the monster's moist face before wrenching the abomination to the left and dodging the parasitic syringe of its mouth. My lungs filled as Lee and Kit pulled the deadweight from me and I rolled away, thick liquid spilling from my face to the carpet as I coughed and gagged. I wiped the wetness from my face and scrambled to my feet.

"*Door*," I wheezed. "Gotta get it barricaded."

"You two get this blocked and I'll meet you out in the kitchen, gotta check the other door."

"Got it."

As Lee raced to the kitchen, a figure wearing a tattered DEFENDERS shirt shuffled from the thicket onto the drive, arms poised and skin mottled with fungus.

"The cabinet," I said, and slammed the door shut before racing to the figurine case by the foot of the stairs. Porcelain animals lined the five shelves, each row cluttered with painted foxes, toads, pigs and cows. I grabbed the left side and pushed, critters shattering as the door unhinged and spilled shards by my feet.

I motioned to Kit, arms straining against the weight of the wood. "Other side, man, other side."

He hobbled to the cabinet and we crab-walked the blockade to the door—just as the *Defenders* man crashed against it. The cabinet didn't budge. "Should do for a while," I panted. "They're not too strong, at least."

Then a slimy arm shot through the siding and grasped my hip.

I yelped and back-peddled, colliding with the stairs as I grabbed the banister for support. The freak pressed against the window as if willing itself through, streaking the glass with browned saliva. It toppled, half-in and sideways, right onto the unforgiving teeth of glass.

"I can't take this anymore," Kit said, and stalked to the monster with open hands. He grabbed the creature's teeshirt and pressed hard, veins rising to the surface of his skin as he sawed the creature into the jagged maw. Dark liquid sloshed down the inner wall as the carpet drank the spreading pool, and then Kit retreated. "Can't get him down any further..." he said, breath quivering, "but I think he's impaled pretty damn tight."

"Out of the way."

I'd had enough. We hadn't made it this far to give up now. We'd withstood too much for our luck to come crashing down. "Move it."

My stomach jittered as I swiped my knife and grabbed hold of the bastard's head, avoiding a patch of what looked like blackened chanterelle. He reached for my legs, weak arms grasping, but I shook off his attack and press the serrated blade to the back of his neck. And then I hacked.

Sinew gave way like old twine, and the stench of decomposed flesh stained the air brown. A gurgle bubbled from the freak's mouth as trapped air escaped and I gagged. His head loosened as the tendons ripped.

"Jesus, Tony!"

As my knife hit bone, I popped the blade out and slammed the weapon home again, satisfied by a *crack*. Kit kept speaking but I heard not a word as I wriggled the blade and repeated the process. With a fourth swing the neck bone snapped completely and I finished the job as fast as possible, fingers slick as oil. The object in my grasp felt like a moulded football.

"I think I'm gonna be sick."

I threw the head and retched as a mess of gore slopped from the neck and splattered the ground. I hadn't noticed Kit return with a coffee-table in his arms, hadn't even noticed him leaving. He slammed the table against the shattered window and completed our blockade of the front entrance.

"Tony, you okay?"

I nodded. "Let's just get this done. How'll we keep the table in place?"

Kit cocked his head as Lee raced in with a hammer and nails. "Kitchen," he said, and relieved Kit of the table weight. "Gonna make some damn amount of noise but I need it done quickly. Tony, double-check the locks in the kitchen for me and pull the curtains." He drove a nail home, smacking it into the plaster with five short pops of the hammer. "The ladder outside leads to a window right above the kitchen, must be a bedroom. Kit, give me a hand here. Tony, *Go.*"

I detoured to the living room and closed the window before racing to the back of the house and double-checked the door— *locked*—then I pulled the blinds and had a moment to catch my breath in the darkened room. The steady *rat-tat-tat!* of Lee bolting the table pulsed in time with a fresh headache as I paced the room, side-stepping the shattered telephone. One of the freaks moaned from outside, drawn by the noise, but apart from pushing down the figurine cabinet or smashing a window, we were safe here. For now.

Lee and Kit returned, both red-faced and sweaty, with Lee spinning the hammer in his fist. "Keeping it," he said. "Good for close encounters. Two of 'em out there now, coming down the drive, but if we keep quiet they might wander off. One's got a growth the size of a shrub. Could chase that fuckin' maniac instead." His eyes found Kit and he quickly looked to his feet. "Sorry."

Kit shook his head. "No, man, he *is* a goddamn maniac." He ran a hand through his wet hair. "Look, I am so sorry, guys. For all of this. I was so fucking sure I saw him in the hallway that night, he came *right out of my sister's room*, I'm fucking sure of it."

"But that's the problem with the freaks," I said, "they all look the same now, covered in all that crap, their movements, the sounds...it's not your fault."

Kit sniffled. "Why the hell didn't he save me or Josie if he knew one of those things had gotten up the stairs?"

I knew a rhetorical question when I heard one, so stayed quiet and allowed Kit to purge the realization his father was a full-blown psychotic. *The biblical butcher*, I thought, and bit my lower lip.

"Fire could draw attention our way," Lee said. And from the hall came the steady *clap-clap-clap!* of hands smacking the cabinet. Lee lowered his voice. "Unless the storm works quick. Then they'd only see smoke."

"My dad will put it out eventually," Kit said in a monotone. "He wants it to be us and him. He's loving this, you could see it on his face. This is his playground now, with no one to tell him no. He's always wanted us dead, deep down...He covered up what he did to me and my sister our whole lives. Even when social came out for a check after Rodgers' dad reported him...he knew how to butter that lady up, sat in a way he never normally did, fuckin' *smiled* the whole damn time...right as rain. He knows that the chains are off. He can be who he always wanted to be."

He winced then, and I instinctively put out a hand but he waved me off. "It's fine, just...hurts like a bitch. My leg."

"Let me see," Lee said, and took a knee as Kit hoisted his jeans. Above his sneaker, purple flesh bulged, swollen and tight like the skin of some fresh fruit. Lee shook his head. "Pain, one to ten?"

"Sev...ten, man, ten, yeah, it's fucking awful."

"Right." Lee pulled the jeans back into place and wrapped an arm around Kit's shoulders. "Let's get upstairs. We'll check out the bathroom and see what's what. Might be something in there to help, maybe even some anti-inflammatories."

I noted the bags beneath Lee's eyes hadn't lessened, like coals in snow now, and waved him off Kit. "You still haven't slept, man. Let me."

As I supported Kit, Lee led the way to the staircase while keeping his presence low. We pressed against the wall as we neared the door, watching the cabinet shake as the freaks slapped the wood. I noted Lee's handiwork with the coffee table, the barrier secured with seven nails across the frame. I voiced my compliment but Lee shushed me as we took the stairs, but not before I swiped my guitar. Having the instrument back filled me with pride. We'd bested the biblical bastard for now.

Lee opened each door on the second floor with his hammer poised. For once, our luck held and we were alone. Rain smacked the windows, the storm giving its all, and I took a moment of thanks to be within solid walls for the first time in days.

"Here," Lee said, and took Kit from me. As the two hobbled to the bathroom, I entered a bedroom to the right, the clean scent of fabric-softened bedsheets alien to my senses and making my nose pucker. The whiteness of the sheets felt *off,* the plump pillows arranged neatly on top, and the purple drapes (matching the walls) were drawn, casting the room in near perfect darkness. My body cried out for rest. I imagined slumping on the blankets but feared I'd never get up, even when the freaks crashed through and fumbled up the stairs, I'd happily die right there on that bed, smelling of fabric softener as my body collected the warmth.

"Tony," Lee called, snapping me out of my daze. "Get in here."

In the bathroom, the hammer sat atop the closed toilet lid, and Lee studied the label of a bottle, an open mirror cabinet by his side. Kit sat perched on the edge of the tub, our mucky footprints the only dirt in the otherwise pristine room.

"Ibuprofen," Lee said with a smile. "Kit, your dad may have inadvertently saved you a lot of pain."

"Thanks, pops," Kit said, and waved for the bottle. He shook out two pills and downed them with water from the sink, throwing his head back and gulping them down. Then Lee pointed to the tub. "Check it out," he said.

I cocked my head. "Water in my place runs off the boiler. We don't light the fire, we don't get hot water."

"It's an *electric shower*, Tony."

The wonders of the twentieth century continued to fascinate me.

"It'll make one hell of a noise, sure, but we plug the drain, we can actually have a shower." His voice jittered with excitement and I couldn't help but smile, too. A fucking shower and a bed? Was this real?

"Why we gotta plug the drain?" I asked.

"'Cause the noise of water running outside will draw 'em. We gotta minimize our presence if we hope to catch up on some rest. Can't do much about the hum of the shower itself, but we'll control what we can, and that's the water draining. Kit needs it. It'll help with his leg, and goddamnit if we don't stink like farm animals."

He had a point, and I almost puked with the sheer excitement thrumming through my system. A night's rest in a secure house with a shower and a clean bed. Even if I slept on the floor with a towel I'd be the luckiest boy alive. Then I recalled the food, the cereals, fruit, and fish in our grocery bag and almost fainted with delight.

"Come on," Kit said, and pushed to his feet before clapping his hands. "You two, out. I'm gonna scrub myself like a motherfucker."

"Right hand for that?" Lee asked, and we all laughed.

As the bathroom door closed behind us, Lee and I stood in the darkened hallway and took a breather, rain pelting off the rooftop but not getting inside. Nothing was getting inside. The freaks downstairs assaulted our makeshift barrier but their attacks grew weaker by the minute. The electric shower clicked and Kit let out an exaggerated sigh that made us both chuckle.

We'd kept the nightmares at bay all by ourselves. If only for the briefest of time. And yet, some part of me felt we'd just entered the calm before the storm.

CHAPTER SEVENTEEN

"**D**ID YOU GUYS** ever do this back in the day?"

I let Kit's question hang and stirred on the floor beneath my duvet, my hair damp from the shower and the scent of soap on my skin just as foreign as the cotton. I'd milked the heavenly shower until the water ran cold, and even then breathed the clean air as my sinuses relaxed before toweling off and dressing in Allie and Nate's son's clothes—clothes far too large, but that worked wonders as pajamas. Lee and I made sleeping bags from spare duvets in the closet and allowed Kit the bed, his leg needing the comfort more than our aching limbs. We'd each taken a dose of Ibuprofen after our supper of dry cereal and fruit, and the drugs now coursed through my system, almost as soothing as a mother's touch.

"Do what back in the day?" I asked, the term *back in the day* making our situation all the more surreal.

"Sleepovers," Kit said. His blankets rustled as he stirred.

"Yeah. I mean, I stayed at Rodgers' every other weekend. All three of us spent weekends in the tree house now and again, once a month, I'd say."

"Huh." Kit wrapped an arm beneath his head, eyeing the ceiling. "I'd never had one before all this started."

"No?"

"Nope. Not with *him* around. He'd never let me stay anywhere, either. Afraid I might tell what he'd done to us if I was gone too long, I suppose. I was planning on running away. Someday." He laughed, a single chuckle to hide the crack in his voice.

"Usually I'd never fall asleep at home, watch TV until the sun came up. Or play my Game Boy."

"Rodgers was the same," I said, and blinked away my blurring vision. "Always the last to fall asleep in the tree house, holding my Game Boy for dear life, face lit up like the fourth."

Kit sniffled. "I'm sorry I picked on him. Even about the food. Sitting here, showered, fed, I feel like an asshole and I wish he'd made it this far. I mean that."

My own voice cracked, and I cleared my throat. "Couldn't have done anything, man. And he'd have forgiven you."

Whether that was true or not, I didn't know, but I knew Kit needed the comfort. We all did.

"I'm gonna check on the barrier," Lee whispered, and climbed from his sheets beside me. He swayed a moment, stretched, and crept to the door, still wearing his filth-covered jeans and leather jacket, hair combed back and damp. He still hadn't slept in damn near two days, and the fact he hadn't dropped by now wasn't lost on me. At sixteen, the kid could push himself more than any adult I'd ever met.

Once Lee left, Kit asked, "he all right?"

"He's fine. Get some rest."

We'd bandaged Kit's leg after slathering it with an expired healing cream, the only remedy possible considering the circumstance. I'd used some of the cream on my meagre cuts and bruises, too, but knew I'd probably bruised a rib or two and nothing but a doctor could help there. After a while, Kit snored, and I clasped my hands beneath my head, savoring the sliver of refuge, knowing full well it would not last.

Rain trickled down the window through the drapes, moonlight glinting off the racing drops. The steady *tap-tap-tap*, like drummers on the roof, caused my eyes to shudder shut, but sleep did not come. In the cinema of my mind, Rodgers fell again and again, face red and streaked with tears. He wheezed as he collided with the earth and a shattered rib or punctured lung caused his eyes to bulge. I imagined one of the freaks (didn't matter which), falling onto him, mouth open in a grimace seconds before the tooth punctured his neck and shot the infection into his bloodstream. I visualized him choking on his own blood, slapping weakly at the attacker's back, grasping handfuls of hair and clothes that stunk of wet dog before another fiend punctured yet another slab of skin. Just to be sure. I wondered if he slipped away without pain, or if he'd lasted long enough to watch the tree house above, regretting every second leading up to the drunken decision, his mistake playing out in slow motion as his brain finally petered out like the battery-dry Game Boy.

You think any part of them knows what's happened? You think something, even in the back of their minds, is screaming out?

My breathing shuddered and my eyes shot open. I pinched the bridge of my nose and counted to ten, relaxing my muscles once more. After fifteen minutes, the slapping rain turned to water-drip torture and I shoved the covers away, rising to my feet.

"Gonna check on Lee," I whispered, but Kit only snored in response.

After removing the fresh clothes, I grabbed my stained jeans and shirt, the grimy texture strangely comforting in its familiarity. I dressed and crept from the room with my fingers working along the wall for direction. At the doorway, my eyes began to adjust to the gloom. Lee stood frozen at the top of the stairs.

"Hey, man...what's up? You've been gone ages."

Lee slowly raised a hand to me, palm out. *"Hush."*

"What?" I hissed.

He shushed me again, and as I noted his intense expression, fingers of fear tickled up my spine.

I listened.

Something creaked outside. Something coming from the back door. Lee took a gentle step down one stair and removed his hammer from the back of his jeans. As he passed a sliver of moonlight, his ashen skin and sunken eyes jolted me with worry. I rushed to his side and grabbed his arm.

"Lee, you haven't slept in *days*, man. *Wait* for me. You should've called me when you heard *anything*. Are you listening?"

He shook his head and whipped his arm free. I kept close, matching him step for step, grabbing my knife. Halfway down, I hissed, "What about Kit?"

"He needs the rest for that leg. Probably a freak from the front of the house, chancing the backdoor. Stay alert, Tony. Keep close."

Stay alert, coming from Mr. Insomniac.

I strained my ears but the pounding rain safeguarded all. We reached the bottom of the stairs, and I eyed the nailed-up coffee table and doll cabinet, both still in place. A harsh wind blew from around both.

"No one at the front door," I said, but Lee didn't listen, and bee-lined for the kitchen. "Lee, wait up!"

I jogged to his side and together we pushed open the door. It creaked on its hinges. The room remained in darkened silence, not a thing out of place. Through the window in the back door, the ladder blocked sight of the yard.

"Anyone out there?" I asked, motioning to the window as Lee crept closer for a better view. He cupped his eyes and squinted through the glass. "One of 'em. Out in the trees way back. Just fallin' about the place. That's not the sound we heard, though. There's gotta be another one around. Give me a sec."

As Lee continued looking, I double-checked the surrounding shadows. The incompetent freaks wouldn't think to hide, but I needed reassurance, all the same. Nothing amiss.

"Not a thing out there," Lee said, his words fogging the glass. "I swear I heard something, though."

"Lee, you haven't slept in days. Now, I trust you, and I think I heard something creak, too, but you gotta sleep, buddy."

To be honest, at that point I wasn't sure if *I'd* heard something other than the bones of the house settling. I wasn't prepared to tell Lee, though.

Lee ran a hand through his hair, chest rising as he took a deep breath. "Maybe you're right, man. I dunno. Ever since Rodgers, I just can't close my eyes."

"I know, man. Me, too. But he wouldn't want you wearing yourself out on his behalf, you know that."

"Yeah. Maybe we should try get to sleep. I'm sorry, Tony. You've really held us together, you know that?"

I decided to take the compliment and gave a sheepish smile before leading the way back to the hall. Though we'd checked the house, my smarts maintained and I still clutched my knife. The front door remained clear, and I detoured to the living room, just in case. A floorboard creaked overhead. I froze.

"I heard it, too..."

Another creak, and another, quicker. Then, full-blown running.

"Jesus!"

We reached the bottom of the stairs as yells and slaps erupted: a young boy and a man. The stairs zipped by beneath my feet and I swung for the open bathroom door—the source of the sound.

"Sonofabitch, I swearta god, I'll kill you!"

Water splashed from the tub as Kit's father's legs frantically kicked at his son who held him face down in the murky water. Veins and muscles popped on Kit's arms, his skin dripping, screaming his throat raw.

"You crazy sonofabitch, this is for her, you hear me? This is for Josie, you bat-shit motherfucker!"

"Kit!"

I raced to my friend's side and, god help me, I pinned his father's legs down. Lee rushed in, and water splashed as he reached into the tub and snatched the man's arms. The water bubbled as he yelled, and, just for a second, his head surfaced. A guttural cry gave me gooseflesh before Kit mercifully smashed his head back beneath the water. Another stream of bubbles overtook.

"Clean!" Kit yelled. "Cleansing time! Can you go longer than thirty seconds, you pig-bastard, can you?"

I bucked and rocked as Kit's father continued struggling but his strength quickly depleted. As power waned from his limbs, our combined panting filled the room, and one more bubble popped on the surface of the water. A grimace remained on Kit's face as his muscles remained taut, keeping the psycho's head submerged. After a full minute, Lee announced, "he's dead."

Kit fell from his dad and collapsed against the toilet, his shaking hands wiping wet hair from his forehead. He cupped his face and cried as his shoulders hitched. "Fuck. Just...*fuck.*"

Lee panted and overstepped the dead man's legs, squatting by our friend. "The hell happened?"

"The window." Kit sniffled. "Woke me when I heard you guys go downstairs. I just fucking *knew* it was him in the house, I fucking *knew* it. Wanna know how many times I've heard that man sneak around to try and get me, huh? It's burned into my damn instincts. I got out of the room and waited behind the door." He nodded to the hiding spot. "He *heard* our fucking plan, man. He was listening to us in the tree house the whole time."

"Jesus..."

I imagined Kit's father stalking the thickets, ears strained as we concocted our escape, a slow smile creeping across his face as he understood our route to the mill. The ladder against the back of the house.

"He opened the bedroom window before we ever got here," I said. "We practically set ourselves up by mentioning it."

Rage boiled as the bastard's trick really registered. Why had we been so goddamn stupid and not checked the window?

Because it's on the second floor. And they *can't climb.*

"That's where he went," Lee said. "After burning the tree house. The sonofabitch."

"He *was* a sumbitch, but damnit, he wasn't dumb." Kit coughed before climbing to his feet. He wobbled a moment. "He had this whole thing planned out. Waitin' for us to be asleep. How fucking sick is that?"

To be honest, after getting to know the post-birthday world, that revelation didn't shock. The dead man leaning in the tub didn't phase me, either, come to think of it. I'd grown immune. "He didn't count on you being ready though, huh?" I said, and gave Kit's shoulder a squeeze. "You outsmarted him, man. You did it. It's over."

Kit nodded, eyes never leaving the corpse. "You're damn right I did."

As Lee blew a breath and sat on the closed toilet, a far-away look sank his features.

"You all right, man?"

"Blindspots," he said. "Worn the fuck out."

"At least you're not denying it."

"Yeah." He took a moment. "You're right, Tony. I do need the damn rest."

"We all do."

I didn't want to say it aloud, but with Kit's father dead, we needed to dispose of the body before the smell rendered the house useless. I remembered when building the tree house, Rodgers' dad stopped for a full two days while complaining about a stench from the forest. We'd found a bloated fox by a towering pine, killed from frostbite. The sweet stench of decay was something I never wanted to experience again. I also didn't want to think about dragging a corpse then, either, and instead silently prayed we at least got a few more hours in the quiet house before madness recommenced.

But Lee said it for me. "We'll have to get rid of him. Before he stinks up the joint."

Goddamnit.

With a quick break, we sent Kit back to bed. He protested at first, stating he needed to be a part of the act. More importantly, though, we needed his leg better, and after he got in my face a couple of times, the rage luckily subsided. He stalked back to bed and left his leg dangling from the mattress. Lee eased the door over to avoid him seeing much.

"Count of three," he hissed. "One...two..."

We pulled the body from the tub and lay it sprawled on the tiles by our feet. Open eyes bulged from their sockets, and brown water slithered from the blue-tinged lips.

Cleansing, I thought, and wondered if Kit appreciated the irony.

"Legs," Lee ordered, and clicked his fingers. "I'll get the pits and we put the bastard out back."

"Think he'll draw attention from the freaks?" I already got to thinking if this could be a plan B for the man. If he failed: draw the neighbors to our location with a rotting scent.

"They're all over the woods," Lee said, "not a chance we're spending an hour digging a hole out there. They'll be on us before we know it. Best case scenario, we dump him by the tree-line and race back inside before any of 'em notice us. Even then I can't say we won't be spotted."

I motioned to the body and on the count of three, we hoisted him. His pants slowly slid from my grasp and I wheezed 'go-go-go' as we crab-walked to the top of the stairs.

"Down, now," Lee said, and lowered his side of the corpse. The body thumped the carpet as we cradled our reddening hands. "Weighs more than I thought."

As I shook out my hands, I listened for movement around the house, but the hissing rain once again cloaked all sound.

"Around this side," Lee said, and descended a couple of steps. "Take an armpit with me, we can pull him down the stairs easily enough."

I wondered if Kit heard any of that, and if he was smiling or crying. I imagined he was smiling, raging he couldn't be a part of the disposal.

We got the corpse down without a hitch after discovering that dragging him by the pits worked better. In the kitchen, I studied the moonlit backyard through curtains of rain, spotting no signs of movement, but knowing full well the freaks littered the woodlands. We'd have to move fast.

I grabbed the door lock. "Ready?"

Lee nodded and worked his sore fingers back beneath the man's arms. "Okay. Do it."

I pulled the door open, amplifying the white noise of rain. As we pulled the corpse over the threshold into the deluge, I stopped just enough to ease the door over (not closed—we'd have no way back inside). The mud slopped beneath our shoes as we shimmied across the lawn and out into the woods, eyes wide with adrenaline while we listened for any nearby freaks.

"Here, here, here," Lee wheezed, and we dropped the corpse by a pine. He paced, shaking out his hands with a sharp inhale. "Fucking fat cunt. Fingers are *killin'* me."

"Lee, quiet." I flexed my own digits as my arms shook with exertion.

He sighed. "I'd take five of 'em on right now. Fucking assholes. Even Kit's dad wasn't a problem, eh?"

"He was, Lee," I reminded, "and if Kit hadn't been quick, we'd all be dead now."

He shook his head with a grin as if I'd cracked one. He needed sleep, and soon. I blamed a dump of adrenaline for his bold attitude, but he wasn't risking my life.

As rainwater dripped from my nose, I said, "let's get back to the house, man." And, as if on cue, a moan slithered from the darkness. A branch snapped, and feet shuffling through soggy leaves sent fear scuttling across my skin.

"Go, go, go."

Lee led the way back to the house, and my heart kicked when he chuckled. Like the new Rodgers, Kit and I were going to have a problem on our hands if Lee didn't rest. We traipsed the garden in record time, and in the kitchen, I closed the door, careful not to let it bang. After re-doing the lock, I shivered in the warmer temperature, again soaked to the bone. So much for my shower.

I wished we could light the fire but the lack of fuel meant smashing apart furniture and signaling our location, or worse, heading back outside for a fuel hunt. Knowing Lee's current state, he'd probably agree to that right now. But the cold house would have to do.

Lee cupped his hands and peered through the window. "Two...three of 'em. Not so bad."

He turned to me, his lack of color alarming. "Got away with it, man. Only three. They'll push off before dawn. And, goddamnit, we have *towels* to dry off. Actual fucking towels." The last part trailed with a laugh and my stomach leaped with fear. He needed shut-eye. His reckless actions made me think of Rodgers playing a video game rather than Lee recognizing the stakes. All things considered, though, the luxury of dry towels was pretty fucking amazing.

"And fresh socks," I added, wanting to remain on his side.

He chuckled. "And fresh socks, yeah. But no damn shower, that's for sure. Can't be bathing in dead man juices."

I smiled at the morbid joke and crossed to the living room, plucking two towels from a pile on the armchair. Beneath lay a summer dress and two crisp shirts, never to be worn again. "Here," I said, and threw him a towel.

The fabric softener instantly calmed me, and, once dry, I couldn't help but share at least some of Lee's hype. We *had* neutralized a threat today. We'd survived being burned out of our home (did I really think of the tree house as a *home* now?), and we'd navigated the freaks with ease. We *could* do this. Once Kit's leg healed, we'd make it to the mill. We stood a chance, provided Lee's sanity maintained, and the smile that spread across my face actually pained.

It vanished when alarm clocks echoed through the woods.

CHAPTER EIGHTEEN

MY HEART JACKHAMMERED and I froze. Above, floorboards banged as Kit scrambled from bed.

"The fuck is that, man? *The fuck is that?*"

The tinny sound continued, joined by another and another, setting my teeth on edge until the woods sang with a shrill copper choir. A freak yelled in response.

"Alarm clocks," Lee said. "Tony, that bastard did something. We gotta go find them."

He raced to the door and as his fingers found the lock I slapped his arm away. "Dude, careful. We can't just go rushing out there without a plan. They'll be coming from everywhere, all of them. It's a goddamn dinner bell."

His eyes narrowed. "Then, what, Tony? We sit here and wait for it all to blow over? Ain't gonna happen. We gotta get out there and shut 'em off, wait for the bastards to go wandering off again."

I clenched my teeth and cussed, blood thrumming in my ears. I imagined Kit's terror right now—*alarm clocks, fucking alarm clocks!*—and his burden doubled my own. "We can't leave him."

"Tony, every second we spend here is a second they're gaining on the house, we have to get out there."

"Fuck!"

I pulled my knife and followed my friend, keeping close as we bolted across the lawn, pelted by the rain. The high-pitched ringing wailed from the darkened thicket, the bobbing branches daring us to enter like beckoning hands of diseased carnies. As three freaks turned tail and gave chase, we broke into the forest.

Wet leaves slopped beneath our rushing feet and as we passed Kit's father, Lee tripped, slapping the soggy earth. I pulled him upright and tried ignoring the alarm clocks but their incessant ringing blocked my concentration.

"My hammer," Lee said in a panic, getting to his knees and flinging around the mucky foliage. In the darkness and rain, the place looked like rancid oatmeal. "I dropped my fucking hammer."

A groan crept through the trees, and in the moonlight, something shambled towards us. Something that blended with its surroundings. I pulled Lee to his feet. "We don't have the fucking time, man, come on! Get up."

"Shit!"

Lee fell through the trees, off-balance and using trunks to pull himself forward, his breathing tinged with a wheeze. I worried how smoking affected him, and his lack of sleep didn't help matters, never mind the fact he was now unarmed. "Up there," he said, and pointed to a glistening pine. Ten-feet up the trunk, bound by gaffer tape, an alarm clock screamed.

"One down," I said, and grabbed hold of the tree, hoisting myself to the first branch. I pulled myself to a higher platform and dislodged water, a curtain of rain hissing down. With a leap, I made it close enough to grab the device and tried ripping it from the trunk. The tape held.

Fuck.

I pulled my knife, fingers shaking, and rammed the handle into the clock face, smashing it to pieces. With a fifth swing, the bells finally fell silent.

"Jesus Christ." I blew a breath before worming back down, leaping from the last branch to the ground.

"I think there's another couple," Lee said, already starting off, moving deeper into the woods. Shapes danced around us, swaying branches, and other, more human movement. I wondered how many freaks peppered the woods at this point, but instead focused on the task at hand. I prayed for Kit's safety back at the house.

"Over there," Lee said, and jogged through the trees, clumsily dodging the reaching branches. He called back, "that asshole left a plan B, man, he fucking *knew* something could go wrong. He *knew* we were coming here. This is sick, this is fucking sick!"

I agreed, but felt no urgency for discussion, and instead concentrated on the shuffling shapes in the moonlight. As he pushed further, slamming past an interlocking gate of leaves, my friend's lack of awareness horrified me. But an argument wasn't going to solve anything, I reminded myself, and followed.

The ringing came from everywhere and nowhere, and I strained to find the source. Lee, on the other hand, moved with complete confidence. Until he froze by a clearing.

"I thought it was right here."

I scanned the open patch of land, rain splashing off rocks and felled greenery. "What are you talking about? Come on."

"I swore it was coming from right here." He ran a hand across his face, leaving a black streak on his right cheek that stood out in high-contrast to his ashen features. "I swore it was coming from right here, man."

The two alarms continued, sounding like mechanical laughter. A freak spilled into the clearing and lost footing, splatting on the moss. It quickly regained its posture and stretched its arms, racing for us with a cry that sounded like a leaf-clogged drain.

"Move, Lee!"

He shook his head clear before following, and I veered right, back in the direction of Nate and Allie's, knowing if we didn't make a break for the mill *right now*, we were done for. Those alarms cackled like psychotic spectators, and our hopes of finding them dissipated by the second. Kit's leg ruined or not, our escape came now or never.

"This way!" Lee said, and grabbed my arm from behind, almost pulling me off my feet. I spun and avoided face-planting a trunk by millimeters before readjusting my path and following my friend, the darkness as thick as a blanket. Moonlight struggled through the glistening overhang. That's the moment I realized: we were lost.

"Lee, it's back there, I know it."

"No, it's not!"

The alarms cut deeper into my brain, forcing me to clench my teeth. I dreamed of smashing their mechanical faces to pieces.

"Lee, follow me, you're going to get us killed!"

With a snarl, he shot off, smacking a tree and agitating a water spill before stumbling and correcting himself. A groan echoed behind me, and my heart rate soared, urging me to *move, move, move.* I knew Lee was wrong, knew he'd taken off deeper into the woods and not towards the house, but I couldn't allow him to race into the night alone. Not in his condition. So, I followed.

"Lee!"

Fat branches swayed before my eyes, trying their damnedest to throw me off track. I had a hard time distinguishing the leafy limbs from the freaks'. I found Lee by a trunk, catching his breath as he scanned the area.

I panted. "You're lost, man. *Follow me.* You're fucking delirious. You haven't slept in days. It's my turn to lead you."

"It's this way." He pushed off and I swiped for his arm, missing by a nano-second. One that proved fatal. "Lee!"

His yelling jarred my legs.

I grabbed the tree trunk and my nails almost pressed through the wood. In the clearing, a shape engulfed the silhouette of my friend. A shape unlike any we'd seen before. A fungal gathering in a humanoid form. Paul Osmond. As more moans responded to the clacking alarms, I swiped the knife from my belt and raced to the struggle.

"The hell off him!"

I swiped a vicious arc and the blade sunk deep into flesh. A yell like a blender full of rocks made me back-peddle, followed by a dull thump as my friend dropped to the dirt.

The shroom-covered monstrosity stumbled away, knife embedded in its shoulder as it spun in confused circles. I grabbed blindly and my fingers worked into Lee's shirt. Then I dragged him back into the darkness. Something warm trickled across my knuckles.

"No..." I dropped Lee by a bush where a sliver of moonlight cut the canopy, giving me a view. Crimson trickled from his neck. "No, man, no!"

Lee clutched the wound, his face tight as sweat beaded down his cheeks. "I'm sorry, Tony..."

"How deep is it? Did he get you? Lee, move your hand."

He gasped. "Went in. Like a needle from Mrs. Bloom. Remember the fuckin' flu shots? Tony, I don't wanna die."

"Fuck!"

I stood and grabbed my hair, stifling the scream erupting from my guts, but barely. Anger consumed me, and I wished I could turn back the clock—*the clocks, the fucking clocks!*—and force Lee to follow my route. Instead, here he lay in a quivering heap, bleeding out as adrenaline reinstated some semblance of sense. Our predicament sure as shit got through now: This wasn't a damn game. All this was for keeps.

"Help me," he cried, and a pang of guilt pierced my chest. "I don't wanna change. Not into one of them, man, no."

Change. It all came down to change. Innocence to sin, dream to nightmare. Youth to death.

"Here," I said, and wrapped an arm around his shoulders, cringing at the heat spilling from his skin. Liquid soaked through my shirt, smelling of crushed metal. "On the count of three, we're gonna run. Got it?"

Lee nodded, but yelled as movement agitated more blood.

"Shit. One, two..."

We shot off, this time racing in the correct direction. Wet leaves tickled my face and I wiped off the excess, veering from the path each time another moan emanated close by. I prayed Kit hadn't left Nate and Allie's already, hoped he had the means to protect himself if he'd stayed. I wondered how many freaks littered the backyard by now. And how many had gotten inside the house.

The wet slush of feet rushing through the foliage increased. Faster and faster, closer and closer.

"Damn it, Lee, move your ass!"

I gripped his midsection and pulled, his weight bogging my speed. He spat a garbled string of nonsense that made my hair stand on end.

"Lee?"

In the low light, his head tilted back, and a tooth slipped from his mouth. A front tooth. Then another, like kernels of popcorn. Bleeding gums glistened in the moonlight—and, god help me, I dropped my friend.

He crashed with a thump, and his back arched. He spat a wad of blood. Seconds later, a rain-soaked freak with a white and fuzzy growth on its back dropped to its knees and enveloped him. I turned, and I ran.

I screamed my throat raw, matching Lee's hair-curling yell as my brain struggled not to switch off, the weight of the world finally bursting the numb dam that protected my sanity. Images of Jack on the first night, pleading for help, pulsated in conjunction with Lee's quivering body as the freaks feasted. I chanced a glance and watched his spasming arm jut from a pile-up of slithering bodies. The endless forest trail spread before me, and I cried when the nightmare didn't end. Just me and Kit now, two kids against a world slowly consuming everything we'd ever loved.

I cried as I caught a break. Rain slapped off my face. Nate and Allie's home appeared through the thicket. More freaks materialized from the darkness, and, pushing my legs to the limit, I cut a direct path for the house.

My pursuers swelled in number, and I imagined half of Riverside on my tail. Fathers, mothers, butchers and drop-outs, each with only my neck in mind. Each with an urge to bite and spread that parasite. To infect.

The back door stood open.

"Move it!" Kit motioned from the doorway, same as our first outing, and I took the yard in strides, avoiding the grasp of a white and fuzzy abomination in a night-robe. Kit slammed the door behind me, remade the lock, and grabbed my shoulders.

"Where is he?" He cried, and I couldn't find the words. "Tony, speak."

"He..." I gestured to the door, to the apocalypse in the woods, but all that came was an involuntary cry before I finally caught my breath. "He didn't make it, man."

"Shit!"

He yelled and barged across the kitchen, swiping aside the curtains. "They're crawling all over the damn place, man, they're everywhere."

A bang on the front door made me jump and Kit shushed me. "Five out front, I've kept count. They've been there ever since you left, one more every couple of minutes. Tony, I need you to get a grip, okay? *More are coming.* Two in the back, the rest in the woods. My dad made 'em swarm us. He's trapped us, and you need to concentrate or we're not getting out of here alive."

That quivering arm...the slopping...Lee...

"We've gotta make a run for it now, I can't do anything about my damned leg. Longer we wait, the more our path gets blocked."

He sucked a breath, steeling his nerves. "Tony. I'm thinkin' the backyard, race past the two on the lawn, get out on the main road, there'll be less of 'em out there. They're all headin' for the woods. Plain sight is our best option."

"Okay."

My guitar, I thought, horrified by the strangeness. *I'll need my guitar.*

And without thinking, I made for the hall.

"Tony, it's here."

My instrument sat propped against the kitchen table, its presence as comforting as an old friend, each crack or grain as familiar as a line or wrinkle on a loved one's face. Kit's gesture took my breath away, and I sniffled as I approached the guitar. "Thanks, man."

A renewed sense of purpose filled me, and as I grabbed the instrument, I was calmed by its weight. "How's your leg?"

"It'll have to do. We've got no other choice." He nodded to the guitar, and the conversation we'd had in my living room remained clear in his eyes. "You need that. I know you do."

"Thank you."

"Look, I got knives from the kitchen. You still got yours?"

"No."

"Okay. Take this. Now let's get the hell outta here."

I riffled through the grocery bag on the kitchen table and pulled my notebook. I stuffed it inside my pants. The food and water were useless now, but I needed the work if I made it out alive. Within those pages lurked my fears and nightmares, transformed to rhythm and rhyme. I could not lose them. With a shuddering breath, I followed Kit to the back door. Once I gathered my nerves, I steeled myself for the run.

Kit counted under his breath, then flung the door wide open.

Two freaks instantly dragged their ruined bodies towards us, green arms reaching as their heads flopped back. Kit raced to the right, to the matting of trees separating the yard from the road, and I slowed my pace to stay by his side. I ignored the incessant banging of the guitar against my leg as the groans of the infected bloomed, and more freaks shambled from the darkness. A sour stench from the burning tree house ghosted beneath the sickening smell of fungus.

Kit smashed through the thicket and we dodged an isolated creep with white strands caking his body like spider webbing. We broke through onto the road, and as my feet touched the smooth tarmac, I imagined a starter pistol cracking for a final home run. We shot off.

Our neighbors shambled in our wake, an unimaginable number of swaying horrors, once with names and homes, now only vessels for a primal purpose. The first-turned had slathered their fresh growths with mucus thick as gel. Dead eyes beamed from the moss of those who weren't facing skyward, and from each mouth crept the same parasitic growth, one white and gnarled and deadly.

"Shit!"

As we broke into a run, I tore my eyes from the orange glow of our ruined tree house pulsating from the far side of the mountain. The acrid stench now filled the air. The town of Riverside chased us as a singular black mass, but with Kit's leg damaged, our speed only just outpaced them. The distance increased the more we moved, but against the cloak of night-sky stood silhouettes in the fields around us, straggling wanderers who would surely intercept us at first sight. Dead bodies with white fuzz and glazed eyes. We couldn't stop for anything.

Among the dead walked Rodgers and Lee, I knew, and their lumbering corpses refused to leave my imagination: Lee's leather jacket, hanging crooked as fungus sprouted from his fresh pores, his neck in ribbons and leaking over a classic rock teeshirt. Rodgers, his unshakable sadness still haunting those empty eyes, now by his father's side and needing revenge on his so-called 'friends' who allowed him to commit such an atrocious act. Friends who'd introduced him to a cruel world full of teeth.

Tears stung my eyes as the mill appeared on the mountaintop, the building now a corpse just as much as our dead town. Thick vines crawled the wire fence, fighting to reclaim the plot for Mother Nature. Mottled spots of growth, like green boils, peppered the faded brickwork. Ahead stood the gate with its 'no entry' warning for those who would be so brave.

A freak grunted as it toppled from a field and tripped a few followers on the road. Their numbers were down by a handful, but still nowhere near few enough. My heavy breathing filled my head, fighting for sonic real estate against my thrumming blood and the symphony of our chasers. A cry erupted from them, and goosebumps rippled across my flesh as we reached the gate. The gate of the damned mill.

Kit worked his hands between the wire mesh, pulling and rattling the frame. "How the hell do we open this thing? Ed tried the other day, it was useless."

The contagious panic of his voice worked through me and I took a deep breath. Then, beside the gate, I spotted cable ties holding the mesh.

My knife.

"Here, hold this."

I passed him my guitar and took a knee, working the blade into the plastic using both hands. The irritating angle made me shake with rage, but soon the first tie popped free.

"Hurry, Tony, they're coming."

"Shut up."

I sawed into the next and the next, ignoring the fact I'd leave a hole of our chasers to follow.

"I got it!"

The final tie snapped and the fence instantly tipped over. I got to my feet and pulled the section out, wrenching it from the hold of the grass. "Gimme a hand here."

Kit worked his fingers into the side of the gate and pulled, too, snapping more grasping blades, and, finally, the entrance parted by a sliver. "We're in."

We squeezed inside the mill yard, and I pulled the gate closed, but with nothing holding it in place, it wouldn't do much. The small section of fence lolled open. The neighbors were getting in, after all.

"Come on."

I led the way through the overgrown graveyard of rusted lumber frames and bins, weeds up to my knees. A matting of nettles stung my shins and I hissed at the pain, biting back the urge to stop and rub the irritated spots as we spilled into a gravel-strewn clearing. Solid brick made up the lower portion of the building, the second half covered in corrugated sheet metal painted the color of rotten spinach. A metallic folding door sat on this side, the chipper's back-end pressed against it for trucks unloading felled trees. Another door, the very same, sat in the front for lorries to carry away the chips. Neither had been opened for some time, and weeds crept along the bottom. Beside the sliding door, an entry to the administrative quarters sat sandwiched between two grime-caked windows. A little elbow grease would work wonders.

"Come on."

The freaks smacked against the fence, rattling the structure as they leaked saliva into the chain-link, too dumb to spot the opening in the gate for now, and actually pressing it shut with their weight.

I tried the handle of the door. Locked, of course.

"Stand back."

Kit rammed his shoulder home with a cry and the frame rattled. He fell back and rubbed his shoulder. I placed my guitar against the wall and joined him, both of us counting before giving another hit, this time using our boots. The first time, we got nothing but a loud bang. The second try was just as futile. On our third attempt, the wood cracked. I responded with another kick.

"One, two, three!"

Crack!

The door shot inward, its lower hinge clinging on for dear life before snapping. The door fell. A plume of dust puffed from the concrete floor, and I coughed before gathering my guitar and knife and then rushed inside.

"A phone," Kit said, and crossed to a dust-covered wooden desk. He lifted the receiver to his ear, dipped the button in the cradle. He shook his head. "Worth a shot, at least."

Graffiti saturated the walls. Tall white letters told me '*Miss Moore is a hoor*', and a stick-figure with a bulging stomach and fairy wings accompanied the title '*Ben Rodgers*'. My guts tightened.

"I'm sorry," Kit said. "Tony, we don't have time, okay? I am *really* sorry. You know that. It was last summer, a year ago. They'd fixed the fence because of it. You know I don't think that now."

I did, but the words still hurt, a leftover memento reminding me of the tumor on our otherwise nice childhood. One put in place by Kit and his friends to spoil our good times.

I made my way to a green door separating the main work building from the office. "How many times have you been here?" I asked, and tried the handle. The door creaked open.

Kit gasped before rushing before me and blocking my way. Panic lifted his features. "Let's get to the front door. We're running out of time. Before they completely swarm us."

"What is it?"

I peered over his shoulder, and he moved from my path, running a hand across his sweating face with a groan. My shoulders slumped.

There stood the chipper. The machine that'd taken my father's life over five years ago. A conveyor belt lay hidden behind the rusted metal hulk of the machine itself, the walls a barrier concealing the sight. On the wall itself, in now-browned paint, Kit had sprayed: THE PIG SLAUGHTER.

"Kit..."

"Tony, I'm sorry, okay? Look, it was years ago. I know that doesn't make it any better but Eddie and Meyer came over and I told them the story of...look, I'm sorry, man."

"You asshole."

I crossed to the machine, kicking aside pebbles of concrete and stirring a pigeon from the rafters. Bird shit covered the chipper walls, the sheer mass and color indistinguishable from the rusted metal itself now, all one lumpy, dull tone. Dust caked a cherry-picker next to the chipper, the platform raised as if untouched since the days the mill operated. I remembered stories of how my father would sit up there as trees were fed along the conveyor, pressing down the wood each time a trunk rose, keeping the vegetation on course for the whirling blades at the far side. On the seventeenth of December, he'd worked overtime for Christmas, just himself and Paul Osmond. Paul had taken a cigarette break, and my dad, confident in his abilities, had climbed down into the conveyor to dislodge a splintered branch. Christmas tunes blasted from the office (I've always wondered which), and when Paul returned inside, humming, he'd kicked the machine back to life, assuming my dad had taken a bathroom break.

Osmond had told all this to the police at the top of his lungs, half-mad within the hour. He'd passed our house a couple of days later and tried our door to apologize, but Richardson had come by and removed him. The guilt consumed him, and the few times we met around Riverside, he'd avoided me like a mangy dog.

Turns out my dad was standing right by the blades when Paul restarted the machine. I imagined they'd chewed into his spine first, the back of his skull...he'd probably managed a scream as Osmond cut the chipper, but by then his brains were probably spilling down the back of his shirt.

"Tony?"

The pig slaughter.

I shook my head and took a shaking breath. Then I placed my guitar beside the machine and put my free hand on the hulk, needing to touch it.

"Tony?"

I made to speak when something smacked the front door.

Chapter Nineteen

THE CORRUGATED METAL rattled as dust puffed from the rollers above.

"They've gotten around front," Kit said, and his eyes darted frantically about the room. "We gotta try the security door before there's too many, they've got us trapped."

I remembered we'd pulled the office door clean off its hinges, and I raced across the room, needing that door closed—just as a shorts and sandals wearing freak shambled inside. Shrooms jutted from its bare legs, its face caked over with white fuzz.

"Shit!"

I pulled my knife with the intent of burying the blade in the bastard's skull. That door needing closing before...another freak lumbered inside. And another. And another. A rotten stench filled the air.

"Tony, Tony, come on!"

Without thinking, I grabbed my guitar and followed Kit in retreat, pausing by the fire-exit next to the rattling gate. Kit pushed down the safety bar, and, stupidly, I cringed, expecting an alarm to blare like the safety-exits at school. The door opened—and instantly slammed shut from the weight of freaks on the opposite side.

"They're all over the place."

Kit backed away as the shambling monsters behind us moaned, the sound reverberating around the empty space and stirring up pigeons from overhead. They cooed and whipped up the smell of dry wood. The office continued flooding with our neighbors. And the fire-exit was off limits...we were trapped.

All except for one place.

"Follow me," I said, and raced for the cherry-picker. The freaks at the office sped as their heads fell back to give a clear sight of the growth. I gritted my teeth as I flung my guitar inside the chipper, cringing as it thudded the conveyor. The sturdy wood survived the throw from the tree house, and I prayed it could take another hit.

With my hands free, I climbed the cherry picker's cab, perching atop the buckled hood. Kit came next, and I grabbed the scruff of his neck before dragging him up beside me, just as a freak swiped and missed his heel by an inch.

More and more neighbors piled in from the office and filled the workroom, the closest smacking the cherry picker, their fungal-covered faces trained on us with dead eyes.

I took a quivering breath before working my hands into the picker's lift, thinking it no more than a metal branch, reminding myself I'd climbed enough trees in my day.

"Follow my lead," I said, and hoisted myself out. I wrapped my legs around the metal, worming towards the chipper, suspended above a sea of death. They reached like believers to a savior, fingers snapping on empty space. As I wriggled further, my palms began to sweat. My left leg popped free and I gasped, foot swinging until I found purchase. My stomach flipped as snapping fingers grazed my shirt.

I trained my attention back to the chipper and kept moving, daring not to look down. Relief flooded as I passed the rusted wall and below lay the conveyor. I let go. I landed with a thud and scrambled to my feet on the filthy rubber, my skin crawling that such a thin metallic sheet separated me from my dead neighbors. The walls of the chipper reached just above my head, so instead of jumping, I shouted, "you okay?"

My neighbors' arms reached above the wall.

"I'm good, man. You okay?"

"Fine. Come on. Think of it as a branch. You've climbed a million before."

Kit groaned, but the creaking metal told me he'd wasted no time in positioning himself on the picker's arm. I screamed as a freak smacked the chipper inches from my face and I stumbled, crashing on the conveyor. Splinters of wood embedded in my palms and I brushed myself clean before pushing upright. The rusted mouth of blades waited patiently at the end of the belt, and my stomach flipped as a movie of my dad's final moments played before my eyes. Did blood still stain the blades? If I inspected close up, *really* checked, would I find some, or had some kind soul washed it clean? What about the belt beneath my feet, did they contain splattered DNA? Vomit rose in my throat and I placed a hand to my chest.

When Kit fell, I screamed.

"Just me, Tony, just me." He scrambled to his feet and brushed wood chips from his clothes. "You all right?"

With the machine separating us from the dead, I took solace in the respite. "Just...never expected to be here. This was the last thing he ever saw, y'know?"

"I know."

"Wondering what he was thinking as it happened, if he thought of me and mom, or if it was all panic and pain. Until it wasn't."

"Well, let's not end up like that, huh? Your dad, your mom, my dad, Rodgers, Lee, Jacob, all of 'em. We're still alive. Let's keep it that way."

The blades pulled my attention, refused to let go, a haphazard mess of razor-sharp teeth like the mouth of some robotic shark. I imagined the conveyor whirring to life as myself and Kit landed smack on our backs and the rubber tongue crept us closer and closer, the sound overwhelming...

"Jesus Christ..." I ran a palm across my sweat-slicked face and took deep breaths.

"Tony, what's wrong?"

Later I'd realize, this is what a panic attack felt like.

My vision distorted, blindspots fizzing and popping in my peripheral as the eager groans of our neighbors dulled, replaced by a thin ringing. My heart used my ribs as a punching bag, and my breath struggled to find a pattern.

"Tony, sit, sit, sit. That's it. Deep breaths. Slow."

I did as instructed, but a smack on the metal jolted me and everything started over. Kit pulled me to the opposite side of the chipper and leaned me on the metal once again, this time with no freaks on the other side. With some rest, my senses cleared.

"All right?" Kit asked. He squeezed my shoulder as his ashen face swam into focus. Then he snapped a finger.

"I'm good," I said, and climbed to my feet. Kit steadied me with an arm as my strength fizzled back. "Never had that happen to me before."

The metal mouth of the chipper mocked me. I looked away.

"I have," Kit said with a nod. "Panic attack. Used to get 'em all the time. You'll be all right."

More voices joined the choir over the wall, but something else caught my attention. The banging on the front gate had lessened. Still a few beaters, sure, but nowhere near as insistent. I told Kit.

"Must be coming 'round front," he said. "Following the others like they did into Rodgers' and Lee's, remember? Like sheep."

An idea stuck, and the adrenaline that hit caused my vision to flicker again. "Still got the slingshot?"

"Yeah, but we've got nothing to shoot. I even used up Rodgers' molar."

Kit plucked the homemade weapon from his pocket and held it out but I shook my head. "You need to do this."

"Do what?"

"Hold on."

I got to my knees and felt around the conveyor, palms grating over splinters and debris. I crawled on all fours, away from the blades, until my palm hit a pellet-sized stone.

I breathed a sigh of relief. "Kit, take this."

Kit rolled the rock about in his palm. "Think it'll work?"

"Gotta try."

His face fell. "Walls are too high for aiming. I gotta jump just to see over. Can't be expected to hit 'em all while in mid-air, man. Ain't a comic book character." He sighed and wiped his forehead. "Besides, took you ages just to find that one. How long would it take to find a whole heap of stones to knock 'em out one by one?"

I grunted in frustration. "No, man. We smash out the front office window, just like we did for our runs, okay? We smash that, it draws the last ones from the fire-exit around. Clears our path."

"But how do we get out to the fire exit, Tony? Can't jump out into their open arms."

"We make the biggest goddamn ruckus you ever heard on the far end of the chipper. Smack the metal, draw them all up that end. Then we run like our asses are on fire down this end and climb out, leave 'em all trapped here."

"We can use the blades to climb over."

Fear punched my chest. "I can't."

"Tony."

"I—"

"—Tony, we don't have time, all right? Listen to me. This could work."

The idea of touching that metallic mouth made my legs weak.

"Fuck," I said. "You're right. It *will* work. It has to. Now, come on, I'll give you a boost."

I kneeled and gritted my teeth as Kit's boot pressed into my spine. He hoisted himself and wobbled a moment, the weight crushing my back. "Got a shot?" I wheezed.

He took a moment, hands on the edge of the chipper. He grimaced as a hairy hand swiped at his face. "Jesus...look, I got a shot. But it's gonna be risky. It's about as far as Lee's place from the tree house, but there's an open doorway to the office I gotta get through first. One of the freaks come out of there at the wrong time and I take them out instead of the window."

I sucked down air, arms shaking. "Well, take it, man, we don't have all the time in the world here."

"Right."

As Kit loaded the slingshot, I could practically hear his conscience tease him about missing his dad as the psycho approached with a lighter and machete. Years later, I'd wonder if Kit had missed on purpose out of a momentary lapse of pity. He'd never missed a target in his goddamn life, yet he'd missed his father *twice*. I closed my eyes and waited.

"Here goes."

Kit took aim a mere second before glass exploded and I yelled in victory. With his arms off the chipper, Kit toppled. He crashed beside me and I helped him to his feet as my back thanked me for the relief. I strained my ears and whispered.

"Sounds like they're coming 'round. Listen..."

The banging slowly petered out as the intrigued freaks meandered towards the damage, drawn by nothing more than tendency. A few seconds passed, and the gate stopped rattling. My hopes soared. The fire exit would be free. A straight run to the forest trail and then the highway. "They took the bait. Come on. We gotta make one hell of a noise."

We raced to the back of the chipper, the metal here rusted and thin. Stars peppered an inky sky in a hole above our heads, a ragged ceiling wound that leaked on the conveyor and ate away the metal. Slimy moss caked the conveyor itself by our feet, and I treaded lightly before banging the metal wall. The sound reverberated, the dead moaning in response, and then they shuffled towards us.

"They're headed here."

Above the wall, swaying heads bobbed in our direction, some crashing against the chipper with a boom. Kit kicked the wall to my right and got an even bigger response, the sound loud as thunder. Rust hissed to the conveyor by our feet. I should've paid closer attention at the time, should've told Kit not to kick so hard, but clarity had been snuffed by a blanket of optimism.

"Come on, you horrible bastards!"

I punched the metal, my blood drumming. My knuckles screamed but I ignored the pain. "Get the fuck over here!"

Pigeons circled overhead, scared beyond belief, and I hammered the wall again. "Come on, come on!"

Kit slammed his boot home, causing another rust shower. "Let's get movin', you fucks! You know you always wanted to get at me, now come on!"

I laughed, couldn't help it, and a great smile lifted my cheeks. I punched the wall again and again, unable to stop, each hit releasing a flood of endorphins and shredding my fists. Kit beat the shit out of the metal beside me, and his laughter matched my own.

All until the *crack*.

A ragged chunk of wall fell outwards and smashed the workroom floor, the edges of the hole marred by rust like the pink skin around a wound, and in that hole appeared Rodgers.

Even in death, my friend's sadness remained.

Tufts of moss jutted from his clothes and caked his face, the parasitic tooth now the length of the others, red-tipped and ready for flesh. I didn't speak, couldn't find the words, and took off running. I bolted for the blades, the rusted life-takers now the lesser of two evils as Rodgers fell inside and took Kit down. Kit yelped and punched the boy, his knuckles coming away slick with saliva and matted with fungus. He screamed his throat raw as Rodgers' mouth eventually found his neck, and pressed down. I stopped by my guitar and scooped the instrument. Next came Lee and Lacey, the youth of Riverside having pushed their way to the front of the group. When Ford and a fat man I didn't recognize spilled inside, my paralysis broke and I dropped my guitar before leaping at the high wall. I ignored the pain in my body. I ignored Kit's screams. The chipper had become my coffin.

My fingers slapped the edge but popped free, burning.

Come on, Tony, come on.

I hopped again and again, but the wall stood an inch too high, teasing me with just centimeters to freedom. I glanced back, pulling my eyes from the quivering body on the conveyor, and saw no hope of rushing through the crowd. They spilled inside like oil from a leak. Their hands would find me in seconds, clamp down, and I'd be punctured by dozens of parasitic needles within seconds.

"Fuck!"

I kicked the wall, prized with a rattle. The metal here held strong, not a trace of the quick-eating rust from the hole in the roof down the other end. And as a couple slipped from the group and lumbered along the conveyor towards me, doom anchored me still.

I'm dead. I'm dead. I'm dead.

"No!"

I spun like a mutt chasing its own tail, the metal walls embracing me and holding me trapped for more on-comers. Until I studied the rusty blades. I had to do it. And yes, a splatter of brown still stained their metal teeth. A brown that had once been wet crimson.

I hadn't looked for fear of seeing that very thing.

With a shake of my head, I grabbed my guitar and flung it out to the work-floor, wincing as it clattered. I'd find a way to repair the damn thing, but I couldn't leave it. I worked my fingers around the sharp metal and hoisted myself up, standing on the sharp blades. My brain projected the image of everything whirring to life, smoke churning from the engine, my body cracking and spurting like some over-the-top movie effect until I was all gone and spat out.

That isn't going to happen. Just move it.

The freaks quickened the closer they got, and as Lee (his face stubbled, still visible) and a man in a bathrobe reached me, I jumped, stomach smacking the wall, but arms going over. I sucked down air and gasped as Lee's fingers tightened around my ankle.

"Lee!"

I kicked, cracking his nose and sending him back a step. Spit overflowed his lips and soaked his jacket, his glands producing gallons of saliva, something Lee himself would've found fascinating. But without dwelling, I pulled myself higher, legs kicking as I struggled. A couple of stragglers still dotted the work-room floor, pausing now I'd come into sight. Nothing I couldn't take. If my legs didn't break once I fell, of course.

Here goes nothing.

I pulled myself up with everything I had, muscles straining and pain biting. My entire body shook but, as Lee swiped again, his fingers only found air. I'd done it. I fell across and smacked the concrete with a gasp, landing next to my instrument. Something burned, but I had no time to inspect any damage. A crack adorned the back of my guitar, but I did not care, I was out with my instrument and that fire-exit called me like an angel.

I swiped my guitar and raced to the exit with my heart punching, each step causing something warm and wet to race down my leg. My teeth gritted and every breath felt like swallowing nails, but I pushed on. Until a red button made me pause.

Dark stains caked the washed-out plastic, the lettering above faded but legible: ON / OFF.

Would the mill still retain power despite being closed for half a decade? Did Kit's rumors hold any truth?

...try get the ol' chipper goin' again!

"Fuck it."

I slammed the button home.

And the chipper screamed to life.

Thick, acrid smoke billowed from the motor as the device jittered and I jumped from shock as the high-whining blades sliced through bodies. The blocked-up pipe vomited a mess of shredded innards and bone across the dust-covered floor. And in it, swam clumps of white fungus.

My mouth fell open as I spotted leather chunks, my friend's infamous jacket floating in the mix. I leaped across the stream and reached the back door as another teeth-clenching *rip!* rang out—another victim entered the chipper. Red and white exploded across the concrete.

I pressed my shoulder against the fire-exit, getting little resistance, and the hinges gave way as I fell out into the backyard. The door slammed behind me, mercifully muting the stream of bodies being chewed up and spat out. The sound, the smell, something would call attention to Riverside.

I sucked fresh air, a wet forest scent tinged by the harshness of burning wood coming from the tree house across town. No flames flickered in the distance now. The rain had finished its job of snuffing the flames. But clouds of moon-saturated smoke still carried through the trees in a fat mist.

I hobbled across the yard, each step drawing a wince as wetness soaked through my sock. I made my way to the old export trail and was surprised to find it clearer than expected. A wooden fence boxed it from the forest, and a vehicle barrier stood this end of the mill. I ducked the barrier to the flattened path, and studied the gravel, already sprouting weeds from lack of use. A bang came on the mill door, followed by another high-whine of the chipper. I wouldn't get all of them, but I got a few, and that felt only right. With the guitar slung over my shoulder, I took off down the trail.

Ten minutes later, unstoppable tears came. The full weight of my luck crashed home the further I made it, and I welcomed the break of my mental dam. I yelled, not a word, just a roar of triumph, screaming at the trees and sky as if they somehow held responsibility. Something in the back of my throat ripped and I didn't care, I swallowed the pain and screamed again, this time from the gut, and I damn sure showed the land who's who.

The rattle and whine of the chipper faded in time, and as ant-sized lights appeared like stars through the trees, my entire body shook with disbelief. I raced the rest of the way, left shoe squelching from a wound, and I muttered a prayer not to collapse now, not with escape so close.

I did not collapse. And a half-hour later, I came upon the highway guardrail.

I placed my hand against the cold metal, sniffled, and studied the painted tarmac as if it belonged to some alien world, one where fungal-covered abominations did not exist. And I supposed it true, in a way. Out there lay safety.

A headache thumped beneath my eyes from dehydration and a lack of food, and I ducked the guardrail before shambling onto the roadside. I began walking the highway, not caring for direction, only praying a car came soon. Now that the adrenaline fizzled from my system, I didn't know how long I could continue before falling flat on my face. I could've stayed put, probably would've made no difference, but something inside me needed to be far away from the mountain. I needed to be amongst tall buildings, smiling faces, and the overwhelming noise of business. I needed not to think.

And then I collapsed.

It happened without warning. My legs buckled and I gasped as my ribs smacked the hard-shoulder. A hollow pang rang from my guitar and I pulled it aside, spotting two broken strings. Then the rain picked up again and hissed all around, matting my hair to my forehead and wafting the stench of my sweat.

I cried, and huddled my guitar. I cried for my mom, seeing her hand in mine years earlier, eating ice-cream and strolling the woods in a sun-soaked haze. I cried for Jacob, Lee, and Rodgers, images of us in the tree house late at night with candles burning as adulthood promised us futures of fortune and happiness, all the while crossing its fingers behind its back. I cried for Riverside, a town full of care and support, one that wanted a prosperous future for its residents. A good, clean and honest home.

I wiped my face with my filthy palm and took a deep, slow breath. Then I slipped off my shoe and sock, my bare foot soaking in the fresh air. Rain took the blood from my skin, dripping to the tarmac before washing along the ditch. I massaged my toes clean as I hiked my jeans to my knee, and eyed a gash as wide as a sinister smile drooling blood across my calf. My fingers shook as I dabbed the wound, and I sucked air between my teeth. A shard of glass had gotten me worse than I thought.

My sight blurred, and bright light encircled my vision. I tried shaking my view clear, but the glare refused to dull.

Then the rumble of an engine bloomed, and my heart sped. That light wasn't from a lack of blood.

The car jittered through the rain, wipers doing their best to clear the windshield. I waved my hands and yelled, unable to stand but creating a ruckus for attention. And as the car approached, my stomach tightened. When it shot by, my entire face stretched with shock.

"No...*no, no, no.*"

Brake-lights came alive and I closed my eyes, laughing in disbelief as the tires squealed to a halt. The door popped and out stepped a figure in a raincoat, an overweight man with a thick, white beard.

He jogged to me and I couldn't stop myself from scanning his face, searching for glistening fungus and a gnarled bone jutting from his gums. I needn't have worried: not only was the man's skin clear, he hardly had teeth at all.

"Boy, what's happened?"

I mumbled something about a police station and my brain registered the jerking motion of being lifted. I half-heartedly mumbled about my guitar and heard the strings ring out as he lifted it, too, and that made me smile. The warm blanket of sleep (or death, I didn't know which at the time), engulfed me, and seconds later, I curled on what I imagined was leather. Country music lulled from somewhere very far away, and I noted a door popping and slamming, the vehicle rocking as softly as a crib.

The man spoke with a baritone, coming from beneath a vast ocean, and I nodded along to where I sensed lay all the right beats. My fingers found the rain-slicked surface of my guitar and I allowed them to rest there, reassuring myself I still had the instrument, if nothing else.

The future lied, I realized. To my youth, it promised smiles and old age and a good job and a thousand other things I thought every grown-up had. With the eyes of a child, I assumed paradise, clueless to suicide and pain and starvation and loss and grief, and a thousand other things I never heard tell of. Until I did.

I cried again. This time for the loss of innocence.

Chapter Twenty

THE CITY BAR sat empty save for five patrons at the counter. They talked in hushed tones as a musician named Peter Laughlin untangled cables by a road-battered PA system. A fireplace crackled in one corner, keeping the December bite from the air, and a stuffed moose head watched over a worn-out pool table. I nodded to the bartender and ordered a beer before easing down at a free booth, away from the talkers, and placed my guitar case by my leg. Peter had an hour set, and a half-hour change-over left plenty of time for me to talk to the man I'd come to see. Provided he showed at all.

I sipped my drink and sighed, shaking the remnants of rain from my shaggy hair after removing my coat, a leather jacket similar to one once worn by an old friend. I kept all sorts of mementos from my childhood, unable to shake the past.

Peter greeted the handful of drinkers while tuning his instrument, and their attention told me he must've released something worthwhile back in the day, even if he only pulled a baker's dozen on an evening in the city. He acknowledged me with a wink, some unspoken link sparking between two kindred souls. Little gestures like that made me feel less alone in the world.

The bell chimed above the door and a cold wind entered along with an elderly man. He shivered and untangled a scarf from around his neck, ordering a tequila as he hobbled across the room. I scanned him over. Long white hair, thinning on top, a thick beard, and a scrawny frame layered in clothes. He thanked the bartender before knocking back his shot and slamming the glass to the counter. Then he smacked his lips and gave a salute, drawing the attention of the other patrons.

Goddamnit, what have I gotten myself into?

He spotted me and smiled, approaching with open arms and a laugh. Then he stood before me and I got to my feet, accepting the embrace. He clapped my back.

"Tony Wheeler!" he said, and pulled me back to arm's length. "Teddy Littleman. Man, I can't tell you how nice it is to finally meet you. Pixelated reproductions can only tell us so much, no?"

"Likewise, yeah. Please, have a seat."

Teddy pulled a stool from a nearby table and seated himself with a sigh. Thick spectacles amplified his overeager eyes, and his too-large dentures called as much attention as breasts in church—for all intents and purposes, he looked like a man wearing a disguise, and I fought not to laugh.

His brow creased. "Everything all right?"

"All good, man. All good. It's nice to finally meet you."

He smiled. "Hey, all that emailin' almost gave me carpal tunnel, I gotta tell ya. But, man, what an exciting day, huh?"

"It really is."

He studied me like a particularly interesting zoo exhibit, slowly nodding. "Right on. Right on."

Peter started into a slow number from the stage, drawing the attention of the patrons. And I cleared my throat. "Teddy, this'll all go how we say it will, right? You're running the site how long?"

He clicked his tongue, running calculations. "Fiii...six years now? Yeah, around there. Dave, the old owner, passed it on to me after he saw how often I frequented the message boards. Man, you've no idea how many folks still wanna defend Duke Wetherell's Nessy photograph, if ya can funk it. People'll believe any old shit, dude. Once hadda try disprove a photo of a mirror the poster said was for vampires. Just a snap of a mirror, askin' me to disprove it, flash and all. How do you even *talk* to people like that? But, hell, I love it. And that site's my life. You know you're in safe hands. They'll believe what I research. They always do."

"Even the Riverside Case."

His face fell, and for a moment, I worried he'd lunge across the table. "Dude, the Riverside Case is the damn Holy Grail of conspiracy. Screw mirrors and Nessy. If you got what you say you got, you're gonna blow everything wide open. Most people in this bar even have a theory, it's not underground fringe shit."

"Damn right about that."

"So, look." He folded his hands, taking a beat. "What I wanna know is why me?"

"Don't want the limelight, Teddy. I don't want anything to do with Riverside again for as long as I live. I just need to make sure the truth gets out."

The Riverside Case, as it'd become known, sprang up just a year after the incident. 1998 saw papers lead with supposed photos taken from forensics of fungal-covered corpses splayed out on metal slabs, one with a shroom sprouting straight from its forehead. The world never knew who took the shots, not even me. Talkshow hosts and late-night newscasters speculated with be-speckled experts, but the consensus always ran in circles. And after a while, the world forgot. It always did.

Except for those on the fringe, those who scoured what the dawn of the millennium brought forth: the internet. Message boards exploded with arguing keyboard-warriors on the validity of the snaps. Even to this day, that photograph ranks amongst the most popular for theorists, most pointing to the fact no mortuary claimed business that night.

After being picked up by Dale Fuller by the side of the road, he sped me to the nearest station. Until a roadblock dampened his urgency. The blue-and-red lights and the overwhelming number of security rubbed ol' Dale the wrong way. He slowed by the barrier and ordered me to lay low. Dale Fuller, I'd later learn, was ex-military. Gulf War. He'd returned with a healthy skepticism of authority, often telling me the role of a true patriot was not to blindly follow, but to question command, and know your heart lay in the right place. Know your reasons. Dale Fuller did not trust the blaring lights, or what he later called the Alphabet Soup Corp.

Dale Fuller raised me for five years.

On weekends I helped at Veteran support groups, PTSD anonymous, placing folding-chairs and making sure we'd made enough coffee. I sat in the back, listening, and learned how to process my own war. I kept my music going, too, and from sixteen played at bars, earning enough to help out. Dale lived alone in a cabin twenty minutes from the city in an area I felt all too familiar with. We'd laid low while paying close attention to the coverage as the years eased by.

Papers led with a viral outbreak, something akin to the bubonic plague, and the world mourned the loss of a town captive to one brave man who burned the place to the ground to ensure no trace of the virus ever escaped. According to journalists, he'd kidnapped every living soul and housed them in the mill before burning the place to ash. No mention of a chipper. No mention of blood. No mention of moss-covered flesh or freakish, gnarled teeth. And no notice of the one boy unaccounted for.

"Dude, you'd get a lot of money doing this yourself, you know. Journalists, hell, even a documentary crew would be climbing up your ass with checkbooks. Can't imagine a little music on the weekends gets you much cash."

I began to worry about how much I'd told Teddy throughout our correspondence but pushed my doubt aside. I still lived in the cabin, the land left to me after Dave moved across state with a lady he'd met. It wasn't much, but I called it home. Besides, I'd made this meeting happen, and I intended to see it through.

"I don't want any of it, man. Just want this thing out there."

He nodded in understanding, then said, "well, let's see it."

"Right."

We'd spoken of my evidence at length, but I still found myself amused at Teddy's reaction when I fished about inside my pocket. As my fingers closed around a Polaroid, I took a breath. "Promise me my name will *never* be attached to this, understood?"

"Already said I do. Silent as a grave, buddy. Silent as a damn grave."

"Okay."

I took a quick scan of the room, assuring all eyes remained on Peter before placing the photograph between us. As I withdrew my hand, Teddy paled, and leaned closer for inspection.

"Dude."

I folded my arms. "Yup."

"Sweet pickled fucks."

His eyes zoomed to the polaroid, and I wondered what thoughts bounced about his brain. In the foreground, a handful of freaks stood forever frozen in time, their lifeless eyes glistening like stars from the flash. Rodgers' shaking hands left a slight blur, but not enough to smear detail. The gnarled teeth remained clear, as did the disfigured faces. Like Halloween masks. Each aspect preserved by a thirteen-year-old boy scared out of his wits and ready to die.

"The mountains in the background, just like they were." Teddy traced his finger along the skyline, a subtle shake to his touch. "Those *are* the Riverside hills. Tony, this is undeniable. That mountain range got forested years ago, I know that for a fact, and don't look so shocked, a lot of people have speculated what a photo from Riverside would look like. I've dreamed of this."

"Complete with the date in the bottom, too, even though that could be easily photoshopped, but a nice feature all the same."

Rodgers, I thought. A boy who felt he had no purpose, now blowing the truth of his hometown for the world to see.

"The trees are still on that mountain, dude," Teddy said, biting his lower lip.

"Exactly."

"And the angle...the back of the house, I've seen photos of the Rodgers' place all burned down and shit, but that's the *actual place* still standing...isn't it?"

"It is."

"Holy fuck, just...holy fuck."

He ran a palm across his head, wide eyes returning to mine. "This changes everything, Tony."

"Good."

The anchor of the past twenty years left with that photo. A picture ready to undo the disrespected memories of my friends and family. They deserved the truth, everyone did, no matter how horribly twisted and gnarled it was.

"I better go," I said. "I'm on stage."

I left Teddy glued to the evidence with his mouth hanging open, and applauded Peter as he finished his set. We shared a few kind words, and then I set myself up and played my own truth, one wrapped in a parcel of rhythm and rhyme. One that made each day a little easier, and that allowed me an escape. If only for a little while.

The world revealed itself to me on that day. A disease-ridden mutant full of hurt and rage. One in which good people didn't always win, in which innocence was butchered until we no longer remembered its face, or cared. It all changed at some point.

But change didn't always have to be bad. I'd taken the first step to making this right, to blowing the doors off the nightmare that haunted me for twenty years. I'd change, too, of course. With time. And I'd do my best not to become a monster.

I first bared my teeth when I turned thirteen, and it all started with a drunkard on a riverbank.

Photo by Martin Sinimägi

MATT HAYWARD is a Bram Stoker Award-nominated author and musician from Wicklow, Ireland. His books include *Brain Dead Blues, What Do Monsters Fear?, Practitioners* (with Patrick Lacey), *The Faithful, A Penny For Your Thoughts* (with Robert Ford), *Various States Of Decay, Those Below The Tree House,* and *Lady Luck* (with Robert Ford). He compiled the award-winning anthology *Welcome To The Show,* and wrote the comic book *This Is How It Ends* (now a music video) for the band Walking Papers. He received a nomination for Irish Short Story of the Year from Penguin Books in 2017, and is represented by Lane Heymont of the Tobias Literary Agency. He can be found on Twitter @MattHaywardIRE or at his website www.sundancecrow.com

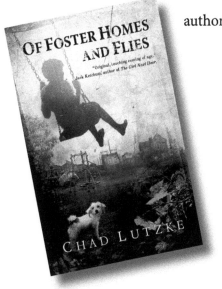

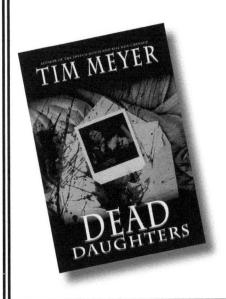